Before I Say I Do

Before I Say I Do

Tara L. Thompson

This novel is a work of fiction. Names, characters, places, and events portrayed in this novel are either the product of the author's imagination or are used fictitiously.

ISBN-13: 978-1496062949
ISBN-10: 1496062949

This book is dedicated to my daughter Sydney. Thank you for the endless love and joy you give me.

Acknowledgements

Wow, I can't believe I am actually writing an acknowledgements page! First and foremost, I have to start by thanking God. I have so much favor over my life. I know I don't deserve it, but I will continuously live to give God all the honor and praise. I want to thank my dad and mom, Pastor W.W. Thompson and Diann Thompson. I am who I am because of you, from my hard headed ways to my persistence and loving nature, you have molded me into this woman. I love both of you with all my heart and I hope that I am making you proud with the things I do. Thanks to my sisters, Tonya and Tiona, who are my best friends and who stay on me to keep going and never give up. I love y'all so much. Tiona, I am so proud of the young woman you have become. Keep allowing the leader inside of you to shine through! Also thanks Tonya for creating my vision for the cover. Continue to follow your dreams sis!

I started this book and journey in 2006, and with life getting in the way and me getting in my own way, I have picked it up and put it down too many times to remember. At one point, I had given up on my dream but God never gave up on me. Once you have purpose and know what God has called you to do nothing or no one can stop that.

I have so many friends and family to thank that if I forget some please charge it to my head and not my heart. I want to thank my close family and friends that always cheered me on with this project…Yolanda H. (who birthed the idea with me), Teresa G., Kim M., Dionne R., Brian W., Omari S., Sherry W., Teetrice D., Brandy V., Mario S., Izell R., Jacqueline P., Jakeisha C., Winter S., Kenshasa M., Temeka W., Laquanya M., ShiQuela M., Na'kia P., Narissa B. and the entire McCrorey Family. I can't put everyone's name because I am too scared I would miss one…too many of you all! But if your last name is McCrorey/Pickett I thank you!

To all my family and friends that read excerpts of my book and provided feedback, I sincerely thank you. To my classmates (Class of 99) that supported and stayed on me about this book I thank you! Thank you for the years of support Tamika S., Meredith T., and Kristen W.! Also thanks to Demorrious Robinson for taking such beautiful pictures for my website!

A special thank you to my sister Sha'Ron Robertson for being there for me and also letting me borrow your laptop for so long(lol). Thanks for the support and being an awesome aunt! You have helped me out too many times to count and I appreciate that so much. Tell Valeria that the book is finally done!

Thanks to my cousin/sister Shuana Davis for all of our girl talks even when I was falling asleep on you(lol). Thank you for motivating me, advising me, and just allowing me to be me.

Thank you to the entire Davis family for being a wonderful family and always showing me so much love. I am a Davis to the core! Thanks to all my family, Thompson, Davis, Scott, and Foote!

A very special thank you to a talented author that pushed me past my fear and rekindled the fire inside me to put this book out. Curtis Little, thank you for your endless support and motivation. Even when I was working your nerves with all my stress and worries, you continued to push me. I admire and cherish you my friend! You are such an inspiration. Great things are ahead! Please pick up his book as well, Unhealthy & Unwealthy: My Battle With Lupus & Life. Also coming soon his second novel, Heart Of A Champion: A Guide To Picking Yourself Up.

Thank you to a wonderful editor, Mrs. Jessica McBride. I appreciate all your hard work on this project.

Also a special thank you to Author Brian L. King and King4Life Publications for the mentoring, advice, and beautiful cover. I appreciate all the help that you have given me.

As I finish thanking everyone I am in tears because this is a dream come true. Thanks to everyone for all the support and there will be a lot more projects in the future. Enjoy!

Love you all!
Tara L. Thompson

Prologue

As he let out a lingering sigh, I opened my eyes and hesitantly glanced at this man on top of me. His body shook once again and I felt his chest rise and then fall as he took another deep breath. Both our bodies were sticky and moist from the sweat that had us bound to each other.

"Are you okay?" he asked, relieved that I had finally opened my eyes.

I looked around the room for a moment, his body weight pinning me to the bed. I tried to form my mouth in order to produce something, but I was speechless. So many thoughts were running through my mind, but none of them made any sense to me right now. Almost simultaneously, we slowly glanced at the gold and black condom wrapper lying on the nightstand.

"Damn," I said, thinking out loud. I attempted to focus on something else, anything else.

The hotel room was dark except for the flickering light from the muted television. Not remembering who had turned the TV on or whether it had been my idea to mute it, I cocked my head to the side imagining what the girl on the Aleve commercial was saying.

The small room contained a queen sized bed draped with a shabby ivory-colored blanket, a TV stand the size of a card playing table, and the tiniest metal desk ever. It captured the smell of sweat, sex, and a mixture of our colognes and gave me such a headache that I wished I had some of the advertised pain reliever.

His damp body still lay on top of mine; his sculpted chest pressed against my heavy bosom as he began to stroke my now wet hair. I could still smell the spearmint gum on his breath.

My muscles relaxed as he carefully pulled himself out of me and rolled over onto the other side of the bed. Lying on his back, his eyes shifted to the ceiling and he exhaled loudly.

"Damn," I repeated again, looking at his muscular dark brown frame, then focusing on his sexy almond colored eyes.

We had just finished a session of love making that lasted for at least two hours, and to my own surprise I wanted more. I wanted to feel him inside me again; pleasing me while I in return did everything I could to make sure he was satisfied.

As we lay in silence, reality slowly reared its ugly head and I remembered the big event that would be taking place in my life in a little more than eight weeks. My wedding day was quickly approaching, and my heart dropped at the mere thought.

The Aleve commercial was gone and two women were now fighting on *The Jerry Springer Show*. One lady who looked like she weighed close to three hundred pounds swung her dirty blond hair back and forth before lunging toward a frail pale girl dressed in daisy dukes shorts and a halter top.

I turned my focus back to the man that lay beside me. Noticing the worried look on my face, he turned on his side and leaned over to place a tender kiss on my forehead.

"Rachel, I will not cause any problems for you, all I want is for you to be happy," he whispered.

I stared at him wondering if he was as confused as I was. I turned on my side with my back towards him and faced the wall. Maybe if I just closed my eyes I would wake up and all of this would be a dream. The room was silent except for his breathing, and even that turned me on. He placed his arms around me and squeezed me tight like I was his and he never wanted to let go. And at that moment I felt like his. I tried to wrap my mind around what had just happened and how I could allow myself to do this once again. This was so *wrong*. So dishonest and devious, yet here I was again, indulging in him once more.

I cautiously turned to face this married man and kissed the tattoo on his right arm.

My lips traveled over each letter of his son's name that was carefully sketched into his skin and I slowly inhaled his scent. Jay-Z's Gold engulfed me and made my nipples harden. I looked deep into his eyes and was honest with him and myself.

"I love you," I whispered, burying my sweat glistened face into his chest, knowing that this one night had changed my life forever.

***

I drove home with the events of the night a blur to me but still fresh in my mind. After riding for about thirty minutes in complete silence, I realized that I had not turned on the radio, which I always do as soon as I get in my car. My shaking hand fumbled around the silver knob as I tried to find a station. My heart stopped when I heard Kelly Price belt out her rendition of "As We Lay". It felt like she knew exactly what I had done and was singing this song for me.

Its morning, and now it's time for us to say goodbye. You're leaving me I know you got to hurry home to face your wife.

I sang along with Kelly and her words cut me so deep that I barely heard my cell phone ringing. I took a deep breath and reached down into my red Ralph Lauren purse.

"Hey, lil' mama," he said in his most seductive voice.

Flashes of him on top of me filled my head and I squeaked out "Hey" without trying to sound like I had a million things on my mind. I tried to remain calm, but my voice told on me. It was the voice of someone that did not know what she wanted anymore.

"Where are you?"

His concern caused a huge smile to spread across my face, but it quickly disappeared as my mind went back to tonight's actions. My voice was a mere whisper as I informed him that I had just crossed the Georgia state line, leaving me with a few more hours to drive.

"Rachel, I understand that we can't see each other anymore. I know that soon you will be a married woman and I don't want to stop you or distract you from your plans."

I swallowed hard. These were the exact words that I needed to hear to get my mind focused on the reality of our situation. My palms began to sweat. My two carat princess cut diamond engagement ring slid around on my finger as I tried to get a good grip on the steering wheel. Just talking to him on the phone made me nervous. Rachel, stay in control, I thought.

He went on about how he realized that our situations would not change. His voice was steady and without feeling when he referred to his own marriage. Usually, I never have any difficulty telling people how I feel and what I want, but for some reason, this man did something to me that made me become a different person. I became someone that listened to her heart without thinking about the "what ifs".

"Are you there?"

"Yeah, I'm here," I replied flatly, my stomach twisting into knots. "This wasn't supposed to happen, we should have just talked," I said remorsefully.

He sighed as silence overtook our conversation. After a few seconds he finally spoke. "I know," he said. "I didn't plan on this happening again. I just had to see you."

Why can't I let him go? I wanted to scream feeling the tears well up in my eyes. My stomach continued to turn and that meant I was going to be sick at any moment. I held my cell phone in my dripping wet hand and struggled to concentrate on the road.

"How do you feel about me?" I asked quickly.

"You know I love you. How could I not love you?"

His answer made the tears fall uncontrollably and I began to tell him what was in my heart. As I began to speak, he cut me off and said the one thing that I did not want to hear.

"Rachel, you know how I feel about you, but I want to talk about the one thing that you have not told me."

He can't know about that.

He can't know my secret. That was the reason for us meeting tonight but I still couldn't bring myself to tell him.

"Sweetheart, I'm sorry," was all that I could manage to say.

"Please tell me the truth."

He knew. He already knew. Before I could say anything else, I glanced at the road and slammed on brakes. I felt the car slide from right to left. My cell phone fell from my hand as I tightened my grip on the steering wheel, trying to regain control of the car, but it was too late. The car jerked forward. Still pressing the brake with all my power, I finally came to a complete stop. I looked up and saw that I was now on the side of the road. Before I could blink twice the brightness of two lights on high beam blinded me. I couldn't move and the lights were coming straight for me.

"Oh Jesus!" I screamed, and braced myself for the impact.

Chapter 1

One year earlier

"What the hell is wrong with you?" I screamed, my eyes blazing a hole right through Corey. My mind was racing as I tried to figure out who this man was that looked up at me. After four years of dating and three months of being engaged, I thought I knew everything there was to know about him, but boy was I wrong. Based on his recent actions, I was starting to question a lot about him. Corey glanced away as if he didn't hear me. He was a terrible liar and I always knew when he wasn't going to be truthful. He would become quiet, avoid any eye contact, and try to change the subject. The wheels were turning inside his head as he tried to think of something to say to get me off his back.

Even though I only stood 5 feet 2 inches tall, I was nothing to play with. My family and friends constantly teased me about my Napoleon complex. I didn't always admit it, but I thought I had the right to say what I wanted and that I was better than most, as well. I was a middle child who had to fight for attention while growing up, but that only made me stronger and more aggressive. I was not going to allow anyone to take advantage of me, not even the man that I have loved with all of myself for the last few years.

Corey slouched down on my brand new white plush leather sofa and dropped his head in his hands. Sweat beads glistened on his forehead. I glared at him as he tried to wipe them off by ducking his head into his black shirt that used to have sleeves, and used to match the black and red shorts he wore. He'd been playing basketball all day with the fellas, as he called them, and I cringed at the thought of him, sweaty and dirty, sitting on my expensive furniture.

His ragged black and red Jordans made a print in my freshly vacuumed carpet. Thank God he only wore them to shoot hoops.

"Man, sometimes it's just too much, Rachel," Corey said without looking up.

I waited for him to finish his thought before I responded. In the past, I use to cut him off before he completed what he was saying and that would always start an argument. I had to learn to wait a few seconds before I began talking. When I was certain that he had finished, I repeated my unanswered question.

"And I say again, what the HELL is wrong with you?" I didn't even try to keep the irritation out of my voice.

Our wedding was ten months away and we had already begun to feel the stress of planning it. Earlier that afternoon, Corey had left a message on my cell phone stating that he couldn't handle all this pressure and maybe we didn't need to do this. That was the entire message. Nothing more. No "Baby I love you but I am stressed out right now." Nothing. I played the message back several times trying to figure out what "this" he referred to. Was he talking about the wedding? Was he talking us?

Now, just hours after that message, he was sitting on my sofa, head in hands, talking, but still not telling me anything. His clothes clung to his body, and even though I loved that "just finished working out" look, today it was just a major turn off, and his funk from chasing the ball around the court was making me nauseous.

"I seriously don't have time for this today," I said lowering my voice from screaming to normal, but irate, and sat down beside him. My head started to hurt. I focused my eyes on his 6"1' frame sinking further and further down into my couch.

"Oh, now you don't have time for what I'm saying?" Corey lifted his head and his voice started to rise. He sat straight up and scowled at me.

"I didn't mean it like that, Corey.

We're both under a lot of stress and I don't understand what you are trying to say at this moment, if anything." I knew I should have left that "if anything" part off, but it was too late.

Corey jumped up and headed towards the door mumbling about how I always want to talk but never listened to what he had to say. The sudden change in his behavior surprised me, but what was more surprising was that I didn't go after him. Once he calmed down he would call or come back over and we would make up. Weddings are stressful and I figured that he was feeling the same tension and overwhelming pressure I had been enduring.

Sad to say, I was actually glad when he walked out the door, although I could have done without him slamming it. I couldn't bear to listen to him gripe about how he wasn't sure about what we were doing. Corey adored me and there was no doubt that I loved him with all my heart, but sometimes I just needed a break from everything, including him.

***

Saturday was turning out to be a very strenuous day. By the time Corey left, it was four o'clock, and I had done nothing on my to-do list. It seemed like every weekend I had so much running around to do for this damn wedding.

Don't get me wrong, I was excited about getting married and dropping the Simms surname to become Mrs. Rachel Perkins, but I hadn't realized there was so much involved in planning a wedding. I had to call the photographer, videographer, decorator, caterer, etc. and make sure everything was done. Sometimes it was too much, so a part of me understood what Corey meant. But he was not doing these things. I was the one planning this entire wedding while he hung out with his friends or traveled place to place with his job. He had very little room to complain.

I had been in the middle of a vigorous work out before I was interrupted by Corey's knock on the door, and after our conversation I was too wiped out emotionally and physically to finish it. My treadmill sat off to the left side of my spacious living room facing my 60 inch wide screen TV that was now showing the soap operas recorded from the previous week. As always, Brooke was sleeping with someone's husband on *The Bold and The Beautiful.*

The minutes were still flashing on my treadmill. I pressed stop on the timer and pushed it into the small corner of my living room that was its home half of the time. Thirty-five minutes, that's not too bad, I thought. I grabbed the television remote that was sitting on my treadmill, turned off my TV, and headed towards the shower. It may be late afternoon but I still had things to do.

Entering my bedroom, I noticed clothes scattered all over my bed. It was time for me to clean up and rearrange my room once again. I was always redecorating. I despised looking at the same things in the same spots every day. My cherry oak queen sized sleigh bed sat in the center of my bedroom. Positioned on the right side of it, was my matching dresser and mirror stuffed with clothes hanging out like they were hostages trying to escape. Pictures of me and Corey at the zoo, the amusement park, and a Japanese steakhouse cluttered my dresser along with unopened mail and papers from the job. I shook my head at how messy I could be at times. Located in the front of my room and at the foot of my bed was my flat screen balanced on a stand, both of which had been Christmas gifts from Corey.

I stood next to my TV and envisioned the various ways I could change my room around. I felt the need to do away with the painting of the couple lying in front of the fireplace on the opposite wall of my bedroom, facing my dresser. The frame matched my bed perfectly and created an ambiance of romance; however, it had been on my bedroom wall far too long.

My brown and red curtains even accentuated the painting and highlighted the room along with my gold, brown, and red comforter set, yet I still longed for something different.

Corey fussed that I was always changing things, whether it was my hair or my job. I would hit him back with, well sweetie you have been around for four years and I haven't gotten rid of or changed you, so that should mean something. My sarcasm had constantly gotten me in trouble when I was younger, but Corey was never bothered by it. Even with my constant adjustments and cynicism, he loved me.

I removed my blue tank top and tossed it in the corner on a pile of clothes that needed to be washed. I stared at myself in the long mirror hanging on the back of my bedroom door. I began to work out about three months ago in order to look spectacular in my wedding dress and I was extremely satisfied at the results.

Over the past few years I had gained a lot of weight and was really unhappy about my size. Being a size twelve without height on my side didn't always make me feel sexy while shopping because it was difficult to find anything to fit. Granted, I had the hips and ass that God blessed most black women with, - round and curvy enough to sit a coffee mug on- but I could do without the stomach and other unflattering things that came along with the extra pounds.

When I met Corey I was a size eight and he loved it. Tiny and petite, he took full advantage of how small I was. Now that I was a size twelve he cherished my body even more and his hands would always somehow end up on my ass. Still, I didn't like being this size at all, so my goal was to walk down the aisle in April, thirty pounds lighter, wowing everybody in the audience.

I removed my Nike sneakers and untied the string on my grey sweatpants. As my pants fell to the floor, I gazed at my entire body, noting every mark from abrasions to scratches when I was younger.

My brown panty and bra set looked impressive on my honey caramel skin. I smiled at the thought of how much Corey favored seeing me in this color. I touched my breasts and thanked God they were still a perky size 38C. My hands traveled over my slowly shrinking stomach and the fading stretch marks that appeared when I started gaining weight. If only we could all have perfect bodies like Halle Berry, I thought as one of her lipstick commercials came on TV.

I pulled my red and yellow scarf from my head, removed the tie from my black shoulder length hair, and ran my fingers through the brown highlights, realizing it was almost time for a relaxer. I made a mental note to call my hair stylist next week. My attention was now on my face and the few pimples that were popping up around my nose and chin, an unwelcomed symptom of wedding stress. I stared at my long eyelashes and big brown eyes that made me look younger than I really was. My friends and family told me that I favored the singer Chrisette Michele, but I didn't see the resemblance.

I unhooked my bra and threw it onto my bed. A woman yelling on TV caught my attention and I turned to see what all the commotion was about. Halle was replaced by a woman in tears on *The Maury Show*, screaming that she knew the man sitting beside her was her "baby's daddy". The lady carried on and on about how the child looked like the guy and he needed to step up and be a father. It's a shame how women sleep with so many men and don't know who fathered their children, I thought. I am glad that I only have one man, even if we are a little pissed at each other right now. Rolling my eyes at the TV, I finished undressing, pulled my hair into a quick ponytail, and eased into the bathroom for a nice long hot shower.

***

The steamy hot water put me in a trance and I was in the bathroom for thirty minutes before remembering time was not my friend today since my future husband had come in and derailed my plans. I immediately stepped out the shower and onto my fluffy orange bath rug. Admiring my French tip manicured toes, I thought about how much Corey loved my feet. My toes always had to be primped and polished just in case he felt the urge to suck them.

I dried off with my towel and suddenly wished that the argument that Corey and I had earlier had never taken place. I yearned for him to be here with me now, waiting for me. A game that he often played while I was in the shower was that he would get undressed and wait for me to open the bathroom door. I would cautiously open the door and peek out knowing that he was going to pick me up and carry me to the bed. Having a strong man had its advantages.

He would take the body oil that I always kept on my nightstand and slowly moisturize every inch of my body, even my smallest toes. He was very careful to make sure he rubbed me from head to toe, slowly and gently, as if I was a fragile newborn that still needed to be handled with extreme care. After fifteen minutes of the oil and gentle massage, Corey would get up and put his clothes on, pretending he was about to go home. He wanted me to beg him to stay and I would always oblige. While dressing and telling me he was leaving I would walk up behind him and start to remove the clothing that he was putting on.

After a couple of minutes of this little game he would surrender and we would end up making love for hours. By far, my soon to be husband was the best lover I had ever had. His touch was so affectionate and loving that I didn't have to instruct him on what to do like I'd had to do men in the past. His hands would journey up and down my body and make me feel beautiful. When we made love, he never concentrated on himself but focused on me and making my body tingle like no one before.

There were times I even had to tell him to stop because the pleasure was so unreal that I was scared I would wake up and it all would be a dream.

My nipples hardened under my towel at the mere thought of Corey fondling me. I unwrapped the towel from my body and threw it on the pile beside my blue tank top. Searching through the clothes on my bed, I found my favorite red and black P.H.A.T Girl shirt and a pair of old tattered blue jeans. I had the rest of my life to make love to Corey, but I had so much to do to get through the day that I could not waste any more time daydreaming.

Chapter 2

"Girl, I had him screaming MY name!" my best friend squealed as we sat in front of the Fruit and Smoothie Café drinking a couple of strawberry and banana smoothies. The name of my favorite spot was not original at all, but since it was in the middle of uptown Charlotte surrounded by Bank Of America, Wells Fargo, and a ton of other businesses, everyone frequented the café on a regular basis. It helped that they also had the best smoothies in the world. It was a small smoothie stand with tables inside and out. Yvonne and I always convened outside so that we could watch and talk about the people that passed by. We sat at a round black iron table as my best friend pulled on her straw, smiled, and talked about her previous night.

Von and I had been friends since sixth grade, and even though we went to different colleges after high school, we still remained close throughout the years. She worked at Gateway Village, one of the Bank of America buildings located across the street from the Fruit and Smoothie Café, while I worked five blocks up the street at the BB&T Building. Since we worked that close to one another, we ate lunch together at least twice a week.

It was a muggy, humid Friday afternoon and Von's tale of how she had some random brother climbing the walls bored me. The June heat was as exhausting as Von's story. I tried hard to pay attention to what she was rambling about while I wiped the sweat from my brow. Any other day I would entertain her just a bit and ask questions about what she did, but today I was in a different mood. I listened to my friend go on and on about how she made some guy feel. I didn't even catch his name. Better yet, I am not sure she knew his name herself.

The spaghetti straps of Von's black cami made an imprint in her smooth dark skin as her royal blue suit jacket hung freely on the back of her chair. She adjusted her shirt every few seconds so any available man walking by could get a glimpse of her protruding bosom.

Von was an attractive and accomplished woman, but her choices in men left much to be desired. I advised her to be a little harder to get, but she always thought I was trying to be high and mighty since I already had a good man, so my words fell on deaf ears. She had no standards when choosing the men she allowed in her life or inside her body. The upsetting thing was that she was such an outstanding woman. Von attended the University of North Carolina at Chapel Hill on a scholarship and received her degree in Business Administration. From there, she earned her MBA from Howard University and was currently a Business Analyst and VP for Bank of America.

Von stood about 5'10, weighed 140 pounds, and her beautiful mocha-colored skin reveled in the sun light. She had a tiny waist and an ass that made most men want to slap their mother and grandmother at the same time. Everywhere she went guys broke their necks to try to get a glimpse of her backside. At one time, she'd worn her jet black hair long - past her shoulders - but as summer approached, she decided on a change and cut it all off. Now she was sporting a short cut that complimented her high cheek bones and strong facial features. Her cut resembled Meagan Good's hairstyle in the movie, *Think Like a Man*, and my beautiful friend could have even given Ms. Good a run for her money. As stunning as she was, she lacked common sense when it came to the opposite sex. A man could come up to her and tell her that it was snowing in June and this heifer would have to think twice about it.

I was only catching parts of her conversation here and there when she finally caught on that I wasn't listening.

"What's with you today, Rachel?" she asked while slurping the last little bit of her smoothie.

"Nothing."

I turned my attention to a couple walking past us holding hands. The guy looked at the girl tenderly and whispered something in her ear. She laughed and softly pushed him as they continued to walk by.

"Yeah okay, tell that to someone that hasn't known you all your life."

"Are you going to church with me Sunday?"

"Is your father preaching?" Von asked, rolling her eyes at me. She knew this was my attempt at changing the subject.

"Yeah, I think so."

My dad was the senior pastor of one of the largest churches in Charlotte, North Carolina. My sister, brother, and I grew up in the church and it just didn't feel right to let a Sunday go by without being there and praising God. No matter what we had done the night before we would always be in church on Sunday morning. We might party up until seven a.m., but come ten o'clock we were in church singing in the choir and worshipping God as if we had been at home reading the Bible all night.

"Now girl you know I can't sit through no one else preaching but good old Pastor Simms." Von laughed as if she had told a Kings of Comedy joke.

"You need to hear someone's preaching after making what's his name jump up the walls last night," I replied. I followed suite and rolled my eyes back at her.

"Bitch, you're in a stank mood today." She looked at me and tilted her head to the side, examining me. "Having the wedding blues?" Von laughed again.

I shook my head at my friend. She was being rather lame today. Then again, it probably was just me and my mental state. Von was my maid of honor and she had been a great aid when it came to getting my mind off the wedding, but for some reason, even she was aggravating me right now.

My ringtone startled me and I looked down to see Corey's face flashing on my new Galaxy S4 Android Phone. I had just recently purchased the phone and was still trying to figure out all the features.

However, one option I took full advantage of was the reject button. I ignored the call and continued to talk to Von about coming to church with me Sunday.

"Who was that and why didn't you answer the phone?" she asked.

"That was Corey and I don't feel like talking to him right now."

"What? Not Miss 'I am so ready to be Corey's wife!'" Von chuckled, trying to make me laugh. "Okay, tell me what happened because it's not like you to just ignore Corey's calls."

I told Von about the argument we had had last weekend and that we had barely talked all week.

"Girl, that is just his nerves," Von said making light of the situation.

"Yeah, maybe, but I don't have time for his nerves to get the best of me," I snapped.

"Child please! In a few months you are going to marry the man of your dreams. Not only the man of your dreams, but a good man that loves you unconditionally, so stop acting crazy and call him back."

Von was getting disturbed with me so I decided to leave the conversation alone. She did have a point though. I glanced at my watch and realized that I needed to get back to work.

"Okay okay, you are right," I confessed.

Von was more than pleased that I was admitting I was wrong and she was right. She had so many nicknames for me, and one was Never Wrong Rachel. I stood up from the table, adjusted my cream colored blouse, smoothed out my gray pencil skirt, and told her that I would give her a call later. I don't know if she heard me. Von's focus was now on a well-dressed brother wearing a charcoal colored suit standing in line ordering a smoothie. She was on the prowl again.

***

Snyder & Lawry Law Firm was within walking distance from the Fruit and Smoothie Café. We occupied space on the seventeenth floor in one of the larger buildings in that area. The BB&T building stood thirty-four floors high with glistening black tile decorating the lobby floors, and beige corridors and walls that listened to every business deal or offer that was made. I loved the atmosphere every time I walked through the massive glass double doors. The hustle and bustle of so many people rushing to get to work, meetings, and lunch excited me. Seeing successful people, especially African American men dressed in suits and ties striving to become more than they were once told they could be gave me a sense of pride.

On the walk back to the office I thought about the conversation between Von and me. She was right. Corey and I needed to sit down and talk, and not just over the phone. Corey lived two hours away in Greenville, South Carolina, so if I wanted to see him I would need to tell him at least a day ahead of time. Most of his weekends were spent with me or his family here in Charlotte, but then there were times he would stay in Greenville to work overtime. He was a district manager responsible for twenty Target stores. Corey accepted the position a little over a year ago and moved to Greenville. He was currently in the process of transferring back to Charlotte. I was anxious to have him back in the same city as I was.

We had both grown up in Charlotte although I didn't meet him until I went off to college. I knew of him in high school since he was a big time basketball player at a rival school. He was rumored to go to the NBA, but a very painful knee injury ended that aspiration.

Corey attended the infamous Morehouse College and I was across the street at the historically acclaimed Spelman College. I met him at one of the many parties that my friends and I attended at Morehouse. He was very laid back and carried himself which so much confidence that all the girls admired him.

Standing over six feet tall, with light honey-colored skin, all the girls competed to get his attention. They wanted him badly and went to extreme lengths to try to get him. He was the quintessential Morehouse man.

Corey had a slender build with just the right amount of muscles, long athletic legs, perfectly sculpted arms that look like they were painted on him, and stunning white teeth that would make a woman say yes to his smile all day. The guys in his fraternity, Kappa Alpha Psi, referred to him as "Catastrophic", because his smile was dangerous to all women. He kept his hair cut in a low fade but every now and then would allow it to grow out and his curls would fall freely on top his head. Not only was he one of the finest brothers on campus, but he was also very intellectual. So of course I was overjoyed when he began to pursue me our senior year of school. We clicked when he discovered that we were both from Charlotte and have been inseparable ever since.

After riding the elevator up the seventeen flights of stairs, I strolled through the front doors of the law firm and frowned at the thought of having to pass the receptionist in order to get to my office. Daria sat at her desk all day watching people travel in and out of the front door, striking up conversations with whoever came within speaking distance.

She was a very hyper and energetic woman in her early twenties, and you could tell this was her first professional job. Her red hair was full of large spiral curls that bounced every time she talked. Daria's shirts were always too low cut for the office setting and her skirts could stand to be an inch or two longer. Her perkiness drove me crazy at times, and whenever she talked to someone she twirled her curls with her middle finger. That bad habit was just another thing about her that irked me.

"Hey girl," Daria said waving at me with her free hand.

"Hey, I'll talk to you in a minute," I said as I hurried past her desk.

I was not coming back out there to listen to her talk about her relationship or lack of one. She had one of the sorriest men around. This one didn't have a job or car, lived at home with his mom and wasn't trying to do anything for her but spend her money. Today was not the day that I needed to hear that. I had problems of my own to deal with.

My office was tucked away down the long narrow hall, last door on the left. It was off on its own, hidden like a runaway child from the lawyers' offices, which pleased me. My office was the size of a large bedroom closet and had enough room for my dark walnut wood desk and a small matching wood round table with two wooden chairs. If I ever needed to actually "knock on wood" in my office, I would have no problems doing so. My cushy black leather chair peeked out from behind my desk. I spent many days twirling around in it letting my mind wander aimlessly.

Located behind my chair was my favorite part of the office, the floor to ceiling window that gave me the best view of uptown Charlotte, from the high rise buildings to the Bank of America Stadium. I spent countless hours gazing out this window and allowing the sun rays, peaceful scenes, and glorious sky to alter my constant gloomy moods brought on by all the wedding stress.

I settled back in my chair and tried to focus on the work that was piled on my desk. This year marked my third year at the law firm as the accountant/office manager. I handled all the accounting functions and basically ran the office. Seven lawyers made up Snyder & Lawry, and for the most part, all of them were very welcoming people. At every job however, you are going to find one or two assholes, and Doug Cranton was that one in my office. He was a competent lawyer but knew nothing about how to run the office and business expenses. Nevertheless, he felt compelled to tell me how to do my job.

When I began working at the firm, his suggestions (at least that is what he called them) would annoy me, but over the years I learned to ignore him and smile at his dumb ass at the same time. Tall and lean with slanted green snake like eyes, he slithered past my office and tapped on my door twice before entering. I glanced up and contained my eye rolling and sigh for a brief moment.

"How can I help you, Doug?" I gave him a fake half smile.

"Ms. Rachel, I have some ideas I would like to go over with you on cutting costs. Do you think you will have a moment sometime this week?" He asked.

"Let me check my calendar and I will send you a meeting request. Thanks." I shuffled through the papers on my desk in hopes that he would get the hint that I didn't have time to be bothered with him.

"Looking forward to it," he said, turning and walking out of my office. This time I didn't control it and rolled my eyes at Doug's back as he disappeared down the hall.

I was crunching numbers and sorting through the payroll for the week when I heard my cell phone ring. I glanced at my phone as it lay next to my computer and saw Corey's face flash across the screen again. I answered the phone this time, anxious to hear his voice.

"Hello, Rachel."

"Hey sweetie, how are you?" I hoped that he realized by my tone that I was over last weekend.

"Baby, do you have any plans for tonight?" Corey asked.

I was not able to tell by his voice if he was still upset, but I was definitely not going to bring anything up at the moment.

"No, I have no plans."

"We need to talk, so I am going to drive up tonight after I get off work. I'll be at your house around nine if that's cool with you."

Grateful that he wanted to see me, I told him that was fine and hung up the phone.

The sudden change of plans gave me something to look forward to after work. I rushed through the payroll and the rest of the work on my desk.

As soon as five o'clock flashed on the screen of my computer, I packed up my things. All Daria saw was the back of me as I ran out of the office, hurrying home to plan a romantic evening for my soon-to-be-husband. My body ached for him. Tonight needed to be perfect and that was just what it was going to be.

Chapter 3

"Move out the way!" I screamed at the guy who was driving a dusty grey Ford 150 truck, as if he owned the road. I knew that I would end up in 5 o'clock traffic, which was the worst coming from uptown Charlotte on a Friday afternoon, but this was just ridiculous.

"Am I the only one who knows how to drive?" I impatiently rolled my windows up and turned on the air in my white Infiniti G37. Traffic had completely stopped, which meant that it would be a good forty minutes before I made it home. I lived right outside of Charlotte in a little town called Fort Mill and it took me fifteen to twenty minutes to get home. Today traffic was backed up more than usual, so that would add another twenty minutes to my drive.

Fort Mill was an up and coming community, and I was extremely fond of the charming scenery it provided. Once I graduated college, I decided to settle down in this peaceful town instead of staying in the over populated city of Charlotte. It was the first town after crossing over the North Carolina line to South Carolina. Small but quaint, it provided a country atmosphere right outside the metropolis of Charlotte. Bold trees with swaying leaves along with vivid arrays of flowers dashed here and there brought this miniature city to life.

Between my road rage and wanting to get home to make sure everything was just right for Corey, I gave myself an excruciating headache. I reached into my briefcase that sat in the front seat beside my purse and searched for my favorite pain killer. I always kept a bottle on me since it seemed like the simplest things gave me migraines these days. Another thing I can thank this wedding for, I thought as I fumbled around in my briefcase, having no luck finding my much needed medicine.

"Ouch! What in the world?"

I yanked my hand out of my bag and stuck my finger in my mouth. Slowly, I released it and examined the bleeding cut, wondering what in my briefcase could have given me such a painful wound. I was accustomed to paper cuts with all the paper that I handle on a daily basis, but I still hated them. I gingerly fumbled around in my briefcase and took out the card that had caused me to cry out.

Traffic moved a little as I tried to focus on the road and the words on the card at the same time. "Terrence Walker, Attorney at Law" was printed on the card alongside the Barker & Retter law firm name. The law firm's Atlanta address and Terrence's work and cell phone numbers were beside his name on the card.

Terrence was a lawyer who worked with one of our sister companies based in Atlanta. I spoke with him on the phone every week about business expenses and reports. Barker & Retter was a very new firm, and although he was a lawyer, he handled some of the company's financial business needs. I'd never met Terrence in person, but had gotten to know him through the conversations we had to go over budget numbers. We were long past the formality of addressing each other by our last names.

After only speaking twice on the phone, my first thoughts of him were that he was a complete jack-ass that I would not be able to deal with. After chatting a few more times and really getting to know him, however, he seemed to be a pretty cool guy. I was supposed to fax him a few documents before I left the office and had stuck his business card in my briefcase to remind me. I guess I was in too much of a hurry today to even remember to do it. I'll just fax it on Monday, I thought, as I tossed the card onto the front seat of my car.

Around six o'clock I finally made it to my apartment building and jumped out the car.

Gable Gates was a reserved, quiet apartment complex that housed older people, with a couple of families with children here and there. I moved into the neighborhood two years ago and was content living here. Even though the apartments were more costly since they were built a year before I moved in, I had no complaints. The neighborhood was particularly colorful today with the radiant summer flowers in bloom, bright green grass spread throughout, and the valiant trees standing high and gallant in the sunlight.

Boys and girls roamed throughout the neighborhood on bicycles laughing, playing, and enjoying every ounce of their summer vacation. I glanced at the kids at the park right across from my building and couldn't help but smile at the thought of me and Corey having a couple of little ones soon to run around the house and keep us on our toes. His dream was to be a father one day and I was going to be the person to make that come true.

I sprinted up the stairs to my door and saw my neighbor, Mrs. Harris coming out of her apartment.

"Well if it isn't the blushing bride. How are you, lovely?" she asked smiling at me. The silver haired woman had moved into the apartment beside mine a few months ago, and I often chatted with her in passing. I told her recently that I was getting married, so whenever she saw me she would ask how the wedding plans were coming.

"I am fine," I smiled back not wanting to hold our usual long conversation. Mrs. Harris was a thickset, short, buttercream colored lady in her late 60's who could always be seen smiling and humming some tune. She lost her husband to lung cancer a year ago and sold her house because she started to feel lonely and wanted something smaller. She didn't have any kids to go live with so she had gotten a little apartment just for herself. When she shared with me the story of how her husband died, I was in tears thinking about all she had gone through. I would be heartbroken if I ever lost Corey.

She was a resilient woman, however, and seemed to be taking the loss of "her John," as she often referred to him, admirably. Sensing I was in a hurry, she continued to smile and mosey down the stairs to her car. I made a mental note to visit her next week to ensure she was doing well.

I put my key into the door and entered my apartment, wanting to turn around as soon as I stepped in. It was in complete disarray. One of the many reasons I chose this apartment complex was how capacious the rooms were. My living room was enormous and right smack in the middle was my oversized white leather sofa and loveseat that I recently purchased. My living room was decorated in shades of white and sage, including white curtains and a sage, lilac, and white area rug that covered most of my living room floor. The beauty of it was hidden today by piles of clothes, papers, and books scattered here and there. It looked as if Hurricane Hugo from the late 80s had visited my apartment, started in my living room, swept its way into my kitchen, and finished in my bedroom.

The black and brown wooden clock on my wall that was given to me as a housewarming present read 6:10. I had to do some major cooking and cleaning before Corey arrived. Good thing my grocery shopping was already done since I would have no time for that with my house looking like a natural disaster.

Corey cherished my home cooking and, because of that, I decided to give him a reminder of one of the reasons he proposed. I retrieved the pack of pork chops from the freezer and placed them in the sink to thaw out. While I waited for them to defrost, I began to clean the room that we would spend much of our time in tonight, my bedroom.

Once I finished gathering the piles of clothes that had accumulated on my floor over the past week, I lit the Apple Cinnamon scented candles that were on my dresser just to give the room that fresh aroma that I loved.

I finished cleaning my room, tidied up the living room, and trotted back to the kitchen to wash the pile of dirty dishes stacked in my sink, and finally prepare dinner.

***

Hearing a gentle knock on the door, I grabbed the biscuits out of the oven and placed them on the table. Corey had called thirty minutes ago and said that he was almost here, which meant I had another hour before he arrived. Like most men, he was not time conscious and seemed to always be late. His tardiness gave me more time to prepare dinner, therefore, I wasn't going to give him grief for being an hour and a half late tonight.

I tossed the oven mitts onto the counter, adjusted my pink lace teddy, and ran to answer the door. I didn't want to keep him standing outside too long. He had a key to my apartment, so I didn't understand why he decided to knock on the door instead of coming in like he usually did.

I opened the door and smiled at what was awaiting me on the other side. Darkening my doorway stood Corey dressed in a pair of khaki pants and a button down light blue short sleeved Polo shirt, holding a bottle of champagne. He would never step out the house unless he looked his absolute best. As soon as he saw me and the little teddy I was wearing complimented by my "stripper" heels, a smile spread across his face.

"Hey baby," I said motioning for him to come in. Corey wiped his brown, square toe, Kenneth Coles on my welcome mat as I stepped to the side so that he could enter my apartment.

"Well aren't you sexy!" Corey replied. A smile that made his eyes squint in the corners stretched across his bright face.

"And you are the most handsome man I have ever seen." I laughed at my own corny line while enjoying the view of my stunning fiancé.

His eyes glowed as he looked around my apartment at all the candles that were lit. The dining room table was decorated with his favorite foods in covered dishes so he would not be able to see what was in them. I put together a mouthwatering dinner that included smothered pork chops, macaroni and cheese, rice and gravy, green beans, biscuits, and for dessert, a peach cobbler.

During my first year in high school, my mother began to drill in my head that no man wanted a woman that could not cook. She taught me all her recipes and divine entrees and although at the time I did not understand, I understood fully now. No wonder she and my dad were celebrating their 40th wedding anniversary this year. Every since I could remember, whenever my dad came home from a long day at work or church my mother had a hot plate of food waiting for him.

I vowed to do the same for Corey so I wouldn't have to worry about another woman feeding my man. One of the ladies at church always teased and said if her husband was at another woman's house eating it wasn't because he was hungry, but because he was greedy. She made a point to always cook for her man.

John Legend's "All of Me" was playing on the stereo since that was the song that Corey and I were going to dance to at our wedding reception.

"Baby, are you hungry?"

"Starving," Corey said turning his focus from me to the table. He looked as if he wanted to devour me instead.

I took the bottle of champagne from him and sashayed into the kitchen. I placed the bottle in the freezer, and suddenly felt Corey behind me. He gently grabbed my waist, pulling me towards him, and began to kiss my neck. As he pulled me closer I felt the warmth of his body and the rise in his pants. I wanted to sit down and eat dinner first, but I couldn't resist Corey's touch. His hands massaged my breasts as he continued to kiss my neck.

His kisses found my shoulders and at that moment I knew that dinner would have to wait.

"I love you so much," I moaned as Corey turned me around to face him.

"I love you too, baby," he whispered kissing me on the lips while he began to take off my teddy.

He led me to the bedroom and laid me on my freshly made bed. I opened my legs wide to display Corey's recently shaven treasure. I was completely naked, ready and willing to make love with my future husband. It took Corey seconds to get undressed and he began kissing me again. We might have argued the week before but at this very moment everything was wonderful. Passion oozed from my pores as Corey's kisses became more intense. I loved that he knew exactly how to kiss me and how I liked to be touched.

I lost my virginity at the ripe age of sixteen to my high school sweetheart. We were both virgins so the sexual learning process was fresh and thrilling to us. While some girls experienced their first orgasm their very first time having sex or soon after, I experienced mine when I was twenty-two years old, almost four years ago, with Corey.

During my years as a single woman I had been with a handful of guys but never really had a full orgasm. I had almost reached my sexual peak a few times, but something inside of me made my body hold back from this. My boyfriend before Corey was a lot older than me and taught me how to satisfy a man on every level. I focused so much on pleasing him that my needs were often missed. He taught me how to do things to men that would make them fall in love with one touch, but the favor wasn't returned.

With Corey, however, I was able to release in every possible way. Corey showed me that it was ok to be "selfish" in lovemaking and that he was content in gratifying me.

Corey's lips parted from mine and traveled to my neck, lingered at my shoulders, and rested on my breasts.

His right hand palmed my left breast as his tongue circled my nipple. Knowing this was my spot, Corey began to suck gently on my nipple, ever so often softly biting and pulling. He went from my left breast to my right breast sucking, licking, and pulling, causing me to moan and squirm. He abandoned my breasts and his kisses traveled down my stomach and continued in between my legs. He buried his head in between my legs and again the kissing and sucking continued. His tongue pressed firmly on my clit causing me to cry out in pleasure. I couldn't take it anymore; I wanted to feel my fiancé inside of me.

"I need you, Corey!" I screamed.

Corey lifted his head and climbed on top of me. His smile was that of a man who was pleased that he had pleased his woman. Before he entered my body, I gently pushed him off of me, wanting to repay him for the satisfaction he had already given me. My mouth longed to taste him. As if he could read my mind, Corey stood directly in front of me, his long, hard, erection beckoning me to do whatever I desired. I slowly caressed him, moving my hand up and down before taking him all in my mouth. Corey's hands rested on my shoulders as I continued my intense sucking, my mouth moving back and forth, faster and faster, like a woman possessed.

"Rachel, you...gonna...make....me....," Corey uttered, his hands now gripping my shoulders.

I didn't want it to end like this, so I released Corey from my mouth and pulled him on top of me. The flavor of me on his tongue mingled with the taste of him on mine as we kissed while he carefully entered my body. I gasped at the delightful pain that he gave me. Corey's slow steady movement made me moan in satisfaction as I realized that he needed me as much as I needed him.

His pace quickened, and in one smooth motion, Corey flipped me over so that I was now on top of him. I straddled him and kept my eyes locked on his, slowly moving my hips back and forth. Corey closed his eyes and tilted his head back into the pillow.

He grabbed my waist guiding my movements and pushing himself deeper into me. Tears of uninhibited joy filled my eyes as I repeated my lover's name over and over again. Corey's grip tightened around my waist as my motions sped up.

"Rachel, I love you!" he exclaimed as he reached his point of climax.

"I love you too," I groaned, releasing seconds after Corey.

I collapsed on top of him, unable to move. After a few seconds of lying there, I rolled over and smiled at my man. He grinned and then suddenly jumped up. Winking and still smiling as if he had just won the lottery, he asked, "What's for dinner?"

Chapter 4

I half opened my eyes and looked around my dark bedroom. The silver and black alarm clock by my bed flashed 4:45 AM. The street light shone outside my bedroom window dimly as if it was about to go out any day now. I had a couple more hours to sleep before I had to get up for church. I twisted and turned my body so that I could free the grip that Corey had on me in order to go to the bathroom. Whenever we would sleep together he always held me tight like I was going to get up in the middle of the night and run away. I reassured him time and time again that I wasn't going anywhere, but this did not cause him to loosen his hold on me at all. At times I felt like Tina Turner from the movie *What's Love Got To Do With It*. Like Ike, Corey would wake up and ask me where I was going anytime I got out of the bed.

I had to use the bathroom badly and couldn't hold it any longer. I finally released myself from underneath his heavy arm and staggered into the bathroom. I felt my way into the bathroom and flopped down on the toilet. My legs were as heavy as lead and my head throbbed from the champagne that we drank with dinner. No matter how I felt, I was not going to let any of that stop me from going to church.

"Devil, you are a liar," I said out loud.

I might not always do what I should as far as living right, but I did know *how* to live right. I tried to live a righteous life and always have, except for sex before marriage. Looking at Corey, I knew I couldn't resist that temptation even if I tried. I was like the many people who went to church every Sunday knowing right from wrong, but still not living that way.

Thinking like that was crazy when there were people dying each day. I bet half of them had plans to get their lives together, too.

That would soon be corrected when Corey and I were married. I prided myself on being honorable and staying out of trouble. I saw enough misfortune from the people closest to me, Von, my older sister Monica and my younger brother, Daryl. They should really listen to me more, I thought. I could steer them in the right direction.

I walked out of the bathroom, pulled the covers back on my bed, and climbed in next to Corey. As soon as I curled up beside him the sound of his vibrating phone resting on my night stand caught my attention. It was close enough that I could see the name Chrissy flashing on the screen. Who was Chrissy and why the hell was she calling so early? My mind began to race as I thought of every possible reason a woman would call my fiancé's phone at this time of morning.

Calming myself down, I recalled that he had a new store to open and maybe this was one of his employees saying that she was not going to be able to come in the next day. Taking a deep breath, I decided not to jump the gun and ask him about it in the morning. As if he could sense my troubled mind even in his sleep, Corey instantly turned over on his side and reached for me, so that I could cuddle back in his arms. My mind was at peace now and I smiled at the thought of spending every night with him snuggled in our bed as a married couple.

"It won't be long," I whispered in his ear, and closed my eyes, drifting back into dreamland.

***

I sprang up when my alarm clock went off. Like I did most weekend mornings, I hit the snooze button and rolled back over to embrace Corey. Instead of wrapping my arms around him, all I felt was my pillow. I opened my eyes and Corey was standing at the edge of the bed buttoning his shirt.

"Where are you going?" I asked, surprised that he was even up this early on a Sunday morning.

Whenever we went to church I practically had to drag him out of bed and make him get dressed.

"Baby, I am sorry, but I thought I told you. I have to be in DC tomorrow morning so I am flying out today."

"No, you didn't tell me," I replied angrily. I didn't want to ruin what had been such a wonderful weekend together, but I was hurt. Friday after dinner we had made love once again, and Saturday we spent the day shopping and enjoying one another. I assumed that we would end the weekend with going to church together, like always.

"I apologize, baby. I really meant to tell you. I guess I got carried away in all the excitement of seeing you this weekend that I forgot."

"I just thought we were going to be able to go to church together. You know that my father hasn't seen you in a while." I was whining now, which Corey hated.

"I promise I will make it up to you," he said as he finished putting on his clothes.

"Yeah, yeah."

I sat up in bed and searched for the remote control that was tangled up in the sheets. Corey watched me, trying to figure out whether I was mad or not, but I avoided his stares. I turned the TV on and pretended to listen to the singers on *The Bobby Jones Gospel Hour*.

"If I didn't have to do this for work you know that I wouldn't go." Corey stood at the edge of the bed hoping that I would understand, but I wasn't going to grant that wish this morning. On most days I did appreciate everything that his job demanded of him, but today I wanted to be selfish. Since we had just reconnected in such a powerful way after almost a week of minimal interaction, I just didn't want to see him go. "Do what you have to do." I sulked. Still not looking at him, I began to sing along with the choir on TV.

Corey disappeared into the bathroom and when he stepped back out, I snuck a quick glimpse of him.

I wanted to pull him back in bed and make love to him all over again, but that was out the question so I calmly told him to have a nice trip.

Suddenly remembering the phone call from last night I asked him who Chrissy was and why she called so early.

"Who?" he stammered.

"I didn't stutter, Corey. Who is Chrissy?"

"What are you talking about Rachel?" Corey asked.

"Some chick named Chrissy called your cell phone last night," I replied attempting to keep my voice from rising.

"Baby, it probably was one of my employees," he said brushing off my interrogation. "I have all of their numbers programmed in my phone. I will call you as soon as I get home. My plane leaves this afternoon, so I have to go home and pack."

Corey sat down on the bed, leaned over, and kissed me. Even though I was still angry, I was not going to stop him. I sighing deeply, not wanting to see him leave, but satisfied with his answer about the untimely phone call. I trusted him, so there was no need for me to worry about a simple call.

"Ok, be careful," I groaned.

"I will. I love you, Mrs. Rachel Perkins."

Knowing that he only said that to keep me from being pissed, I couldn't help but smile.

"I love you too," I said as I watched him walk out the door.

***

"Don't you look good girl!"

I wiped my tan Nine West heels on Von's mat that read "Bless All Who Enter" and walked into her house. Dressed in a black and tan two piece jacket and skirt set with a black Nine West purse hanging from my shoulder, I smiled at her compliment.

My shoulder length hair was full of body and highlighted curls, and the little bit of makeup that I did wear was flawless.

Dangling from my ears were a set of pearls, a birthday gift from Corey. My heels added almost four inches to my height, which I was thankful for, and made my legs look even sexier with my skirt that stopped right above my knees. I took pride in always looking my best for church. The Lord had blessed me and I was grateful.

"And you are glowing," Von laughed as she put on her silver earrings that were a little too big for church, but I didn't dare tell her that. Von lived in Charlotte, off of Arrowood Road near my dad's church; therefore, I picked her up most Sundays for service.

"Girl, Corey came over this weekend." I walked into her bedroom and stood in front of her dresser mirror applying a little more lip gloss to my already perfect lips.

"Figured that," Von smirked. "That is the only man that can put that stupid grin on your face."

"And the only one that ever will," I replied. I sat down on the bed now, watching Von put on her makeup. The silver bangles on her wrists clanked together as she applied her blue eye shadow.

"Oh Lord! Girl, everyone knows that Corey is the only man that you will ever look at. I do not hate at all, but you have been crazy about that guy since you all met."

As always whenever she talked about me and Corey, Von was correct. The first time that Corey even spoke to me I was wide open and I have been that way since.

"There is nothing wrong with being in love," Von continued, "but I want you to have a little fun before you get married and enjoy your last months as a single woman."

"I do have fun!"

"I am talking about doing things that Ms. Goody Two Shoes wouldn't normally do," Von said as she stepped into her silver and blue pumps that matched her low cut powder blue dress.

"Ok, if I tell you that I will party a little before I jump the broom, will you come on so we won't be late for church?" I asked impatiently.

"That's all I wanted to hear," she said, grinning devilishly.

***

"When praises go up, blessings come down!" My father's powerful baritone voice boomed over the church speakers and rocked every pew in the temple. The church shook with cries of amen and hallelujah. Pacing back and forth across the pulpit, Pastor Robert Simms raised his hands toward the ceiling causing his black and red robe to hang loosely from his body. He was a slim man of average height, in his early sixties, with salt and pepper colored hair. His presence and spirit was one of a God fearing, holy, and honorable man. He lived for God and stood by his word. He was known all over Charlotte for his radiant smile that could light up a room. Anytime someone would see Pastor, the first thing they would notice was his smile. Even through trying times, he always had the same grin that people grew to recognize and love.

Pastoring at New Zion Baptist Church for almost thirty years, the congregation and entire community respected him. He was a handsome chestnut-colored man, and even in his early sixties, the women still flocked to him, vying for his attention. My mother, however, was not going for that. She made it a point to stay by his side and travel to every church or church function he had to attend.

Most people just saw it as being a supportive wife and half of that was true, but the other half was that she was not going to let any of these women too close to her husband. I didn't blame her one bit for that. Just because you are in church doesn't always mean you have the best intentions. Many times, I have seen women flirting with men who were too blind to figure out what was going on until it was too late.

I glanced at my mom, sitting on the front pew where she sat every Sunday. She was a beautiful woman that exuded poise and class.

First Lady Deborah Simms was the same height as my father and a very voluptuous woman. Raised in the small country town of Fargo, Georgia, she was no stranger to hard work and her hands told of that story.

My sister, brother, and I use to tease all the time that we would rather get hit with a belt or switch than my mom's hands. Even though she was raised in the deep South and picked cotton as a child, you couldn't tell that by looking at her now. Makeup perfect on her dark bronze skin, her smile was just as dazzling as her husband's. She was dressed in a black suit with a long jacket and long skirt. Like most Sundays, she had on a hat. This Sunday, she wore a black hat trimmed in gold. She clapped her hands and shouted amen as she gazed at my dad in admiration.

New Zion Baptist Church held close to eight hundred people, and on most Sundays the church was filled to capacity. My dad had developed a small church with three hundred members into a flourishing church, daycare, and community center that was growing more and more each year.

I was swollen with pride at my dad's accomplishments and even more pleased that I could call this valued man my father. I held my head up high when someone recognized me and asked that all too familiar question, "Hey, aren't you Pastor Simms' daughter?" If I was the child of President Obama, I could not have been more proud.

My father finished his sermon and motioned to the choir director to begin singing. Cedric, the choir director, pointed at Jerome, the newest member on the choir. Jerome quickly got out his chair, preceded to the microphone, and stood in front of the church waiting for Cedric to begin playing.

"Girl, who is that?" Von asked, her focus now on Jerome.

"Oh, he is new to the church and choir. He just became a member a few Sundays back," I informed Von, who was staring at him.

Drool seeped from the corners of Von's mouth and she looked as if she was ready to attack Jerome at any second.

"Wait until you hear him sing." I grinned.

Jerome was a tall muscular brother that looked like he had just stepped out of a GQ magazine. He was as dark as Wesley Snipes and he had the smoothest skin I had ever seen.

His eyes were a fascinating light grey that held the mystery of who he was. There was only one world that could truly describe Jerome: Gorgeous.

Jerome began to sing and Von's eyes lit up. The words, "I've had my share of ups and downs, times when there was no one around," flowed from Jerome's mouth as amens and shouts filled the church. Not only was this man just plain handsome, he had an incredible voice as well.

Von leaned over and whispered in my ear, "Is this guy married and if not why didn't you tell me about him?" Von's eyes were set on Jerome and I knew she planned to approach him after church.

"He is not married and he is real cool. He is engaged though."

Von's smile widened like she had just laid eyes on the man of her dreams. My second sentence hadn't meant anything to her.

When Jerome first appeared at the church, all the women, young and old, were in awe of him. Church women are the most aggressive, and every Sunday there was some woman in his face. My father introduced me to him the Sunday that he got baptized and sang his first solo. Everyone was astonished at his stellar voice. Following his solo, I commented on how wonderfully he sang. Ever since then we would speak and hold conversations after church.

Jerome was just as excited as I was about getting married.

His future wife lived in Chicago, attending Medical School there. She was one semester away from graduating, and they planned to be married soon after that.

He talked about his fiancé with such love that I felt close to him since I talked about Corey with the same emotions.

"Von, don't bother that man." I shook my head and frowned at my friend. I didn't want her messing up the good relationship he had with his fiancé. "He is in love with his girl so just leave him alone."

"So you say," was Von's simple reply as she watched him take his seat among the choir. "So you say."

***

"I can't believe you said that to him!" I yelled. I was ashamed but shocked at the same time at how bold my best friend was. A wicked smile spread across Von's face.

"He liked it!"

Not only was she bold, but cocky, too. After service, I greeted Jerome, gave him a hug like I do every Sunday, and introduced him to Von. She took one look at him and asked him if he sounded as good screaming as he did singing. My face turned bloodshot red as Jerome smiled and told her that he really didn't know since he didn't do a lot of screaming. What Von had already said was bad enough, but to make matters worse, she replied, "That's because you've never been with a woman like me."

I was too embarrassed at this point. I asked Jerome to excuse my friend and told him that I would talk to him later. Snatching Von's arm, I pulled her away and scolded her for saying something as vulgar as that to an engaged and saved man – in church no less. Her rebuttal was, "But he is still a man."

I must admit that I was a little jealous of how upfront and aggressive Von was, but not of her awful decisions and actions. I was the type of woman that waited for men to approach me, but Von was the complete opposite. Whenever she saw something she wanted she went after it and nobody got in her way.

Ninety percent of the time she got what she wanted, but this time would be different. Jerome was a God fearing man that loved his future wife.

***

I walked into my apartment exhausted from last night's activities and being up early this morning for church.

After changing into a pair of blue yoga pants and an oversized black t-shirt, I plopped down on the couch to watch television for a while, or let it watch me. I positioned myself comfortably on my sofa and heard my home phone ring. Thinking that it was Corey, I reached for my cordless phone on the floor beside the couch.

"Hello," I sang not even looking at the caller ID.

"Well hello, Ms. 'I'm too busy to hold a conversation with my mother.'"

Damn, I should have looked at the ID on the phone, I thought. For the last few months, every time my mother called all she talked about was the wedding. She never asked how I was doing, or asked about any other things that were going on in my life. It was always the "wedding this" and the "wedding that". I couldn't remember the last time my mom and I held a conversation that had nothing to do with my upcoming nuptials. My mom's obsession with my wedding even caused me to stop visiting her as much. Every time I went to my parent's house my mom was shoving another damn wedding magazine in my face.

I remained silent as I listened to my mother talk about how she didn't get a chance to chat with me today at church and she had some things to go over with me about the wedding. I sighed heavily over the phone hoping that my mother would detect that I was tired and really didn't want to talk about my wedding.

"You all really need to think about how you want everything to be set up and what food you want to serve," she said.

"Mom, I really don't feel like talking about this now," I said calmly interrupting her discourse over serving ham or chicken.

"Rachel, you need to talk about it. That's what's wrong with you and that's why we can't get this stuff taken care of," she said harshly.

At that moment my calmness flew out the window. "Sorry I am not consumed by this wedding like you are, but I refuse to talk about this today.
I will call you back later Mom," I said in one breath.

I clicked the phone off and tossed it on the floor. Seconds later the phone rang again but I was not going to answer it. Those few minutes on the phone with my mother had soured my entire day and made me even more ready to get this wedding over with. I knew I had been rude, and I planned on calling my mom back and apologizing, but right now all I wanted to do was lie on my couch and sleep.

Chapter 5

I stared out of my office window at the different shades of blue and suddenly wished I was somewhere or somebody else with no concerns or worries. The sun brightened the tiny room and for a second, I felt at peace. For a second, I forgot about the conversation that my mom and I had and the nasty message she left on my voice mail this morning. The moment did not last long because I scanned my desk and saw all the work that I needed to get started on. My mood from last night had trickled over and I was sitting in my office on a Monday morning with the same sour attitude.

The only thing that would cheer me up would be to hear Corey's sweet serene voice telling me how much he loved me. He'd also left a message that he made it to DC safely and to give him a call when I got a chance. After my mother's call, I hadn't felt like talking to anyone else, so I turned my ringer off and went to bed. I twirled back around in my chair to face my desk and reached for my office phone. I dialed Corey's number expecting him to answer the phone with an "I love you" or silly little comment he always had for me.

"Yeah, what's up?" He snapped.

I glanced at the phone to make sure I had dialed the right number. The number was correct, but Corey didn't seem too pleased to hear from me.

"Hey baby," I said hoping to put a smile on his face so he could return the favor.

"Hey Rachel, what's going on?"

"Are you busy?"

"Not really," he answered quickly.

"Baby I had an awful day yesterday and I am not doing too well today. My mom called and we sort of got in an argument."

"Was it about the wedding?"

"Of course!"

"Rachel, you know how to handle your mother and you know this is our wedding."

This conversation was not going as I planned. Instead of making me feel better I was starting to feel worse.

"Baby, I know but it gets frustrating," I whined.

"I don't know what you want me to tell you, Rachel."

I sensed anger in Corey's voice so I opted to change the subject. "What's going on with you?" I asked.

"You called me about nonsense and I got real issues on this job. My boss is on my ass right now so if you have something important to tell me, go ahead. Otherwise, I have work to do," Corey huffed.

"I didn't know that you were dealing with things, Corey. You should have said something when I asked were you busy."

"Like that would have mattered," he mumbled.

That was the straw that broke the camel's back.

"Corey, I have had a rough night and morning and I was looking for you to cheer me up but I see that is not going to happen so I'll talk to you later," I said in the nastiest tone I could muster up.

"Whatever Rachel," was all I heard before the phone became silent.

I wasn't shocked that Corey hung up on me since he tended to do that lately whenever we argued, but the fact that I could not even turn to him when I was feeling down troubled me. I swung my chair back around and stared out the window again. Regardless of how I felt the sky was still just as exquisite as before. I took a deep breath and exhaled loudly as I heard my desk phone ring.

"Rachel Simms speaking." My tone was somber. I hoped that the person on the other end did not recognize this.

"I see you forgot all about me."

"Excuse me?" I steadied myself as I tried to figure out what man's deep raspy voice had me repositioning in my chair.

The man laughed to himself and even that was as enticing as his voice. Something about it calmed me.

"Guess you had a good weekend seeing as how you don't even know my voice now. Just forgot about my papers on Friday, huh?" Terrence continued to laugh.

I hit myself for not being able to pick up on his voice. I spoke to him every week so I should have known who he was from the beginning.

"I apologize Mr. Walker," I muddled, trying to hide my shame. I shuffled through the stack of papers on my desk attempting to find the ones that I should have faxed to him on Friday.

"We are being so official today, Ms. Simms," he said, still laughing to himself. "I apologize for my un-business like teasing."

"Wow *you* are in a good mood." I recalled our first couple of conversations when he acted like an ass on the phone. Even though I talked to him every week, his soothing voice caught me off guard today.

"I am alive, so that qualifies me to be in a great mood."

I left the papers alone for a second and turned back around to stare out the window again as Terrence continued to talk about his family spending the weekend in Baltimore. Through our talks I knew that Terrence was married. He spoke of his family every now and then, but not often. Whenever we talked it was pretty much me enlightening him on the never ending wedding plans.

After a couple of minutes of listening to him talk, my spirits were lifted a bit. I shared with Terrence how my weekend went and why I sounded like I had an attitude when he called. He listened carefully and I realized that this was the longest conversation that we'd ever had.

When Snyder & Lawry began to help their Atlanta-based company, I told Terrence I was getting married and he would ask how that was going every so often, but I never went into detail about my feelings until today.

Something about his voice made it easy for me to open up to him. I could tell he was actually paying attention to me. I finished rambling on about my frustrations and felt a sense of relief come over me.

"Don't think about what is going on now, just focus on the outcome. You are marrying someone you love and after the wedding none of the other stuff will matter," Terrence said.

Terrence's words made me feel much better, and he was right; after the wedding I wouldn't have to agonize over any of this.

"Don't let anyone steal your joy. You might think that your fiancé is not going through anything, but believe me, he is, so just be patient with him," he said.

I smiled for the first time today. "Mr. Walker, I really needed that. Thank you so much."

"Anytime Ms. Simms, now let's get down to business."

***

I left the office still feeling energized from the conversation with Terrence. Instead of running on my treadmill I chose to relish in the fresh air and jog around my neighborhood. Being out in the elements, feet pounding on the pavement and gravel, would provide a better work out and help me reach my goal even quicker. I texted Corey before leaving my office and told him that I was sorry he was going through things and that I loved him. He replied back that he loved me, too. Terrence's advice was working already.

Usually, the middle of June in the Carolinas would feel like the devil's kitchen, but today was a rather cool day. It was still hot and humid but not the heat stroke sizzling weather that was often associated with summers in the south.

I laced up my blue and grey Nikes and started out with a light jog around my block. After five minutes of jogging, I saw a familiar sky blue Nissan Altima driving up slowly beside me.

Von's brother lived in the apartment complex about a mile down the street from mine and I often waved to him in passing. He was ten years older than me and Von, and I've known him as long as I've known Von.

Kevin's copper skin and seductive lips made him ooze sex appeal. He was a fairly decent looking guy, but the fact that he carried himself with confidence and had the cutest dimples ever created added to his charm. He was shorter than most men, standing at 5"7, but from his chiseled frame one could tell that he stayed in the gym and was very health conscious. Growing up, he often joked with me and said that he was going to marry me when I got older. As a little girl, I was infatuated with him. I thought he was the best looking guy in the world and I caught myself daydreaming about him while in school. Von knew that I had a huge crush on her brother and she wasn't bothered by it. Kevin moved to Texas with his wife when we were in college, but they had recently gotten a divorce so he moved back to the Carolinas to be with his family.

As the car got closer, I slowed down and tried to catch my breath. Kevin stopped and rolled down the windows.

"Hey there Ms. Rachel," Kevin smiled and winked at me, tapping his finger on the steering wheel.

"Hi Kevin," I said bent over with my hands on my knees gasping for air.

"You working out a little?"

"Yep, just trying to get into shape," I replied standing up straight and taking notice of Kevin's smile and his sexy dimples.

"Your shape is looking good to me," Kevin said winking again.

I blushed and looked away. Even though I was a lot older now I still felt like a little girl whenever I talked to him.

"So are you coming with Von to the cookout at my mom's house?"

"I didn't know about the cookout, but I am sure that Von will tell me about it," I said turning to look at Kevin again.

"Make sure you come so I can try to tempt you before you get married. See you later, Ms. Rachel." Kevin laughed and drove away before I had a chance to respond. That boldness definitely runs in the family, I thought to myself.

I didn't know whether to be turned on or offended by his remark. Did he really think I could be tempted by him? Before I met Corey, I used to tease Von and tell her that one day I was going to find out what her brother was working with. However, my childhood crush on Kevin was long gone by now.

I finished my run and planned to relax for the rest of the night. I ran my bath water, poured two capfuls of lavender bubble bath in the streaming water and thought about all the things that I needed to do for the wedding. Just the thoughts frustrated me. I removed them from my mind, climbed in my garden tub and slid down into the warm bubbles.

My thoughts went to Kevin and the comment he made. I smiled knowing that another man wanted me and envisioned flirting with him a little more at the upcoming cookout. I loved to flirt and put hope within arm's reach for guys, but they all knew that my body and heart belonged to Corey.

The entire time that Corey and I have been together cheating never crossed my mind. I enjoyed the interest from other men like most women, but flirting is the farthest that it would ever go. Corey also never gave me a reason to even think about being unfaithful. He kept me satisfied and paid so much attention to me that adding someone else into that was unheard of. I couldn't imagine making love to someone other than him.

My mischievous thoughts that led to my hands disappearing under the bubbles and sliding between my legs were interrupted by the phone ringing. I prayed it wasn't someone that would put me back in the bitter mood I had experienced earlier.

I stood and stepped out the tub to see who was disturbing my peaceful time. Glancing at the caller ID, I saw that it was my sister Monica. Monica and I were not just sisters, but best friends, and we talked at least every other day. We had a very special relationship that I cherished.

"Hey girl," Monica mumbled as I answered the phone.

"Hey, what's going on?" I asked.

"Nothing much. Just trying to get this man out my house," Monica whispered.

Another day with Monica and her drama. I dried off, wrapped the towel around me and got comfortable in my bed fully aware that this phone call would last at least two hours.

Monica was six years older than me but functioned like she was still in her teens. She and her boyfriend Tony had been dating for nine months and living together for three. They met one night when Monica stopped at the gas station next to her house and he was standing outside smoking a cigarette. I warned her that she didn't know anything about this guy and she was skeptical, too, until they slept together. Once he put it on her, she was at his every call. This girl would get up in the middle of the night and pick him up from his cousin's or sister's house, wherever he might be at that time. He didn't have a car and he was, as he said, "between places". In other words, he didn't have anywhere that he could call home, either. I guess he hit the jackpot when he found my simple sister.

After a few months of dating he moved right into her place and started living off of her. He claimed that he had a job but for some unknown reason he was laid off and now he was in the process of looking for something else. Tony sat in the house all day smoking weed, and when Monica came home, he expected her to cook his food. Monica considered all of this "cute" until other women started calling her house. Now all she wanted was to get him out and claimed she didn't know how to do it.

I felt sorry for her because she was so naïve and believed everything that men would say.

But, there comes a time when all women have to wake up and get rid of the men in their lives that are holding them down or not bringing anything valuable to them.

"You there sis?" Monica asked.

"Who are you talking to now?" Tony screamed in the background.

"Girl, do I need to call Daryl and come over there?"

Daryl, my younger brother, was two years younger than me and he hated Tony just as much as I did. Even though we despised him, we both knew that Monica had to live her own life. My dad even knew about Monica's situation and every Sunday he would pray for her at church.

"I just have to put her in God's hands now," he would say whenever we told him the latest happenings with Monica. He didn't meddle in our lives like most parents, or like my mom. He accepted the fact that we were grown, with the exception of the night we all thought Tony had hit Monica. My dad and Daryl hopped in my dad's beat up red pickup truck and gunned it to her house faster than the roadrunner on *The Looney Tunes*. That was the only night that my father "laid down his religion" as older folks would say, grabbed his antique shot gun, and rushed out to protect his child.

Thank God it was just a false alarm and Tony had not hit her. She had screamed and dropped the phone that night. My initial thought was that he struck her, but he just slammed the door and left. She could be so dramatic at times, but no matter what, Monica, Daryl, and I stuck together. No one was going to lay a hand on one of us without answering to all of us.

"No, don't call Daryl!" Monica whispered loudly.

"Then why are you whispering?" I was trying to be there for Monica but was slowly getting irritated at her trying to hide that she was talking to me from Tony.

"Sis, I am going to call you back," Monica said, and slammed the phone down.

Another night of this. I slid out of bed, threw on a pair of jeans and a t-shirt, unwrapped my hair, and brushed it back into a ponytail. I stood by the phone for a moment debating on whether to call Daryl or not. The alarm clock by my bed read 8:30 and that meant he was still at work.

I wouldn't bother him tonight since he would be ready to kick ass. I would have to handle this on my own. I grabbed my keys from the kitchen table and ran out of my apartment on my way to Monica's house.

Chapter 6

Monica lived in Charlotte off of Freedom Drive, twenty minutes away from my place. Her neighborhood was definitely not the safest and I wouldn't dare travel over there late night or early morning by myself. I begged her to move many times but she seemed to like it. She was the ghetto one in the family anyway; the loudest one and the one that was always in fights growing up. The hood one.

I pulled into Briarstone Apartments and choked on the smell of beer and marijuana smoke that seeped through my halfway rolled down window. I thought of the Goodie Mob song, "Cell Therapy" as I punched in my sister's code to the gate. The part where they say, "But every now and then I wonder if the gate was put up to keep crime out or keep our ass in," came to mind.

Monica stayed on the back side of the apartment complex. I dodged and swerved to miss the numerous potholes that lined the streets leading to her place. All the buildings were a dingy grey tint and looked like they were crowded around one another like buzzards on a piece of fresh raw meat. Damn, I need to get my sister out of here.

I parked next to her black Toyota Camry and dashed up the one flight of stairs to her apartment. I knocked on apartment 203 and noticed that it was awfully quiet compared to all the noise that was in the background when she called me only thirty minutes ago. After waiting a few seconds, I put in my key that she had given me, and unlocked her door.

Monica sat on the floor in her living room beside her couch. She was positioned with her knees to her chest and her face rested on top of them. She rocked back and forth as she silently sobbed in her hands. My sister, at the age of thirty two was a very alluring woman.

She was "thick", as men in the South liked to call women that had an ample chest and a large booty, and she carried all that very well. She dressed her age and kept her hair in a simple short cut. We both had the same light caramel skin and resembled one another, but she was a few inches taller than me. Her height was the only way that most people could tell us apart. I acted older and I admit at times I was the bossier one. Even though Daryl was the youngest, he looked older, and was taller than both me and Monica. Out of all of us he favored my dad the most. He was slender like my father with the same complexion as me and Monica. All three of us looked alike; and it was obvious we were siblings.

"Monica?" I walked in and sat next to my big sister on the floor. She looked at me, leaned over, and buried her head into my chest as she started to cry again. After hanging up the way she did, Monica knew that I would be right over. Every time they argued and she called me, I came over to make sure my big sister was alright.

"Sis, what happened and where is Tony?" I asked. I knew that they probably argued over something stupid and she told him to leave. She was good for demanding that he get out but he would come back in a day or two and she would allow him right back in.

"I asked him to leave," she said sniffing in between cries. I lifted her head up and wiped her tear-filled eyes with my hand.

"What happened this time, Monica?" I tried to show her that I was concerned, but frustration got the better part of me. Monica stopped crying for a moment and stared at me.

"You know Rachel everyone doesn't have a picture perfect relationship like you think you have," Monica said glaring at me.

Shocked by what I was hearing, I began to get pissed. I was trying to help my sister get over her sorry excuse for a boyfriend and now she was attacking me.

"I don't think that I have a picture perfect relationship but I do know that Corey respects me and I don't take any mess off of him."

I got up from Monica's hard floor covered with the ugliest rust colored carpet ever, and sat down on her dingy brown sofa.

"Oh, and I guess Tony doesn't respect me," she replied. She sneered at me like I was the one that had walked out on her and not Tony.

"Well, you are the one sitting on the floor crying like the world has come to an end," I smirked.

"Rachel, if you came over here to be all superior like you always are then you can leave, too."

Monica was hurting but she never talked to me like that. We had our little arguments, but she was being rather harsh tonight.

"Okay, Okay. I came over here because I was worried about you. You know that I almost called Daryl."

"Oh my God, that is the last thing I need. The two of you hovering over me like I am going to lose it."

"Where is Tony?" I asked again trying to find out what happened.

"I told you I asked him to leave." She got up off of the floor and sat on the couch beside me. Her grey tank top was torn at the bottom and I wondered if they had fought before he left.

"Monica, if you are alright and you don't want to talk about it then I am going home," I said standing up and reaching down to retrieve my keys from the floor. I was already tired and Monica seemed rather defensive tonight.

"Sis, please stay. I am sorry, I am just hurt about what he has done this time," Monica pleaded.

Waiting for her to go into her usual long drawn out spiel, I sat back down on the couch and dropped my keys back to the floor.

Monica began to tell me how one of Tony's ex-girlfriends called her and left a message on her phone that she had been sleeping with Tony and was now pregnant with his child. At first she didn't believe this woman, but when Tony got home she played the message and he didn't deny that she was pregnant. They began to argue and he said that he planned to tell her whenever the time was right. He had gotten her pregnant when he first met Monica. This woman was nine months pregnant and was due any day now. He claimed that they were not sleeping together anymore and he found out that she was pregnant two months ago. Of course Monica did not believe his story so she threw him out.

"I need a drink," Monica declared.

My sister hopped off the couch and went in her kitchen. She poured two shots of vodka and brought the bottle and shot glasses back into the living room.

"Take a shot with me, little sis," Monica said trying to smile after spending the last few minutes crying.

"Do you believe him?" I asked. I took the shot glass that had Atlanta printed across the bottom out of Monica's hand. Normally I wouldn't drink during the week, especially the beginning of the week, but my sister needed me and I wanted to be there for her.

"Part of me does believe him, and then part of me thinks he has been screwing this broad the whole time. Regardless, he is about to have a child and you know that is something I can't give him."

Two years ago Monica discovered that she could not have children. She was dating a guy named Brent for three years and everyone in the family adored him. He longed to have a child, and instead of Monica and Brent getting married first they set their sights on having a baby. After a year of trying and nothing happening, they sought assistance and went to the doctor.

After a battery of tests, Monica learned that she was infertile.

It was heart-breaking for them and eventually was the factor that ended the relationship. Brent wanted children more than he wanted Monica. After Brent, her standards lowered, well pretty much went into the gutter, and along came Tony.

Monica talked on and on about not trusting Tony. I tossed my head back and swallowed the shot in one gulp. The liquor stung the back of my throat and sent a burning sensation throughout my chest. That was all I could handle for the night.

"I don't know what to do now," Monica said, downing her shot and pouring another one.

"I am not going to tell you what to do, but don't let Tony run all over you. Stand up for yourself."

"I know, but I love him. Why does this always happen to me?" Monica blubbered, starting to cry again.

Before I realized what I was saying, "Stop finding men in the gutter and maybe you wouldn't go through this," came out of my mouth. I didn't mean to say something so insensitive to my sister. She was in so much agony, but this was one of those times that I spoke before thinking. Monica's tears suddenly stopped and she glared at me once again.

"I can't believe you just said that, Rachel." Monica's voice was filled with rage and her eyes were overcome with pain. "I would like to be alone now."

"Sis, I didn't mean to say that," I implored.

I pleaded with my sister to understand that I didn't mean to hurt her feelings but her voice remained calm as she asked me to leave again.

"I know that you are in love and you would never ever hurt Corey, but everyone isn't as perfect as you." Monica sniffed as she stood up and marched into her bedroom. "Lock the door when you leave!" she shouted right before she slammed her bedroom door.

Chapter 7

Three weeks passed and Monica was still not talking to me. This was the longest amount of time that had gone by without my sister and me speaking to each other. I went over the conversation in my head a million times and each time I felt worse and worse for basically implying that she deserved what was happening to her. Over the last few weeks, I'd called Monica many times, at least twice a day, but it went to her voicemail. I called Daryl to see if he had heard from her and of course she told him how uppity I was acting. I had to admit that I did think my relationship with Corey surpassed most. We had our fights and arguments from time to time, but we always made up and he never disrespected me. With the exception of the last few weeks, I could count on one hand how many times Corey and I had actually quarreled. But now that we were planning this wedding, disagreeing had become a ritual between us.

I woke up Friday morning after taking another gut wrenching phone call from my mother the night before and figured the only way to get her off my back was to make at least one decision about the wedding. Choosing something as simple as the cake would not be dreadful. Corey loved sweets so he should not have any problems helping me with this one simple task. At least that is what I was telling myself when I got out of bed.

I arrived at my office around eight. Corey went to work at five in the morning, so I decided to give him a call to see if we could spend the weekend together and pick out a cake. I dialed his number and opened the blinds in my office to let the radiant sunlight in and give the room the luster that would help lift my spirits.

Corey answered the phone cheerfully singing, "Hey baby."

"Hey sweetheart," I replied. I glanced at the ceiling and thanked God that he was not in the nasty mood I always seemed to catch him in.

"What's going on, sexy?"

"Nothing much. I was just calling to see if you were coming this way tomorrow so we could spend some time together."

"Sorry babe," Corey said in mid yawn. "Derrick is having a party for all the bruhs at his place in Augusta, so I am heading to Georgia for the weekend." Corey would never turn down hanging with his fraternity brothers just to select a wedding cake, but I wanted to try anyway.

"So I am not going to see you at all?" I asked.

"Nah babe, we can get up next weekend if that is cool with you."

"Not really. I thought that we could pick out our wedding cake tomorrow," I said half pleading and half whining. I swung my chair around to face the window and closed my eyes. Please don't let this be another argument.

Corey sighed. "You can handle that without me right?"

"Well since it is *our* wedding I figured it might be nice if *we* picked out *our* cake." My pleading and whining turned into straight sarcasm at this point.

"Rachel, don't start. Please. Not today. We can pick out wedding cake next weekend."

"Don't start what?" My voice rose as I swung my chair back around and jumped up. I walked over and closed my office door so no one else could hear the fight that was about to happen.

"Rachel, don't start the bullshit today," Corey said. His voice was calm and nonchalant which only frustrated me more.

"I don't ask you for all your time, Corey, but we are getting married in nine months and I need some help."

"You don't need me. You have your mother and everyone else that is begging to help you. I could care less about the wedding plans. Just tell me where and when and I will be there."

"Well contrary to popular belief I am not superwoman!" I screamed. I lowered my voice after I realized that someone in the hall may have heard me yelling into the phone even through the closed door.

I glanced up and looked through the small window of my office door. I saw Doug creep by.

A fierce pain struck my forehead like lightening striking a tree and splitting it in half. Another wedding headache. I searched for my faithful medicine bottle, barely able to see.

"Whatever, Rachel. I love you but I am not going to get into it with you over this."

Before I could really let Corey have it like I wanted and needed to, I heard that all too familiar click at the end of the phone. My heart felt like it was on The Drop Zone at the Carowinds amusement park. The ride took park-goers up 100 feet and then dropped them; talking to Corey had my heart floating in the air and one argument sent it crashing to the ground. I sat down in my chair and leaned back, trying to get my thoughts together. I was so upset that my temperature rose and sweat was starting to trickle down my neck. I removed my white blazer and unbuttoned the top button of my purple blouse. I did not want to cry, but I was so fed up of Corey carrying on as if he didn't care about the wedding and everything I was going through that I felt tears threatening to fall.

Rachel, don't cry. Too late. One single tear fell on the yellow folder that was on my desk. I sniffed and tried to get myself together. Another tear found the first one and joined it, making a home together. I laid my head on my desk and cried until I had no more tears left. All the misery and distress that I had endured for the past month came out in a puddle on the stack of work that had to be completed by the end of the day. How could I be getting married in a few months and feel like everything was on me to do?

My head was still throbbing and my eyes began to swell.

I reminded myself of where I was and all the work I had to do. I needed someone. I needed to feel like I wasn't doing this all by myself. The one person that I was supposed to go to for love and comfort was not there and I didn't even know if he felt the same pain that I was feeling.

The sound of my desk phone startled me and I carefully lifted my head from my desk. Taking a deep breath I answered my phone on the third ring.

"Rachel speaking."

"Of course it is," the voice on the other end said.

"Hello, Mr. Walker."

"Okay, stop with the 'Mr. Walker'," Terrence said, laughing.

"Excuse me, Terrence, how are you?"

"No, the question is how are you? You sound like something's wrong."

"Same ole same ole."

"You want to talk about it?" he asked in such a sincere tone that a part of me wanted to tell him what happened. I suddenly remembered our last conversation and that he had to cheer me up. I didn't want to make that a habit.

"Not today."

"Okay, whatever the lady wishes. I am here to help."

"I doubt anyone can do that at this moment," I sighed as I thought about Corey.

"I tell you what, I will actually be up your way in a few weeks to visit my father. He just moved to Charlotte and I have not seen him in a while. I also have to come by your office to pick up some reports, so why don't we do lunch or something?"

"That would be nice," I said trying to put some sort of excitement in my voice.

"Great, I have talked to you for so long and I would love to put a face with that voice."

"Are you ready for the report?" I asked.

I wanted to hurry up and get off the phone with Terrence so I could call Corey back before he became too busy at work.

If Terrence noticed the sudden change in my tone, he didn't say so.

"Sure thing," he said.

***

I dragged myself into Von's house and collapsed on the couch.

"I know that is not what you are wearing," Von said. She examined me like I was a model about to walk the runway.

"Uh, yes ma'am and what is wrong with this?" I sat up on her couch and glanced over my outfit.

"It's sad that you even have to ask," she said turning her nose up and walking back into her bedroom.

We were going to her mom's cookout and since I considered her family my family, too, I had on a pair of black jeans and a yellow short-sleeve shirt with the words SPOILED ROTTEN written across the front in white letters. Nothing special. I even bought a new pair of white Nike Air Max sneakers to wear to the cookout. I was very comfortable and that is all that mattered to me.

I wasn't in the mood for Von today and I thought about not going to the cookout at all, but I needed to do something to take my mind off of Corey. I was not able to call him back and he hadn't even dialed my number since hanging up on me yesterday. He was now in Georgia partying, and living it up with his frat brothers and not giving a second thought to his soon-to-be-wife.

Von strutted out of her bedroom in a beautiful brownish gold halter sun dress. The dress stopped right above her knees and showed off her exquisitely fit slender legs. I wondered why she got so glamorous for a cookout at her mom's house.

"I didn't know that there were going to be Charlotte Bobcats and Panthers players at the cookout," I said.

Her outfit made me glance over my clothes once again.

"Haven't you realized that I am dazzling everywhere I go?"

Von posed in front of me with her hands on her hips as if she was taking pictures for a swimsuit magazine.

"Don't worry girlie, we are going to do something about your outfit," she announced.

"Von, come on now. You know that I am not in the mood to go anywhere, and on top of that you are going to make me change my clothes."

"Yes, I am! You are 26 years old looking like you are 62!" Von laughed and grabbed her gold clutch so that we could get going. "We have some time on our hands, you know that black folks are always late no matter what. We can swing by the mall and get you something to wear so you can show off that little figure that you have worked so hard to get."

"Guess I really don't have a choice in the matter," I sighed. I pulled myself off the couch and followed Von out the door.

***

"Damn, Rachel you wearing the hell out that dress," Kevin whispered in my ear giving me a tight strong hug. I walked off smiling. Damn right I am wearing this dress. After fussing with Von about every outfit she picked out, I finally settled on a lilac sun dress that complimented my honey skin tone. It was strapless and clingy, hitting all the right places on my body perfectly. Von threw up her hands in the middle of Macy's and shouted, "Thank God!" when I pranced out of the dressing room. The salesgirl gave us an evil glare as I twirled around in the dress and Von screamed, "Work it girl!"

I must admit, buying that dress and seeing all Von's male cousins and friends watch my every move when I got out of her silver Yukon truck and sashayed my way across the yard boosted my spirits a hundred percent.

"You know my brother still wants you." Von once again gave me her famous devilish grin as we went into the kitchen where her mom was cooking. I ignored her.

"Don't you look pretty," Ms. Mary said, giving me a hug.

Von's mother was the same complexion as Von, a beautiful dark mahogany, and was slender just like Von. She was in her early sixties and her short black mixed with strands of silver hair made her look not a day over forty. She carried herself with such dignity and pride that you just had to respect her. Ms. Mary separated from Von's father about three years ago and after that she went through a total transformation. While we were growing up, Ms. Mary was conservative and the true "wife" type. She waited on Von's father hand and foot for thirty-five years. After many years of obeying his every command and being the best wife she could be, she found out that Von's father had been unfaithful several times over the past few years and was still doing so with a woman he had been in a relationship with for twelve years.

When he refused to give up his girlfriend and be devoted to Ms. Mary, she immediately filed for divorce and moved out of the house where they had raised Kevin and Von. Ms. Mary now lived in a peaceful suburban area on the outskirts of Charlotte. She owned her own catering business, Mary's Delights, and her vibrant charm flowed into her dishes, making her food dance on your tongue after every bite. Her cuisine was out of this world, so of course she was going to cater me and Corey's wedding.

"Thank you, Ms. Mary," I said. I cut a small piece of her honey bun cake and devoured it in one bite. Today would definitely have to be my day off my diet.

"Baby, you ready for your big day?" Ms. Mary asked.

"I am getting there." I forced a smile, but anyone could tell it was not genuine.

"You don't sound so sure." She glanced at me while putting the finishing touches on her potato salad. "I know you love Corey and he is a wonderful young man but if you have any doubts, communication is the key. Sit down and discuss everything you are feeling with him before you walk down the aisle. Marriage can be amazing, but it is also hard work."

"Yes ma'am," I said, taking in Ms. Mary's advice.

"Hopefully, Ms. Thang over there will settle down one day." Ms. Mary pointed at Von who was sitting on a stool at the bar about to dig into the potato salad her mom had just finished.

"Nothing wrong with hoping," Von giggled, putting a spoonful of potato salad in her mouth.

Chapter 8

"Yeah, she seems like a handful," Jerome said shaking his head. I was apologizing again for letting Von loose on him a few Sundays ago.

"It's cool, Rachel. Believe it or not, I have had a lot of women approach me the same way," he said with a stunning smile that showed all his dazzling white teeth. His mustache and goatee were lined perfectly, as if he had just hopped out of his barber's chair.

Youth revival was going on this week at my church, and I bumped into Jerome on the way to the restroom. He had just sung with the choir and was getting a quick sip of water.

"So how have you been lately? I know that planning a wedding can get stressful."

"Ok I guess." I tried again to force a smile.

"Believe me, it will get better."

"Yeah, I hope so," I sighed.

"If you ever need someone to talk to, I am a great listener." Jerome brushed past me and allowed his hand to touch mine while heading to the water fountain.

I glanced back and smiled at him as I opened the bathroom door and walked in. I would be in a world of trouble if I was single. The more weight I lost the more my confidence grew and I was starting to realize that others saw this, too.

***

"So Friday it is," Terrence said with a hint of enthusiasm in his voice that I had never heard before.

"Sure," I replied.

I hoped that Terrence's conversation during our lunch meeting on Friday would once again take my mind off Corey and the funky mood that he was still in.

It was Wednesday afternoon and a week and a half since Corey had gone to Augusta to hang with his frat brothers. He had not made any plans to come and help me with the wedding cake or anything to do with the wedding for that matter.

Worse, he still had not brought up the subject of coming to see me. I even offered to drive to Greenville to see him, but after so many excuses from him I declined my offer. Our conversations had become very bland and the calls between us were only made out of routine. I got off the phone with Terrence and started to crunch numbers for the weekly budget meeting. Nothing like hard work to take your mind off of what is really going on in your life, I thought as my desk phone rang once again.

"Rachel Simms," I answered. I didn't care how I sound on the phone at this point.

"Girl, cheer up! We are going out this weekend!" Von shouted.

"What are you talking about now?" I groaned. Maybe Von would be the one to pick up on my attitude. I needed to vent about Corey and what was going on with our relationship and who better to dump all my feelings onto than my best friend.

"I am talking about the jazz festival that they are having downtown this weekend!"

"That's cool," I said. I was surprised that Von still hadn't picked up on the depression in my voice.

"Oh Lord, Ms. Drama Queen, what is wrong with you now?"

"Corey again, girl."

Von cut me off as soon as I said his name. "No, we are not going to do this today. I know that you are going through a lot but being this stressed out is not cool. Whatever it is, Rachel I can't believe it's that serious."

I sighed and decided not to even talk about Corey today.

Maybe I just needed some time to focus on some other things.

"Ok you are right," I said.

"When am I ever wrong, girl?"

I smiled. "So when are we going shopping for this festival?"

***

Hours became days, days became weeks, and in no time a month had come and gone. Eight months until the wedding of the year, as my mom often called it, and I was still so stressed out that my hair had begun shedding terribly and was slowly falling out.

Corey finally made time to come down one Saturday to select the wedding cake, and even though we spent the day together, things were still somewhat tense between us. He didn't spend the night like he usually did when coming to see me, due to his work schedule the next day. He went back home right after we left the baker, giving me a light kiss and telling me that he loved me. We didn't make love or hold one another; just a simple peck and a bland "I love you".

As he left, I thought about the way brides and grooms planned the wedding together, looking lovingly into each other eyes, ready to become husband and wife. Somehow that sweet vision was not the reality that I was living. I still kept that small ray of hope that, no matter what happened between Corey and me, when I walked down the aisle on our wedding day he would gaze at me with tears in his eyes and love in his heart, knowing that I was the one that made his life complete.

Chapter 9

"I am so sorry that I have to cancel our lunch today," Terrence said. His phone cut in and out and I could barely make out the muffled words. He had rescheduled the first lunch meeting since his dad's plan for moving was put off a month. This was his second time cancelling on me. He informed me that he would still be on the road traveling to Charlotte when I took lunch and he wouldn't make it in until that evening.

"Believe me it's fine, I understand. I was going to leave work early anyway."

"Hold on, let me call you right back," Terrence said just before his phone completely died.

I was glad that he had to miss lunch since I was going to take a half day and leave at one. Ten minutes later my desk phone rang again and Terrence's number appeared on the caller ID.

"Okay, I can hear you now. Sorry about that," he said, apologizing for the bad reception on his cell phone. "You were leaving early today?"

"Yeah, I am going out tonight and I wanted to do a little shopping and get some rest."

"I will be up that way later this evening. You mind if I give you a call so you can tell me what hot spots I need to check out? I haven't been to Charlotte in a very long time."

"Sure," I said. I leaned back in my chair and recited my cell phone number to Terrence.

The last few weekends, Von and I had gone out to various clubs and bars, and even though I didn't want to admit it, I was really enjoying myself. I loved the attention that I was getting from men.

I delighted in watching their smiles turn into frowns as I told them that I was engaged and getting married in a few months even more.

This Friday night we were going to a club that only played Reggae music. Crystals was a popular club in Charlotte that Von frequented, but it would be my first time going. I fancied dancing to Reggae music as men looked longingly at me sway my hips back and forth. We planned to meet a couple of guys Von worked with and before we got there, Von told me that the guys were treating us to whatever we wanted all night. It had been a while since I was really tipsy so tonight was going to be my night.

I deserved it since I was still planning my wedding without Corey. I had to listen to my mom carry on about what she wanted and liked, and then, to my dismay, Corey's mother began to chime in with her thoughts and feelings about the wedding. I adored Corey's mother like she was my own, but she was very opinionated and used to having things done her way. We were a lot alike and that was one of the reasons that Corey loved me so much, but both mothers had to understand that this was our wedding and we were going to do things the way we chose. Or the way I chose, since Corey didn't want to have much input.

After spending an hour watching Von do her hair and adjust her dress so that just enough cleavage would show, we finally made it to Crystals. Unlike Von, who was in a killer red Donna Karen dress and Christian Louboutin red bottom stilettos, I had decided to go simple tonight. Dressed in a pair of Calvin Klein khaki linen pants that hugged my ass just right, a white tank top, and tan BCBG pumps, I felt comfortable enough to be on the dance floor all night.

The parking lot was packed with Mercedes, Range Rover and Cadillac trucks, and other expensive cars. Von's eyes lit up like a kid on Christmas when she spotted a black 2014 BMW 740 sitting on black and chrome rims near the front door of the club.

"I am going to find the owner of that car," she said, her eyes sparkling.

The bouncer waved his handheld metal detector over us, from head to toe, and we went in to pay our twenty dollars. My eyes adjusted to the darkness of the club. It was extremely packed.

Crystals was a rather large club with two levels. The semicircular bar was located downstairs, and the open dance floor was upstairs. The club was lit with multi colored lights sprinkled all over the floor from the bar to the VIP sections located near the back. The lights looked like skittles tossed throughout the club. Von and I headed straight to the bar so that I could get my first drink of the night.

"Vodka and cranberry juice," I told the cute bartender.

"Starting off a little rough, huh?" Von asked. She squinted and searched the club for her friends.

"Might as well," I shrugged. "I need to loosen up and have some fun." I grabbed my drink and swallowed it in one gulp.

"Damn girl, slow down!" Von laughed at my twisted up face. She took the empty cup out of my hand and placed it on the bar. "My homeboy got some of that loud so I know you gonna get on that with me, right?"

I was not a true weed smoker at all, but in college I had my moments like most people where I took a puff here or there. Von was a regular smoker and she had friends that provided her with the best marijuana in Charlotte. I was constantly on her to stop smoking, but Von is Von and she will always do what she wants. I was tired of being good and doing the right thing so, if only for tonight I wanted to be someone different.

"If it's that good stuff, I'm in." My drink started to kick in as I tried to get the bartenders attention so I could order another one.

"Rachel, trust me, if I'm getting my lungs dirty you better believe it's going to be the best stuff in Charlotte," Von laughed and tossed her arm over my shoulder. "See, this is my girl. I hate to see you all stressed like you were before."

Von spotted her friends on the top level of the club, and once I got my drink, pulled me towards them. We walked up the multi-colored stairs and approached two guys standing in one of the VIP sections closest to the dance floor.

"Glad you all could come out," Chris said. He grabbed Von around her waist and squeezed her tight.

Chris was one of the team managers that worked in the same department of the bank as Von. He was a short stocky guy that could pass for a light-skinned version of Omar Epps in the movie *Love & Basketball*. His tan double breasted sweater complimented his hazel eyes, and as he hugged Von, I noticed the gold Citizen watch that graced his wrist.

Standing beside Chris was his friend who seemed to be taking a great interest in Von. Derrick was literally staring at Von like he was in a daze and couldn't snap out of it. She didn't seem to mind him doing so, either. Derrick's cocoa butter complexion, black v-neck sweater and black jeans forced me to do a double take on this extremely attractive man. His dreadlocks reached halfway down his back and were neatly braided to the back. Usually the guys that rocked dreads were a turn off to me, but I had to give it to Derrick; his were very neat and well maintained. Von loved dreadlocks and immediately began to flirt with him. That snapped Derrick out of his stupor.

"So what are you ladies drinking?" Chris asked.

"My friend here is sipping vodka and cranberry and you can get me the same," Von said. She turned her back to us and continued to flirt with Derrick.

Chris bought me my third drink of the night and I was definitely feeling it by this time. By now, both Von and I were on the dance floor shaking and stirring our bodies to the music, making every man that looked want us. Before we knew it the time slipped away and it was three o'clock in the morning.

"You all want to go grab something to eat at IHOP? My treat," Chris asked as we walked outside the club towards my car.

"You rolled yet?" Von asked.

"Oh yeah, lets hit it in my truck," Chris replied.

We all piled up in Chris's black Escalade truck to smoke before we went to eat. As we sat in the parking lot of the club and passed around two blunts I was at ease and forgot all about the pressures of my wedding. After the last blunt was smoked, Von and I hopped into my car and followed Chris and Derrick to IHOP. By the time we arrived at the restaurant, I was completely relaxed. My tongue was loose and anything was bound to come out of my mouth. Not only was I very tipsy, I was high as well, so all the jokes that Chris was telling that would have seemed corny to me at another time seemed like the funniest in the world.

As I was devouring the last little bit of my divine cheesesteak and fries, my phone started to vibrate in my pocket. I wondered who could be calling me at this time of morning. That could only be one person: Corey. To my surprise I didn't recognize the number.

"Hello," I said, half screaming into the phone after realizing how packed and loud IHOP had gotten.

"You still at the club, huh?"

The liquor and weed in my system kept me from recognizing the voice on the other end. "Hello," I repeated a little louder this time.

"Uh, hey Rachel, this is Terrence."

"Oh hey!" I said laughing in the phone like he had told a joke of his own. "I am at IHOP, where are you?" I asked. I tried to hide the fact that I was really messed up but I could tell it wasn't working.

"I'm at my dad's. I got into town a few hours ago and I remembered that you said you were going out. I figured that you were still out now. I hope I am not being disrespectful by calling so late."

"Damn you sound sexy." Oh no, did I just say that?

"I guess you had a couple of drinks tonight." Terrence laughed.

"I am so sorry. Please don't pay me any attention." My embarrassment brought me down a little from my high.

"You are fine," Terrence replied still chuckling.

"Come and join me and my friends at IHOP."

"How about I just meet you somewhere so we can talk?" Terrence asked.

I was surprised that he would suggest us meeting this late at night but I was too intoxicated to think about it.

"Sure, why not." I gave Terrence directions to a store fifteen minutes from my house.

"Give me about thirty minutes," he said before hanging up the phone.

Von was so engrossed in a conversation with Derrick that it didn't matter much when I told her I was exhausted and ready to go home. I didn't want my friend to ask a million questions, so I decided not to tell her I was on my way to meet a man that I had only talked to over the phone. She would surely think it was more than just two friends having a nice chat.

"Girl, get some rest. I will catch a ride with Derrick and Chris." Von waved at me while playing with one of Derrick's dreadlocks. I smiled at Von, and laughed to myself because I already knew what she would be doing for the remainder of the night.

Chapter 10

I sat in my car and watched every vehicle that drove up beside me, half expecting to see Terrence jump out. Even though I had no idea what he looked like, for some reason I was imaging a charcoal-colored brother on the heavy side. That is the picture I had developed in my head based on the sound of his voice. The clock on the dashboard flashed 5:15 as a midnight blue Honda Accord pulled up beside me. The guy in the car looked at me and then promptly turned his head. He was a skinny dark-skinned man that wore an old pair of brown plastic framed glasses that were way too large for his face. He reminded me of the comedian Ricky Smiley's character Lil' Daryl. I could almost hear him saying "We so hungry. You got some milk?" I laughed out loud at the thought.

This can't be Terrence. I became irritated at the thought of being out at this time of night to see a man that was not remotely attractive. I didn't even know why I was here in the first place but the fact that I was intoxicated and high played a large part in me sitting in a parking lot waiting on a man that I had never seen before.

The guy remained in the car and glanced at me every few seconds, poking at his glasses with his finger, and turning away when I looked at him. This was definitely not safe, so after ten minutes, I decided to go in the store and call Terrence's cell phone. If Terrence was the guy in the car and answered the phone I would simply say that I was unable to make it and stay in the store until I saw him leave. I was too wasted at this point to make small talk with anyone that was not even appealing in the least little way. I hopped out my car, and went in the store, heading to the very back. I dialed the number that he had called me from earlier. No answer. Enough was enough.

I walked out of the store and noticed that the temperature had dropped a bit since me and Von left the club. The wind whipped across the front of my thin tank top and I felt my nipples awaken from their sleep. I paused for a quick second as I noticed a man leaning on a Burgundy Acura parked beside my car. I continued to my car as if I didn't see him.

"Ms. Simms?"

My heart skipped a beat as I examined this stunning man that stood in front of me. Dressed in a pair of dark rinse blue jeans, a royal blue t-shirt, and matching blue and red Atlanta Braves baseball hat he stood about 5'9 and was one of the most beautiful men I had ever laid my eyes on. He had skin that looked like it had been dipped in Hershey's chocolate, and a smile that could make the devil stop torturing souls and stare. I was mesmerized.

"Terrence?" I asked nervously.

"Well hey there," he replied grinning.

I gave him a quick hug while trying to hide my apparent attraction to him. His touch was warm and I breathed in his invigorating smell. What was that cologne? I wondered. He took a quick look at me from head to toe and noticed that my nipples were standing at full attention.

"It's a bit chilly out here so why don't we sit in the car." Terrence walked around to the passenger side of his car and opened the door for me to get in.

"Let me get my jacket first," I said. I unlocked my car and grabbed my denim jacket out of the front seat. I giggled as I thought about the dreadful guy with the glasses that was long gone by now.

"What's so funny?" Terrence inquired.

"I'll tell you later," I said as I turned to face him. I looked into his sexy hypnotic eyes and couldn't believe this was the man that I talked to every week on the phone. I climbed in his car and breathed deeply, taking in the scent of his cologne that filled the Acura.

"So we finally meet," he said smiling once again.

"Had fun at the club tonight?" he asked settling into the driver's seat.

"I had a great time." I was still very intoxicated so I sat straight up in the seat and tried to pull myself together. I wiped my hands across my face in an attempt to sober up.

"Yeah, I can tell that you did," Terrence said laughing.

Terrence's laughter made my nipples harden even more underneath my jacket. This liquor had me thinking things that I normally would not even dare to imagine.

"So, are you ready for the big day? Ready to make that step and become someone's wife?" Terrence took a quick look at my diamond engagement ring then up at me, staring into my eyes.

"Huh?" Alcohol, weed, and a handsome man were not a good mix. I was embarrassed that I couldn't even focus on what he was talking about.

"What were you drinking?"

"Vodka and cranberry juice," I slurred.

"Must have been a lot," Terrence chuckled still looking at me.

"You are not what I expected," I blurted out.

Since I was in an impaired state, I knew that this conversation would be an honest one. Not that I had a habit of lying to men, or anyone for that matter. But the ones that I wasn't familiar with, I would never let close enough to me to involve them in my life, what I was thinking, and how I feel. At the moment, Corey was the only man that I felt the desire to tell all my feelings and secrets to. Our relationship was built on honest communication, or so I thought.

"What do you mean, not what you expected?" he questioned. Terrence's puzzled look made him even more irresistible.

"I guess from talking to you I didn't expect you to look the way you do." Oh man, did I really say that aloud? This has got to be the last time I drink.

"Wow!" Terrence looked shocked.

"I don't mean that in a bad way." I stumbled over my words not wanting to offend him.

I thought about the guy in the other car and laughed once again. I told Terrence about the man that had pulled up beside me. I told him how I thought that it was him and if so, I was going to get in my car and drive away without looking back. He thought this was as humorous as I did and all of a sudden I felt really comfortable with him. Maybe it was the alcohol, among other things in my system, but I felt at ease with him which is something that I have never felt right off with anyone.

I pushed my seat back a little, rested my head on the headrest, and slouched down. Our conversation jumped from family, kids, the job and finally having a little "fun" before settling down and getting married.

"I'm not trying to tell you to go out there and just get buck wild, but if you feel the need to have a little fun before you make that step, I would advise you to do it now."

I didn't know what he meant, but tonight was about the wildest I was going to get. "And when you say 'fun', what exactly are you referring to?" I asked.

"What I mean is anything that you can't do as a married woman."

Terrence had maintained eye contact with me all night but as he said this he glanced away and stared out the window.

"I don't think I am looking for that kind of fun. And even if I was, I wouldn't be able to trust any of the guys out here. Really, who would be cool with just having a little 'fun' and leaving it like that? No strings attached, just fun."

Terrence looked back at me and didn't say anything for a while. "Someone that is in an unhappy situation that they could not get out of. Someone that knew it could only be just fun and that's it. I doubt that you would have a hard time finding someone, as beautiful as you are."

His compliment caught me off guard, and for the first time that night I didn't know what to say. We sat in silence for a few moments.

Terrence looked out the window once again and I examined this familiar stranger that sat mere inches away from me. He removed his hat and rubbed his bald head as if he was in deep thought.

He was even more gorgeous than when I first laid eyes on him, and I was shocked by how attracted and drawn I was to this man. He had a certain spirit about him that gave him this regal manly feel. He looked like the type of man that took care of his family and did everything to make sure the people in his life were content. But there was also a mystery about him. In his eyes there seemed to be some type of hurt, something that I couldn't put my finger on.

"Really, I never gave it much thought, but if I did just want to have fun with someone he would have to be someone that would not expect anything from me, maybe just a friend. I wouldn't want to take it too far though. I have not had a lot of experience with men like that."

I hoped that Terrence understood what I was saying. I wanted to let him know that I have never been the type of female to just jump in the bed with any and everybody, especially those that were already taken.

Von always talked about messing around with married men, but that was something that I just couldn't see myself doing. I was about to take that step in a few months and knowing how sacred marriage is, there is no way I could interfere with that.

I loved Von like she was my own flesh and blood, but the fact that she had affairs with married men made me think less of her. She never listened to my lectures and just continued to do whatever she wanted. Any time I slept with someone, they were my man; no one night stands, no jump offs, no meaningless encounters, - it all meant something to me.

Terrence was looking at me differently than he had all night and I could tell that something was on his mind.

"What?" I asked.

"Nothing, nothing at all," was his simple reply.

He looked at me as if he wanted to say more but once our eyes locked neither of us mumbled a word.

I shifted in my seat uncomfortable that I was so turned on by this man. I glanced at my cell phone and blinked twice when I realized the time.

"Do you know it's 8:30?"

Even though it felt like we had known each other for years, I was so embarrassed that I had sat in a car with a man I hardly knew through the wee hours of the morning. We both looked at the time on the dashboard then again at one another. Neither one of us wanted to end the conversation we were having.

"You need to get some rest," Terrence said reluctantly. I could tell he didn't want to leave and neither did I.

"Yeah, I guess you are right. I need to put some gas in my car. Will you follow me to the gas station right down the street?" The pumps at this ancient gas station were long gone along with any hopes of getting gas here.

"Sure, I need to fill up myself," he said, once again giving me that award winning smile.

I got out of his car and felt his eyes still on me as I hopped into my car and motioned for him to follow me. I pulled into the gas station and drove up to the pump with Terrence pulling up to the pump beside mine.

The temperature was now a scorching 75 degrees. Sweat began to form everywhere on my body. I shrugged off the denim jacket that had kept me warm and had covered some body parts last night I did not want Terrence to see while we were sitting in the car. I threw my jacket in the backseat and dug around in my purse for my debit card.

"Want me to pump for you?" Terrence asked when I finally got out of the car.

"Sure," I said. "And to think I used to think you were an ass when we talked on the phone every week."

"Wow, that hurt," Terrence replied making a pitiful little puppy dog face.

"Well I said used to!"

Terrence stood with his hand on the pump as I walked in front of him to pay for the gas with my card. For the second time our bodies were mere inches away from each other. My hand shook as I slid my debit card into the reader and entered in my PIN. I could feel the heat from his body as I gave him the perfect view of my ass. It took everything in me not to turn around so that I could be face to face with this sexy stranger who had my panties wet all night from just talking to him.

I took a deep breath and stepped away from Terrence and towards my car. As I watched him fill my tank, I thought, I'll bet that is not the only thing he can pump. Why was I feeling this way when I hardly knew this man? Had to be the alcohol. Couldn't be anything but the alcohol or weed or a combination of both. My heart and body belonged to Corey and no other man had ever made me want to disrespect that.

"You are all set," Terrence said turning towards me.

"Thanks!" I began to get nervous again as he walked up to me and gave me another hug.

"It was really nice talking to you," Terrence said softly. He touched my trembling hand and again gave me that same smile he had used all night.

"And it was nice finally meeting you in person," I said so low that it sound like a simple whisper.

He opened my car door and I got inside. "I will talk to you later, Ms. Simms."

Buckling my seat belt, I waved once again at Terrence and drove away. It took me ten minutes to get home and as I was about to strip and get into my bed that was ever so softly calling my name I glanced at my dresser mirror. I looked at the goofy grin that was frozen on my face and thought about the man that had put it there. I thought about the conversation we had about having 'fun" before the wedding and the apparent attraction between us. My head filled with fantasies of him being the one that provided that fun, but they were just day dreams and would remain that.

***

I picked up the phone and dialed Monica's number, once again hopeful she would pick up for me this time. I had been calling Monica at least two to three times a week and texting as well, but she still was not talking to me.

"Hello," Monica answered dryly.

I was relieved that my sister had finally answered her phone. Maybe now I could apologize and make up with her. It was after seven on Wednesday evening and I wanted to try to talk to Monica or get her to talk to me. It had been over two months since we talked and I missed my sister dearly.

I saw her on Sundays at church but she would do her best to avoid me so she wouldn't have to speak. I knew how she was so I gave her space to cool off, but it was time to get past this. To break the ice I would invite her to go with me to her new favorite restaurant. Merlin's had just opened in uptown Charlotte and Monica could not get enough of the place. They served the best crab legs around, which were Monica's favorite. To make it up to her I would treat her to whatever she wanted.

"Hey Monica, its Rachel, you busy?"

"I saw your name on my caller ID so I know who it is," she snapped.

"You want to go get something to eat, my treat?" I asked ignoring her comment.

"Only if you take me to Merlin's," she replied. She knew if I wanted to talk to her again I would take her anywhere, even if it meant paying for an overly expensive meal.

"I was just going to suggest that. Be there in an hour."

Elated that I was finally talking to my sister again, I took a deep breath and thought about all the apologizing I had to do. Since it was mid-week I didn't want to stay out all night, but I was willing to sacrifice a few hours of sleep just to get back in my sister's good graces.

I contemplated telling her about the new friend I had found in Terrence.

Ever since our meeting Friday night he had been on my mind and I found comfort in thinking about the conversation that we shared. Monday mornings were usually slow and dreary for me, yet this week I had been eager to go to work. I was delighted at the chance to talk to Terrence again. When we went over the weekly numbers, I could tell by the sound of his voice that he was just as pleased as I was.

After pondering it for a while, I settled on leaving my new friend out of the conversation with my sister for the night. To Monica, it might not have seemed all that innocent. As much as I talked about loving Corey, I didn't think Monica would understand just having a male friend to talk to. It wasn't even my style to have any male friends. Besides, I commented so much on what Monica and Von did that I didn't want them remarking on me.

I better stick to apologizing and listening to the latest happenings of the Tony saga. I slipped into my heels, took a quick glance in the mirror to make sure my hair was not a mess, and headed out the door to begin my night of pleading with my sister to forgive me for thinking that Corey was God's gift. That wouldn't be difficult tonight because my flawless man that I held on a pedestal for so long was coming down and displaying his true colors. This saddened me and I frowned at the thought that maybe he was never that perfect from the start.

Chapter 11

"Here you go again with that same nonsense. Do you ever get tired of talking about this damn wedding?" Corey's voice rose higher and higher as the conversation continued.

What started off as a somewhat pleasant conversation was ending on a very bad note. I was not surprised at all anymore. Another weekend went by and I finally decided on the invitations, but I wanted Corey's input on them. Down to seven months and bit by bit things were being completed. Corey wanted informal invitations; however, since my dad was such a prominent man in the community I thought formal would be best.

"You don't want my input on those invitations so please don't give me that," Corey said in one breath.

"Why would you say that?" I whined. I was hurt that he believed I didn't want his advice. I pleaded with him for months to help and now he thought I didn't want his input.

"Every time I give you my opinion you don't take it. You have always done whatever you wanted to do so just continue to do so."

"Corey, I value your opinion and I want you to be a part of this," I begged. His words were cutting deep. I wanted to reach out and tell him how much I loved and needed him.

"Listen, I did not call you for all this. Lately, whenever we talk it gets so heavy. I miss just being able to talk to you without talking about this wedding."

"I miss that, too, and once we get the wedding over with we can go back to being easy," I explained.

"I hope so, but honestly I just really don't care about this wedding," Corey sighed. "My focus is to make sure I can provide for us after the wedding.

I have been going through hell lately on my job, and if you weren't so consumed by this wedding you would know that."

We were having this exchange on a Friday night after I spent all day with my mom going to ten different bridal stores searching for the perfect invitation. My regular routine on a Friday night would have been hanging with Von, but she had a date with one of her men and I was too exhausted to go anywhere. I was lying in bed, where I would remain for the rest of the night, flipping through the TV channels. Even though it was only 9 pm, I had already taken my bath, with just a towel around me seeking a peaceful conversation with my future husband. My gut told me that would be damn near impossible.

"Corey, I understand work is stressful. I also know that planning a wedding is frustrating, but you have to think about the outcome." I thought about what Terrence told me on the phone the day I was feeling awful. I wanted to cheer Corey up the same way Terrence was able to do for me.

"Maybe we just rushed into this," he snapped.

My heart stopped and I let Corey's words sink in.

"Rushed into what?" I asked softly, afraid of his answer. This was the second time that Corey was saying in so many words that he was having doubts about the wedding.

"All I am saying is that it shouldn't be this hard. We have been together for a while so you would think planning one day would be simple."

"I know baby, but it will get easier."

"Well, I hope I am around to see it," Corey huffed.

Taken aback by Corey's comment, my feelings of sadness for him and the idea that he didn't think his opinions mattered flew out the window right along with the low tone I had used the entire conversation.

"Hope that you're around? You trying to tell me you're going somewhere?" I screamed in the phone.

"First of all, don't scream at me, Rachel!" Corey yelled. "You have been getting beside yourself talking to me like this and I am tired of it!"

Before I knew it I began to cry which Corey despised even more.

"Please don't start that," he said.

He was irritated with me, but no matter how hard I tried to stop crying it didn't help.

The tears kept coming and I continued to sob in the phone. I couldn't understand it either; I had never been this emotional before. Now the smallest things made me break out in tears.

"Corey, I am not trying to make this complicated, I am just not feeling loved right now. We have not spent any real time together in weeks and I need you to be here with me."

"You know that I can't just be there, Rachel. We are about to spend the rest of our lives together so you would think that I could get a little freedom now," Corey said.

"Well excuse me if I just want to be with you," I said as my crying turned to sniffles.

"Why do you have to be so dramatic? You know that I love you, but I just need some space. You going hard with this wedding and my boss always riding me is too much for me to handle right now."

"I can give you all the space you need!" I screamed. I ended the call and hurled the cordless phone across the room. It hit my bedroom wall hard and landed on the floor.

I knew that it would be only seconds before my phone would be ringing again. Sure enough, the ringing began. I let my voice mail pick it up. I didn't feel like arguing with Corey anymore tonight. I watched the top of my phone light up indicating there was a message waiting. It wouldn't be the nicest message ever left by Corey, so I was in no hurry to hear it.

I reached over and grabbed my vibrating cell phone that was charging on my dresser. Thinking it was a message from Corey I started to ignore it but instead I decided to listen. Instead of it being a message from Corey, it was just a text message from Von that read, *Hey girl,* followed by a phone number.

Now my pain had turned to anger.

I was tired of feeling so drained and unloved every time I spoke to Corey. I dialed Von to see whose phone number she texted me.

"Hey chick!"

"Whose number is this?" I asked

"Were you asleep?"

"No, now just tell me whose number this is," I said impatiently.

"Oh, sorry, that was Kevin's number."

"And why are you giving it to me?" I snapped. I was getting aggravated that Von was not plainly stating her purpose for giving me the number.

"Rachel, I don't know. I saw my brother today and he told me to give it to you so you could call him. Just call and find out what he wants."

"You want me to call him now?" I asked, amazed that Von was actually giving me another man's phone number, even if it was her brother.

"Girl call him if you want and if you don't, then don't. I will call you back."

Before I could ask her another question about Kevin the phone went silent. Why would I call Kevin? I climbed out of bed, grabbed my towel that was somehow jumbled up in my sheets, and wrapped it back around me. I glanced at my cordless phone that was still lying on the floor. I might as well listen to the message. I sighed as I walked over to the phone and picked it up.

"You have one new message," the recorded voice informed me. I heard the anger in Corey's voice and I knew I was not going to like the rest of the message.

"Rachel, that was really unnecessary but if you want to act like a child then so be it. Whenever you grow up, call me back, but I am sure that won't be tonight. I will holla at you later."

A child? He had the audacity to say I was acting like a child? Corey always hangs up on me when we argue, but now I was a child for doing the same thing?

All I wanted to do was spend time with him.

"I will not cry again, I will not." I repeated this over and over but that didn't stop the tears from falling once more. I just needed some cheering up and maybe Kevin could provide that for me. I figured he was a safer option than Terrence. Turning to other people when Corey upset me was becoming too common place. I dialed his number and waited for the phone to ring.

"Hello."

"Hi Kevin, this is Rachel."

"Well hello, Ms. Rachel. I didn't expect to hear from you," Kevin said unable to hide the enthusiasm in his voice.

"And why not?" Part of me wanted him to notice that I was upset and the other part just wanted to talk and take my mind off things. Maybe he could lighten my mood the same way Terrence had done. All I needed was for someone to reassure me that, no matter what, me and Corey would live happily ever after.

"I just figured that you were busy with the wedding coming up. Your fiancé's not there to keep you company tonight?" he quizzed.

"No, not tonight," I said sadly.

"Everything alright?"

"Yeah, I guess," I replied. I didn't want to tell him that I was feeling lonely and vulnerable but at the same time I wanted him to make me feel better.

"Have you eaten yet, Ms. Lady?" Kevin asked.

"I am not hungry."

"Would you like some company? I have some movies we can watch and maybe I can get you out that sour mood."

My first reaction was to tell him no, but I refused to sit at home and cry all night.

"Okay that's cool. We can watch one movie, but I don't want to stay up too late," I said, unsure if I really wanted him to come over.

"I have no plans of keeping you up, Rachel. I will be over in a few."

I hung the phone up and removed the towel so that I could put on some clothes before Kevin arrived. I didn't want to entice him in any way, so I slipped on a pair of black work out pants and a beige t-shirt.

I walked into the living room to make sure that everything was neat and in order. As I examined the kitchen, I noticed a bottle of vodka sitting on the top of my refrigerator. A little sip might loosen me up a bit. I poured a shot and downed it as quickly as I had poured it. Kevin was a regular comedian and I was sure he could lift my spirits. He was also my best friend's brother, so I would be safe inviting him over. Just like family, I thought to myself. I clicked on the TV and sat on the couch waiting for him to get here and make me laugh at least once tonight.

Chapter 12

Did he think this was a date or something, I thought to myself, as Kevin wiped his black loafers on my welcome mat and entered my apartment. Dressed in a crisp white oxford button down shirt and a pair of black jeans, in one hand he held a stack of movies and in the other a bottle of wine. If he had thoughts of getting me drunk, he had another thing coming. I almost laughed out loud since I was on the line between tipsy and drunk already.

While waiting for Kevin I had taken several shots of Vodka, from a bottle Corey had left at my house months ago, and felt the need to call him back to tell him what I thought of his "child" remark. The first two times went unanswered; however, the third time was the charm. He picked up and asked what I wanted and why I continued to call him. Another fight ensued and it ended with Corey informing me that we needed to call the wedding off because we couldn't get along now and he was just tired. I was heartbroken.

I began to once again scream and cry, and like so many times before, Corey hung up on me. Call the wedding off? Was he serious? I could not fathom why he would even suggest something as irrational as not getting married. He had treated me like I was the best part of his life for four years, and now he made me feel like I was not even wanted.

I needed to feel wanted. I needed to feel desired. I needed to be held. After sitting on the floor and crying for several minutes, I finally picked myself up and sucked down two more shots before my company came over. I almost called and told Kevin not to come over, but my hurt had transformed into anger. Corey would be furious at the thought of me having a man at my house that liked me in the least little way.

He wasn't here and wasn't trying to be here, so he shouldn't care who was keeping me company.

Kevin walked in and gave me his usual tight hug. It only took him one look at me to know that I was plastered. My eyes were low and my balance was off. It was hard for me to even walk straight at this point. He sat the bottle of wine on the kitchen table.

"You think you're going to be up for watching a movie?" Kevin asked. He made himself comfortable on the couch while allowing his eyes to dance around the room and inspect his surroundings.

"Yeah, I am good." I attempted to gain my composure as I sat next to Kevin on the couch. I was unexpectedly glad I had invited Kevin over. He was not a stranger, by far. I had known him since I was little. We always mocked and teased with each other and he already knew everything about me. On top of all that, he respected me.

"What movies did you bring?"

Kevin handed me the stack of movies. "*Best Man, Players Club, Friday, Vampire in Brooklyn,* and *Poetic Justice,*" he called out. "They are all old movies but I hoped you wouldn't mind. Which one are you in the mood for?"

"I can do without seeing a wedding movie, so *The Best Man* is definitely out," I scowled.

Kevin chuckled then looked at me and saw that I was dead serious. "Come on now Rachel, it can't be that bad. If I was marrying someone as incredibly beautiful as you I would be a happy man."

"Thanks Kevin, that's sweet of you to say," I said forcing a smile.

He was trying to cheer me up, but the fact was that Corey was not happy right now and no matter how hard I tried I didn't know what to do to get him back to that place.

"So how about my all time favorite, *Players Club?* This movie should have won an Oscar," Kevin joked.

"Yeah, all men feel that way. Okay, *Player's Club* it is." I stood up and tried to steady myself.

Kevin laughed as I slowly walked over to the TV and fumbled with the movie trying to get it to work. "I don't think it's the DVD player," Kevin teased.

"Has to be," I said. I was beginning to feel better already.

"Can I get whatever it is that you are drinking?"

I balanced myself again and walked to the kitchen to fix Kevin a drink.

"A shot or mixed drink?" I opened the fridge to see if I had any juice left.

"Mixed, please." Kevin squatted on the floor and put the movie in the DVD player since I was having so many problems out of it. He started the movie and sat back down on the couch.

"Here you go," I said, handing him a cup filled with vodka and peach mango juice. I sat down beside him on the couch leaving some room between us.

We watched half of the movie making jokes out of everything that was said and done. Both of us were rather tipsy and I was amazed at how fun he was to be around. Although I grew up with Kevin and I was his little sister's best friend, we had never been alone together, especially now that I was older.

"Oh here comes the best scene in the movie," Kevin said, referring to the scene where the character Diamond stripped on stage.

"I think that's the only part that men like in the entire movie," I said.

Kevin revealed the silliest grin, gawking as Diamond twirled around the pole.

"I bet I could do that," I blurted out without thinking.

Kevin turned his full attention on me and gave me a sneaky look. "Show me."

The idea of me stripping made tears come to my eyes, this time from laughing so hard. "I'm only joking!" I exclaimed.

"Well I am not," Kevin said. "Ever strip for your man?"

Stripping was something that I had talked about doing for Corey, but never got enough nerve to actually do it. As I thought about Corey and the conversation we had just had, I began to get furious again. All Corey seemed to be doing these days was hanging out with his friends and working, and he wanted to call off the wedding when I was going through so much to make sure the day was perfect for us. He wasn't concerned about me, so why should I be worried about him right now? I was hurting and he didn't care. Rage coursed through my veins as I realized that my fiancé didn't even call me back after stating that we should call off the wedding and hanging up on me. But Kevin was here and he wanted to be here. My emotions were all over the place.

I got up from my spot on the couch, stood directly in front of the television, and imitated the scene where Diamond first appeared on stage. I rolled my body as my hands traveled over my breasts, stomach, and then down between my legs.

"I could if I wanted to," I said, laughing. I lifted my shirt just a bit to show my belly button. I knew I was only doing this because I was angry at Corey, but I was drunk and just didn't care anymore.

"Girl you better stop before I have to apologize to your man," Kevin laughed along with me as I fell back down on the couch beside him.

"Right about now, I doubt he would care," I said somberly. I was so upset at Corey that my heart felt like it was made of stone.

"Why would you say that?" Kevin asked.

I told Kevin about the disagreement Corey and I had that night and how I had been feeling unloved for the past month. I even disclosed to him that Corey had called off the wedding. I felt relieved telling someone that actually knew me how vulnerable I was feeling. A tear crept from my eye. I tried everything in my power to hold it back. Suck it up girl.

Kevin turned to me and our eyes locked.

His hand carefully moved toward my face and wiped the tear that was now on my cheek. I smiled at the warmth of his hand. I smiled at his familiar face. I smiled at a man showing sympathy for what I was going through.

"Rachel, you have always been my sister's friend but there is something different about you. I haven't been able to put my finger on it until now." Kevin leaned in closer until I could smell the vodka on his breath.

"That's just one of Ronnie's hoe lines." I turned my head to watch Diamond and Ebony arguing on the movie and to avoid Kevin's eyes. At this moment he was the sexiest he had ever been.

"Am I making you uncomfortable?"

"No," I replied quickly. I was lying. I didn't know why I said no. The truth was that he was making me *very* uncomfortable.

Being that close to someone other than Corey made me nervous and the fact that I couldn't stop my body from getting aroused had me perturbed. It had been a while since me and Corey had sex. My body was use to getting satisfied often, but I wasn't supposed to be turned on by another man, especially not Kevin. I guess I still held on to the fantasy that I was only aroused by the man that I loved. My body had proved that wrong in the car with Terrence and again tonight.

"Do you mind if I give you a massage?" Kevin asked. His eyes moved up and down my frame, and I knew his hands wanted to follow.

I turned around so that my back faced him, answering the question without words. I had to stop drinking. Drinking was becoming too habitual. Going from maybe once every blue moon to every weekend and sometimes during the week was clearly way too much for me.

His touch was unfamiliar but pleasant as his hands massaged my shoulders and upper back. He was careful not to get too anxious and not to let his hands roam. A part of me would not have minded an "oops" or "sorry I went to low" from him.

"I want to take your mind off everything you are going through," Kevin whispered in my ear.

"You are doing a good job of that now." I moaned as his grip became stronger and he continued to massage my aroused body.

"No, I want to make you feel as beautiful and sexy as you are to me," he mumbled.

My head swam as the effects of the alcohol and massage took over. "If it is anything like this massage, I am game," I purred.

After I realized what came out my mouth, it was too late to take it back.

"Turn around," Kevin instructed.

I turned to face him. He motioned for me to lay back and place my feet in his lap. His hands gently massaged my feet. It felt like I had died and gone to heaven. I moaned once again and rested my head on the arm of my couch.

"Here you go," Kevin said, handing me a small pillow from my sofa to lean on.

His hands made their way up my legs and stopped to massage my calf muscles. Please let me be able to tell him to stop. He cautiously traveled up my leg and massaged my thigh. No, this is not right. I wanted to tell him to stop but I couldn't. My body wouldn't let me. My mouth wouldn't open to permit those words to come out. His hands inched farther up my thigh as he kept his eyes steadied on mine.

"Please let me know if you want me to stop," Kevin said without taking his eyes off of me.

I remained silent. My body was saying one thing; my head another, but neither one was speaking out. Okay, Rachel, say something. Tell this man that you are getting married and he needs to get his hands off of you! My mind screamed in silence. But I wanted his hands on me. I needed his hands on me.

"Please let me know if you want me to stop," Kevin repeated.

His hands continued up my inner thigh.

One of them found what he was going after and rested between my legs. He looked up expecting at any moment for me to tell him to move his hand; but I remained quiet, frozen like I was a mute, unable to talk or move.

His touch was different now from the firm massaging he had just done. He took his finger and moved it across until he found my clit. He gently massaged it with his finger until he could feel my wetness through my clothes.

"Rachel, I want to taste you," he said in such a low tone that I barely heard him.

Nothing. I still could not say anything. A part of me wanted him to get his hands off my stuff, off Corey's stuff, but another part of me that was fighting to get loose yearned for his hands to be everywhere. This man desired me and that was what I needed. I needed him to want me.

Kevin suddenly stopped and removed his hand from between my legs. He delicately put both hands around my waist and took off my pants. It was like I was having an out of body experience. I was floating over these two people on the couch watching this man stripping off my clothes and saying nothing. After my pants came off without any resistance, Kevin paused again and stared at me. He then repeated what he had done to get my pants off in order to get my panties off as well. I laid on my couch naked from the waist down. All I could think was that for the last four years there had been only one man that touched me and this was not him.

I watched as Kevin's head disappeared in between my legs and his tongue found the spot that his fingers had been just minutes earlier. His tongue lightly moved up and down. He went from licking to gently sucking my juices as his moans mixed with mine. Did this man have his degree in eating a woman? I wondered.

My eyes closed and my head nestled deeper and deeper into the pillow. He adjusted his body so that his knees were on the floor and he was facing the couch in a praying position but never raised his head. His tongue never left my body.

He turned his body sideways and licked me from left to right and front to back. I twisted and turned to try to get away from his mouth but he pulled me back into him.

His grip was strong as he wrapped his arms around my legs and thrust me back into his mouth. Where did he learn this from and why didn't he teach a class on it? I thought as I watched him practically stand on his head to bring me so much pleasure. He switched positions every few minutes and by the time he was seated back on the couch in his beginning position I could not breathe. The moans and screams that had filled my apartment were now gone along with my voice.

He lifted his head for a moment, my juices dripping from his mouth. "Why are you holding back? I want to taste all of you." Kevin's eyes filled with hunger as he realized that I had not climaxed yet.

He went back down and again focused on my clit, adding pressure with his tongue. I didn't want him to taste me. I didn't even want his mouth on me but I couldn't stop him. I was not going to give him the bliss of making me have an orgasm. I situated myself in a way that made me overcome my longing to let go. Kevin noticed this and lifted his head up again.

"I want to feel you," he whispered.

He stood up, unbuckled his jeans, and as I watched them fall to the floor I felt nauseous. He bent down and retrieved a condom out of his pocket and slipped it on like he had done this a thousand times. My head throbbed. I wanted to tell him no, please put your pants on, but I had no sound.

Kevin climbed on top of me and as soon as I felt his thick short dick enter my body I couldn't take it anymore. At last I was able to speak.

"Please stop," I whispered so quietly that at first I didn't even hear myself. Great time to tell him to stop Rachel, I thought. "Please stop!" I repeated forcefully and louder.

"Rachel, are you okay?" Kevin frowned as I pushed him off of me and sat up on my couch.

"Where are my pants?"

I rummaged around on the floor until I found them near the edge of the couch.

"Please leave," I said while trying to slip on my pants so he wouldn't be able to see anymore of my already exposed body.

"Rachel, are you ok? What happened? I don't want to leave you upset like this."

"I wasn't ready for this," I mumbled.

"Rachel, I am sorry. I didn't mean to make you do anything you didn't want to." He reached out for me but I didn't want to touch him. His short fat dick was limp now. I felt disgusted just looking at it.

"Please put your pants on and leave," I said once again, still not looking at him.

Those same sexy eyes that I stared at moments ago were what I wanted to avoid more than anything now.

Kevin finally understood there was nothing else to be said and silently pulled up his pants, heading towards the door. He turned and called my name once again. I sat on the couch motionless, still, quiet, like I had done when his head was between my legs. Once I heard the door close I looked up and saw darkness all around me. Immediately the tears started flowing.

Chapter 13

I woke up to my alarm clock screaming its loud obnoxious song. Saturday morning was here and I had forgotten to turn my alarm off the night before so it would not wake me up at my usual 6 o'clock time. Wow, that was a horrific dream! I yawned and ran my fingers through my unwrapped hair. I sat straight up in my bed as flashes of the dream rolled around in my head. Wait until I tell Von I had a dream about her brother; she is going to laugh so hard. I stretched, reaching towards the ceiling as I let out a much louder yawn. The alcohol had given me a severe headache and my stomach felt queasy. A few more hours of sleep would help me feel better. I loosened my twisted and tangled gold, satin sheets from around me tossing them to the side so I could reach for my cell phone that was at the foot of my bed.

Two missed calls and two texts appeared on my phone. Had to be Corey. The argument we had wasn't a delusion and I remembered every word that was said. That's weird, two texts from Kevin. Why would Kevin text me? As I read the messages I sadly recalled that last night had not been a dream. It was a terrible nightmare.

The first message read, *I apologize if you feel I took advantage of you last night. That was not my intent. Please call so that we can talk about this.*

That message was left at 12:30 am. The next message simply asked me to please call. That message was left at 1:15 am. The two missed calls were also from Kevin. It was now 6:00 am and the night came flooding back to me like a tsunami rushing through my brain. Images of the top of Kevin's head in between my legs were crystal clear.

No matter how hard I wished that this had never happened it did and I could not take it back.

For four years I was committed to Corey. No other man kissed or touched me and now all that was gone. I was marrying the man of my dreams in seven months and had been with another man. How could I do this to him? Did this one act mean that I didn't love him? Should I tell him what I had done? I didn't love Kevin. I didn't want to spend the rest of my life with him. I remembered lying on the couch watching his head in between my legs, sucking on my juices. The juices that belonged to Corey. I had to tell Corey. How could I look into his eyes and lie to him?

"Hey Rachel," Corey said picking up on the second ring.

"Hi sweetheart." I attempted to hide the pain in my voice.

"Rachel, I am sorry for getting into it with you last night. We have not been on the same page since we started planning this wedding and I want to try to fix that. I don't want to cancel the wedding. I was just frustrated. Please forgive me."

If it was only that simple. I saw Kevin's head in my mind. Bobbing up and down back and forth, I just couldn't stop seeing that image.

"It's okay Corey. Maybe we need to spend some time together."

I probably wouldn't have been as willing to overlook the fact that Corey called off the wedding if it had not been for my actions with Kevin. I knew in my heart that I had no right to give Corey a hard time, even if I wanted to.

"I agree," Corey replied. "How about I come over tonight and we can go to church together in the morning. How does that sound?"

Any other day, spending time with Corey would have made my heart soar but this morning I was feeling different. I didn't know how I would even face Corey. Still, I knew I couldn't miss the chance to see him.

"Baby, that sounds great," I said.

"I have to run a few errands first but I will see you tonight around eight. I love you."

"I love you back," I said hanging up the phone.

Kevin was still on my mind and I couldn't stop myself from thinking about him. I could still feel his tongue on me. Still feel his lips in between mine. Head moving from side to side, up and down. I needed to tell Corey, but how could I hurt him like this? I looked down at my phone and saw another text message. It was Kevin again.

Are you ok?

I turned my phone over, fell back on my oversized bed and stared at the ceiling. I wanted to dig into my skin and start scratching and tearing until I removed any traces of him. I felt dirty, revolting, like I had been having sex with a stranger all night.

Another text message. This time Kevin asked if I felt like talking. It was going on seven now and I wondered how he knew I was up. I rolled over, reached down to grab the remote off the floor, and turned the TV on. Good old cartoons. I watched a little of the roadrunner being chased by the coyote until I dozed off.

My annoying default ringtone made the sound of a million waves crashing against rocks and woke me from my restless slumber. I glanced at my phone lying on my pillow beside me as if it had been asleep as well and prayed that it was not Kevin again. Thank God it was just Von.

"Hey girl, you still asleep?" Von asked after I said a groggy hello.

"I was trying to sleep." I yawned and pushed myself up into a sitting position. My eyes adjusted to the sun that was now shining thru my blinds into my once dark room.

"Girl, wait until I tell you what this low down dirty dog did this time."

Thinking that Von was going to tell me about what's-his-face or whoever she was sleeping with, I told her that I didn't want to hear her fussing about some man that she was dating right now.

"Oh this is no man, this is a dog named James Singler."

Once Von said that name I knew she was upset and was talking about her father. Ever since Von's mother had left her father because of his infidelity, Von had no relationship with him. He called every blue moon to check on her, but he had so many skeletons in his closet that she didn't want anything to do with him.

"What's going on with your father?" I asked, glad that I didn't have to sit on the phone and listen to Von talk about some unimportant guy.

"Girl, I need to come over for this one."

"What time is it?" I stirred around in bed to wake myself some more.

"Rachel, it's noon. I am surprised that you are still in the bed."

"Yeah well come on over. I had a rough night, too," I said. Images of Kevin came back into my head; however, I did not plan on telling Von how her brother ate me out before I kicked him out.

"I'm on my way."

As soon as I pressed end on my phone another text message came through. It was Kevin again.

Can we talk?

If I wanted him to leave me alone until I got my thoughts together I would have to respond to him. After a moment, I replied back.

Please not right now. Let me clear my head and I will call you soon.

That should buy me some time, and hopefully keep him quiet until I had a chance to figure something out. Another text message flashed on my screen.

Ok, but we really need to talk about this.

I struggled to get up and shower before Von came over. She knocked on the door twice and then opened my apartment door with the key I made for her. She was one of four people that had keys to my place.

I knew that Von, Monica, Daryl and Corey would come get me at the drop of a dime if I ever needed anything or was stranded on the side of the road. I was sitting on my couch half watching *The Parkers*. Nikki was chasing the professor around the table telling him how much she loved him.

"Hey," Von said.

She plopped down beside me on my couch and immediately took off her black open-toed heels. Dressed in a pair of skinny blue jeans and a flowered peasant top, she wasn't the glamorous Von that I was accustomed to but she was still pretty. Her hair wasn't the usual fresh out the chair salon look she took pride in. It looked as if she had run her fingers though it all night and then woke up and just combed it down. Her short hair was one step away from being matted on her head.

"What's going on?" I asked noticing how swollen and red Von's eyes were.

"See this is why I don't trust men to begin with. They act as if they are going to love you forever and all that commitment and good stuff but the first time a new piece of ass comes along they jump at it and forget that they have a wife or girlfriend."

Pain swept over Von's face as she continued to rant and rave about how no man could be faithful and no matter how much they loved you they couldn't stand by their promises. As she was talking I thought about the commitment that I was about to make to Corey. I was just as bad as all the men that Von was fussing about.

"You listening?" Von asked giving me a nudge.

"Yeah, sorry, I was just thinking about what you were saying."

"Now Rachel, I am not trying to freak you out because you are getting married. Corey is different. He is not like the men that I am talking about and he is definitely not like my father."

"So what did your dad do?"

"Well, I will just say that there is another one of us now."

Von hopped off the couch and walked into the kitchen. She opened the refrigerator and poured a glass of peach mango juice. My mind went to Kevin again and the mixed drink I had fixed him last night.

"Another one of you?" I asked as she paced around my kitchen.

"I didn't stutter!" Von walked back into the living room, glass in hand and sat beside me on the couch with one leg underneath her. "She is older than me and younger than Kevin so that means that my dad had been cheating on my mom years before she actually found out. He has been hiding this woman for 33 years!" she exclaimed.

Tears formed in her eyes as she went on about how her dad came to her and told her that she had a sister that she never knew about. I reached out for my best friend and hugged her. She rested her head on my shoulder and let the tears flow. I patted her back and told her that it was going to be okay, not necessarily believing my own words.

"So why did he tell you now?" I asked.

"Oh, girl, his excuse was that he wanted to right all his wrongs and he had to come clean with everything that he has done. Just a bunch of bull to me."

"Where is this woman? Do you know anything about her?"

"Nope, and I don't care to know," Von responded quickly. "Kevin wants to know all the details, but I don't."

As soon as she said her brother's name I saw his face again. His head. His mouth. I quickly hid my look of disgust from Von.

"How is he handling all this?" I asked.

"My dad called me and said that he was unable to reach Kevin last night so he ended up telling him this morning. Matter of fact, before I came up the stairs I saw Kevin's car parked right in front. One of his friend's lives in your building so he was probably visiting him. Knowing Kevin, he was with some female last night, too."

Von's words repeated over and over in my head.

Why would Kevin's car be parked out front? He left last night, so why would his car still be here? He texted me when I woke up this morning like he knew when I was awake and when I was sleep. This just was not making any sense. I had known Kevin for years and I never took him as the stalker type. Maybe I was just jumping to conclusions.

Von was now staring at the TV in deep thought. I jumped up from the couch and told her that I would be right back as I ran into my room.

"Girl, you okay?" Von asked.

"Yeah, I just remembered something," I shouted from my bedroom.

I peeked through my blinds and out of the window that was next to my bed. Sure enough I could see Kevin's car but, he was nowhere to be found. I reached for my cell phone and sent him a quick text asking him where he was. I waited a few seconds for his reply but I got nothing.

WHERE ARE YOU? I typed, urging Kevin to respond back to me. Still no response.

I marched back into the living room convincing myself that I was just thinking too hard about all this. Kevin was not some stranger that I knew nothing about. He was someone that I could trust and maybe he was over here just visiting one of his friends.

"How do you feel about all this?" I asked sitting down beside Von again.

"Rachel, I am confused, I feel betrayed, and I am just lost. I have a sister that I know nothing about and I am just expected to be fine with this but I am not."

My phone vibrated. Kevin finally responded to my text message.

Are you ready to talk or do you want to wait until Von leaves?

So he was somewhere around here.

Can we wait until she leaves? I replied back.

"Who are you texting?" Von asked.

"Who else?"

I knew she would think that I was texting Corey and would not ask me anymore questions.

"Should have known. You want to go get something to eat or just get out of the house? I need some kind of distraction," Von said. "Actually, let's call Kevin and all of us can go out to eat. I am pretty sure that he is feeling the same way I am right now."

"No!" I screamed.

"Um, why Rachel?" Von asked, shocked that I had screamed out. "I know Kevin has a little crush on you, but you don't have to worry about him making any moves on you. He knows that you are getting married. Besides I need my best friend and brother right now." Von dialed Kevin's number and asked him did he want to go get a bite to eat with us.

I could hear him through the phone tell her sure and that he was already over at my apartment complex so he would just meet us outside. As soon as she hung the phone up another text message came through on my phone.

Did you tell her?

No, and I am not going to tell her. I replied back.

Cool, flashed on my phone. I dropped it into my purse and prayed that this lunch wouldn't be too much for me to handle.

Chapter 14

"Stop looking at me like that!" Sickened, I turned my nose up at Kevin. We were having lunch at one of my favorite Italian bistros and I couldn't even enjoy my chicken marsala because of him. Kevin's smile that I thought was so damn sexy just last night made me want to vomit now and his stares were irritating the hell out of me. His eyes had bags underneath as if he had not slept all night and he looked worried. He had on the same white oxford shirt and black jeans he wore to my house last night, leading me to believe he hadn't gone home at all.

"Like what, Rachel?" he groaned, glancing at the bathroom door for his sister. "You are the one that won't say more than two words to me and who's acting all nervous around Von. I think we just need to be cool until we are alone and able to talk about this," he hissed.

"You just don't get it," I said shaking my head. "The thing is I don't want to be alone with you."

Kevin looked hurt. "I wish you would stop treating me like I have this contagious disease or like I am trying to do something to you."

"Were you watching my apartment today?"

"What?" he asked, watching Von come towards the table.

"Why are you two looking so serious?" Von asked.

Kevin stood up and pulled out his sister's chair so that she could sit back down. I poked at the mushrooms on my plate with my fork to avoid looking at Von.

"Bro, you haven't been making moves on an almost married woman have you?" Von teased.

"Of course not!" Kevin sat back down and smiled at his sister.

After an hour of talking about Kevin and Von's new sister, lunch was finally over and I was relieved.

I couldn't stomach looking at Kevin any longer. Every time he glanced at me I thought about how he made me feel, how he made me scream, and how I cried after he was gone.

The time had flown by and it was five already. Corey said that he would be here at eight so I wanted to make sure my apartment was presentable for him. I still had not decided whether I was going to tell him or not, even though my heart wanted to. How could I tell the man that I was going to marry that I had been unfaithful just because I was lonely and needed someone? The reasoning didn't make any sense to me. If it didn't make sense to me, how could I ask him to understand? My phone rang, displaying Corey's picture on my screen.

"Hey baby," I said.

"Hey, Rachel," Corey said in that all too familiar tone.

"Where are you?"

I didn't expect to hear from him until about 7:30 when he was almost here, but the way he sound let me know that something was wrong.

"Baby, please don't get mad," Corey said.

Whenever Corey started with that line I knew that the plans we had were going to change.

"Don't tell me you are not coming," I insisted.

"Baby, something came up."

"That's all you have to say?!" I shouted through the phone. "So what is more important than your fiancé this time?"

"Hold on Rachel, first of all you need to calm down." Corey's soft voice disappeared and now he was shouting. "Something came up and I'm not going to be able to make it tonight but I was going to tell you that I can try to make it tomorrow."

"Oh, so I guess you can try to spend an hour or two with your fiancé just to keep me right where you want me?"

I paced around my kitchen mad as hell and seeing double. I wanted to shout some more to let Corey know just how upset I was. I was tired of everything being more important than me.

"I am trying, Rachel," Corey sighed.

"Trying to do what exactly?" I yelled. "Are you trying to spend time with me and get things back on track? Are you trying to make me your top priority? Are you even trying to help me plan this damn wedding?"

"I know where this is going but I am not going there with it," Corey said, hanging up the phone in my ear once again.

I stood still in my kitchen for a moment shocked at the conversation that I just had. Not once did Corey say why he wasn't coming. All he said was that something came up. What was something and why didn't he feel the need to tell me what this something was? Those three words, "something came up", swirled around in my head as I tried to process what had just happened.

My fiancé, the man that I was going to spend the rest of my life with couldn't come see me because something came up. Corey had changed from the caring, loving boyfriend that he use to be, and I couldn't understand why. It had been almost three months since Corey and I had been intimate and all he could tell me was "something had come up". Tonight I was going to pour my heart out to him and ask him for forgiveness for what I had done but I would not be given that chance because "something came up". Something that was more important than me.

My stomach was cramping and that meant that I was starting my period. Not only did I have to deal with Corey, but now I would also be in a horrible mood for at least five days.

I needed a drink. I got myself together and walked over to the cabinet that held all my recently purchased bottles of liquor. Alcohol was the one thing that I could count on to make me feel better. Grabbing the knob I exhaled loudly, opened the cabinet and reached for my favorite bottle of rum. The lightness of the bottle told me that I was getting low.

Corey would definitely not be keen with the amount of alcohol I consumed, nor the frequency with which I consumed it, but then again, he was not around to see it.

I had no desire to even call him back and find out what his "something" was. No matter what he said, whatever he was doing was more significant than me. And the fact that he thought that he could make up for it by going to church with me tomorrow only insulted me even more. Yes, church meant a lot to me and I loved when me and Corey praised God together, but he thought that coming up with that resolution would make it alright to not spend time with me. I was used to going to church alone or with Von lately anyway. This was going to be another Sunday without Corey. My dad didn't even ask about him as much anymore.

I looked at my phone sitting on the edge of my kitchen bar. It was 7:15 - too early to go to bed. But I didn't want to go outside of my apartment walls and face the world right now, I didn't want to call Von and have to answer questions about why Corey was not here, and I did not want to have that inevitable conversation with Kevin.

I headed to my bedroom and peeked out the window to see if Kevin's car had magically reappeared. The blue Altima was nowhere in sight. Great, I thought before clicking on the TV and throwing myself on my soft down comforter. I lay on my back and stared at the ceiling. Once again my thoughts went to Corey.

As soon as I thought about how unimportant I was to him the tears began to fall. I had cried so much over the last few weeks that it was hard to determine when I wasn't crying. Get it together, I told myself wiping my eyes and sitting up on my bed. Even though it was early, I climbed underneath my sheets and got comfortable. Flipping through the television channels, I settled on a rerun of *Martin* before I dozed and then fell into a deep sleep.

***

"So where is everyone headed for dinner?" Jerome asked smiling and showing his gorgeous white teeth.

Service was over and I was standing around with a few choir members chatting and catching them up on my wedding plans.

"Oh, you are eating with us today?" Samantha asked giddy, and wide-eyed. Samantha was a heavy set, pretty woman in her mid-thirties who had led most of the songs the choir sang before Jerome joined. I would often go out to eat with her and some of the other choir members after church.

"I figured I would invite myself since no one else was going to ask me," Jerome said, once again showing off that million dollar smile.

"Now you know that you can come with us anytime," Samantha joked.

"You mind if I catch a ride with you, Rachel?" Jerome asked, winking at me.

"Sure." I was a little caught off guard by the fact that he wanted to ride with me, but I didn't have the energy to analyze that now. I would just enjoy his company. Maybe he could give me a little insight on men since right now I had no idea how to deal with Corey.

"I am starving so let's ride," Samantha said.

"You seem like something is bothering you today." Jerome stared at me with those piercing grey eyes as I unlocked the passenger door so that he could get in.

"I just have a lot on me right now."

"You want to talk about it?" he asked.

Jerome placed his hand on top of mine as I was putting the car in reverse. I glanced at him and looked away before I became hypnotized by his alluring eyes.

"Rachel, I know that you don't know me all that well, but I understand how stressful it is to plan a wedding," he said removing his hand from mine.

"I will be okay."

"I know you will, but there's nothing wrong with having someone to listen to you or give words of encouragement."

He grabbed my cell phone that was charging and saved his number in it and then called his phone and saved my number as well.

"Thanks," I said smiling at him. I appreciated his concern. His fiancée was a very fortunate lady to have someone like him in her life.

***

I arrived at home around four and as soon as I turned my key and opened my door, my phone vibrated, letting me know I had a text message.

Have you had enough time now? Flashed on my screen and Kevin's name appeared underneath.

I sighed deeply, kicked off my heels, took my dress off, and threw it on the back of the sofa. I stretched out on my couch with just my slip on. I had to talk to him and I couldn't keep putting it off.

Yeah

Can I come over now?

Knowing that this could be a huge mistake, I told him yes anyway.

Be over in ten minutes, flashed on my screen.

I pulled myself off the couch and went to my room to change into a pair of jeans and a t-shirt before he came over.

"I understand what you are saying, Rachel, but I never set out to make you feel that way. The only thing I was trying to do was help you feel better. Your fiancé is a very lucky man and he should know that. Matter of fact, where is he now?" Kevin sat on the edge of my couch looking straight at me, his eyes begging for my mercy. He still had on his black and blue Carolina Panthers jacket, which I preferred because the last thing I wanted was for him to get comfortable and stay a while.

"My fiancé is not the focus right now," I answered calmly.

"Has he made *you* his focus lately?"

"Is that any of your business?" I snapped.

"Rachel, just the other night you were crying on my shoulder about him and your wedding and now since we were intimate it's none of my business?" Kevin smirked.

"We were not intimate," I said looking around the room. I wanted to look anywhere other than at Kevin.

"Rachel, how can you say that?"

"Being intimate with someone is having feelings for that person. What we did was not an intimate act," I insisted. I placed my hands on my hips and met Kevin's glare this time.

"Hey, don't let your guilt berate what happened between us and how I feel about you," Kevin said as he stood up.

"Huh? How do you feel about me?" I asked, puzzled. I was shocked that Kevin had any feelings for me at all.

"Does it really matter?" he asked, heading for the door. "Maybe one day you will see it for yourself."

He walked out of the apartment door, closing it behind him, leaving me alone again. Alone in my apartment and alone in my heart.

Chapter 15

"Rachel Simms speaking," I answered the phone in an unusually cheerful voice. I saw the Atlanta area code before I picked up and that meant it could only be one person calling me on this Monday morning. Terrence.

"Hey there, pretty lady," Terrence said.

"Hey yourself," I said feeling all giddy inside.

Every since our first meeting that night at the gas station I always looked forward to talking to Terrence on Monday mornings. The phone calls went from once a week to maybe three times a week and sometimes he would call just to see how I was doing. He even began to email me encouraging words every now and then. I was so flattered by the attention that he was giving me and even more thankful that it was strictly in a friendly manner. Although, I was attracted to Terrence, our conversations never crossed any lines or boundaries.

"How are you doing today?" he asked.

I enlightened Terrence about the events over the weekend regarding me and Corey, leaving out the Kevin part.

"I promised myself that I wouldn't cry and so far I have not," I said.

"And there is no need to cry either," Terrence replied.

He then told me about his weekend and the time spent with his family. In the past few weeks, Terrence had revealed to me that he and his wife of five years were having problems. This was his second marriage and he was more determined than ever to make it work. He loved his wife very much but was upset at the fact that the drive she had when they first got married was not there anymore. They had three kids in all, two together and a son he had from his first marriage.

Terrence told me how simple talks between him and his wife would turn to arguments.

He was really unhappy in the situation but he loved her and he would do whatever it took to make things better. My heart went out to Terrence and we would spend most of our phone conversations either talking about his marriage or my soon-to-be marriage.

"I have to go to a conference seminar for my job in two weeks in Greensboro. How far is that from Charlotte?" Terrence inquired.

"Probably about 2 hours I would think," I said, not sure where Terrence was going with this.

"The conference is going to be Thursday, Friday, and Saturday. I think it ends early on Friday so would you like to come up and have dinner with me? I hope you don't think I am being too forward but I really enjoy talking to you and it seems like you could use some time to get away."

"Sure, I will just come up after work Friday," I blurted out without giving the invitation much thought. I felt comfortable enough from talking to Terrence and this would be a nice change from the bar hopping that I was doing with Von on Friday and Saturday nights.

Last night after Kevin left, I texted Corey and apologized for getting loud with him and not allowing him to explain. He responded and said that it's okay and he was sorry as well for canceling our plans. Neither one of us called the other. He needed time to calm down and so did I. He hadn't said anything about coming to see me and I was pretty sure he wouldn't try to visit in the next two weeks, either. I needed a break from the constant arguments, and I was sure he did as well.

"Great!" Terrence said. "We can hang out, just chill and have some fun." He laughed and I caught myself laughing right along with him.

"Guess I need to get back to work," I said, ending the conversation that was making my heart flutter.

"Alright, Ms. Rachel, talk to you soon."

I hung up the phone and thought about how attracted I was to Terrence. Would it really be a good idea to drive two hours to have dinner with a married man? We were friends, and after the Kevin episode, I would not dare put myself in that situation again, but was this really okay to do?

The pre-wedding planning Rachel would never do this. She would never even talk to Terrence as much as she was doing. I noticed that I was doing a lot of things now I wouldn't have done in the past. The words that Von recited to me played in my head on a daily basis. I could hear her saying over and over again, "Have fun, Rachel! Do things that you would not normally do!" I wasn't married yet but my actions were like those of a decrepit married woman. Five or ten years from now would I look back and regret the things that I had done or didn't do?

Terrence was a sweet guy and I did want to see him again. Really, what harm could this do? I rolled my chair towards the window and gazed out of it. One little dinner would be a welcome distraction from all the stress I been under for the last couple of months.

***

Two weeks came and went, and by this time, Corey and I were on speaking terms again. I resolved to keep what happened between me and Kevin to myself and just ask God to forgive me. I vowed to never let anything like that happen again. Even though we were talking now, I had not seen Corey in almost three months, and he still had not made any plans to come see me.

On the advice of Von and Monica, I went to an adult novelty store and bought some toys to keep me occupied and relieve any stress until I was able to get my hands on my fiancé. I didn't want to start any arguments with him, so asking to visit him or when he was going to come see me was out of the question.

I hoped that he would feel the same sexual tension I was feeling, but he never said anything about it, so I left this subject alone, too. We were even getting to the point where we could discuss details of the wedding, and I definitely didn't want to rock that boat.

It was finally Friday and I was rather excited about seeing Terrence tonight. The plan was for me to leave Charlotte at five, right after work. I anticipated working the entire day, but when noon rolled around, I had finished all my work and ended the day early.

Terrence called that morning to see if I was still coming up, and although I was just as nervous as the first time I saw him, my answer was yes. Von called also to see if we were doing the usual and going out tonight, but my answer to her was no. I made up a lame excuse about not feeling well and just wanting some time alone. Of course this did not go over with her and she had a million questions, but I just ended the conversation by telling her that I would talk to her later.

I showered, shaved my legs, and sprayed myself with one of my favorite perfumes, Nude by Rihanna. I slid on the lilac sundress that I had worn to Von's mom's cookout that got me so much attention and a pair of open toed silver Michael Kors heels. The shoes were a gift to myself for meeting my monthly weight goal and losing an extra five pounds. The dress fit me even better now and I knew if Von saw me she would be pleased. I heard my cell phone ringing and reached over to pick it up off my bed.

"Hello," I answered still admiring myself in the mirror. I twirled around and examined how sexy my ass looked in the dress. Any man would be tempted to reach out and grab a handful if he saw me.

"Hey, you are out of the office?" Terrence asked.

"Yeah, I left a little earlier." I smiled at the thought of him calling my office to see if I was still there.

"I called to see if you like seafood. Someone told me about a restaurant a few blocks from here."

"I love seafood," I said.

"Great, call me when you get on the road."

***

We intended to eat dinner at seven, so around five I popped in my Fantasia CD and coasted along I-77 to Greensboro. I directed Ghost, my white Infiniti, towards I-85, set my cruise control to 70, rolled my windows down, and let the wind rip through my freshly permed and layered hair.

The ride would be about two hours - one straight shot there. I listened to Fantasia sing her heart out as she asked where would you be without me, and cleared my mind of all the worries that crowded my world in the last three months. I cherished riding and freeing my thoughts. I was going to enjoy every little moment of this drive.

As Fantasia was about to get into the side effects of you, my phone began to ring. Corey's face and number flashed on my screen, and all of a sudden, I became tense. Hoping that he was not going to surprise me and try to come see me, I hesitantly answered the phone.

"Hey, baby."

"Hey, Rachel, where are you?" Corey asked.

"I am in my car driving," I replied nervously.

I didn't want to tell Corey that I was heading to Greensboro to have dinner with another man. We were just friends and nothing was going on between me and Terrence, but there were some things that I felt were unnecessary to share, especially at the fragile state that we were in right now. Another change for me, the Rachel before the wedding planning told Corey everything.

"I was calling because I was thinking about you and wanted to tell you that I love you," Corey said.

"Baby, that's so sweet. I love you, too."

I was still hoping that he didn't ask me where I was going.

I refused to lie to him, but I also didn't want him asking and that lead to more problems.

"I know that you are probably hanging out with Von tonight so I won't bother you. Have fun, baby."

"You too," I said. "I will give you a call later."

I hung up the phone thinking how strange it was for Corey to call me out of the blue just to tell me that he loved me. That was something that he use to do months ago, but I had not heard him sound like that and say those things in a long time.

I was on the road for about an hour and a half when my cell phone began to ring again. This time it was Terrence.

"Hey you," I sang into the phone.

"Hey yourself," he said laughing. "Where are you, pretty lady?"

"I am about thirty minutes outside of Greensboro."

"Did you get the directions to the hotel I emailed you?" Terrence asked.

"Sure did," I said.

"Just call me when you get to the lobby and I will come and meet you."

***

Everything in my body was screaming *BAD IDEA, VERY BAD IDEA*, when I watched this stunning man get off the elevator and come towards me. Wearing a pair of black slacks that looked like they were tailor made just for him and a cherry red button down dress shirt, Terrence was a sight to behold. His bald head was glistening under the hotel lights of the lobby and I could tell he had recently shaved.

Maybe it was the fact that I had seen him in just a t-shirt and jeans the first time we met in person, but he looked even more handsome that I remembered. The thought that I had not been touched by a man in almost three months, with the exception of Kevin, crept into my mind.

I should have at least played with a couple of toys before coming here. That way I could focus on the dinner and not worry about my twins peeking over my dress trying to get out.

"Damn, you are even more beautiful than I remember." Terrence smiled, making my heart melt.

"Thank you," I muttered. I tried to remember that this was a married man. Nevertheless, he was still making me hot in places that he should not.

"I am starving," he said. He took my hand and ushered me out of the front door of the hotel.

Over dinner, we shared more relationship stories and he continued to tell me about his wife and the problems they were facing. He told me how she could not keep a job and she knew that she really didn't have to work because he made enough to support the family by himself. What seemed to bother him most was that she was an extremely intelligent woman, but after their kids were born, she was more focused on being a house-wife and the ambition she once had disappeared. She had a nursing degree she never used, although before they were married she was anxious to go into the healthcare field. He attempted to talk to her on many different occasions about this, but her feelings were easily hurt; therefore, he resolved to see what would happen.

Throughout dinner I was amazed at how attentive Terrence was. It seemed as if he was hanging onto my every word. There were moments when he would just look at me and smile and my thoughts would go to Corey and how we used to be this way. But thoughts of Corey would soon disappear as soon as Terrence would open his mouth.

"What are you thinking about, miss lady?" Terrence asked wiping his hands on his napkin and placing it in his empty plate.

"I still can't get over the fact that I thought you were such an ass before," I said, giggling.

I took another sip of the vodka and cranberry juice that I ordered and hoped that drinking was not a bad idea.

I twirled the tiny straw around in the glass in a circular motion as if I was still mixing the drink and grinned at Terrence.

"See, there you go hurting my feelings again," Terrence said making the cutest puppy dog face.

"Whatever! I doubt that I could do that."

Our eyes met again. I tried to look away like I had done the entire night whenever we would glance at each other, but this time I couldn't. His eyes were spellbinding and I was in a deep trance.

"It's amazing how I feel like I have known you for years," he said, finally interrupting our stare and the thoughts that were going on in both our heads.

"I feel the exact same way."

"You are beautiful." Terrence leaned back in his chair and folded his arms across his chest.

"Thank you," I replied my face turning red.

I again swirled the ice around in my glass that was now empty. I had not finished eating all of my shrimp alfredo, and even though it was delicious, the damn butterflies that were nesting in my stomach made it quite difficult to enjoy.

"You want to stay and get a few more drinks?" he asked.

"Sure!" I was already past tipsy and on my way to feeling really good.

"Oh no, I remember that look from the first time I saw you," Terrence said, winking at me.

As he lifted his hand and slightly waved at the waitress to come back over to our table, I glanced at the gold band shining on his ring finger. He ordered another cranberry and vodka for me and Hennessey and coke for him.

For the next two hours we talked about everything from his ex-wife to the first boyfriend I ever had. Before we knew it, the time was 11:00 pm and my eyes were heavy. Terrence's eyes were a bit slanted as well, but he seemed to be able to drink a lot more than I could.

Terrence stood up from the table, pushed his chair under and moved around to my side.

"You want to head back so that you can get on the road?"

"Yeah, it's getting late," I said trying my best to stand up without stumbling over.

The worst thing that you can ever do is get drunk while sitting down. The affects of alcohol gave standing a whole new meaning.

"Are you okay?" Terrence asked grabbing my waist in order to keep me walking straight instead of sideways. His hold was strong and firm but tender at the same time.

"Of course," I said trying to get myself together.

Terrence removed his hands from my waist and then reached for my hand. Our eyes locked as he said the same words that I was thinking.

"Holding your hand just doesn't feel wrong to me."

I prayed the alcohol would wear off soon so I could not only walk but think straight as well.

"Rachel, I really don't think you need to drive like this," Terrence said pulling his black Explorer into the parking lot of the hotel. I had been expecting to see the burgundy Acura that we sat in at the store that first night, but Terrence informed me that was a rental car and this truck was one of his favorite possessions. The leather seats in his truck were so comfortable that I had almost fallen asleep on the ride back. With my hand on my head I was in no position to disagree with him.

"How about you come up and get a few hours of rest? Just sleep off that alcohol and then get on the road. I wouldn't want anything to happen to you," Terrence insisted.

I reluctantly agreed and allowed him to help me out of his truck. We walked into the lobby and he gave me the key to his room while he went to the front desk to order something. Not even concerned with what it was he went to get, I staggered into the elevator and pressed the button for the third floor.

Room 309 was an executive room furnished with a king size bed positioned in the center, made up perfectly as if no one had ever slept in it. Covered with an olive green comforter, the bed was large enough for three adults to sleep peacefully.

The room's green, pink, and red flowered curtains were pulled closed showing only a sliver of a sheer dingy beige curtain underneath. The room was dark except for the small lamp light over the cherry oak desk that was nestled in the corner.

Terrence's laptop sat open on the desk, showing a screensaver of three kids. Two boys and one girl. From our conversation, I knew that Stacy was the girl's name and Brandon and David were the boys. Terrence had spent a great deal of time talking about them at dinner. The little girl was smiling hard and showing off the space where her two front teeth used to be. She resembled him the most. The two boys were smiling but not as wide as the little girl. Terrence's kids. This was his family, with the exception of his wife.

I sat on the edge of the bed for a moment and grabbed the remote. As I pushed the big green power button, I kicked off my heels and positioned myself cross-legged on the bed.

After a few minutes, I lay back and waited for Terrence. By the time the second commercial came on, my eyes were shut tight and the alcohol had me in a night time coma.

Chapter 16

Startled, I jumped up and looked around, unsure of where I was. I blinked several times trying to get my eyes to focus through the darkness of the room. Terrence sat at the desk working on his laptop and as soon as he heard me he rushed over to the bed.

"You okay?" he asked.

I ran my fingers through my hair so that I wouldn't look a complete mess and glanced around the room once again. Those ugly flowered curtains were still pulled together but closer than before so that the sheer piece was not seen. I recalled falling asleep on the bed on top of the covers, but now I was tucked neatly under the comforter.

"Oh man, what time is it?" I asked.

"It's only one," Terrence said noticing my obvious confusion. "You have only been asleep for about an hour and a half."

I rubbed my eyes attempting to focus and fully wake up. Yawning, I ran my hand through my hair again. Terrence sat on the edge of the bed a few inches away from me, staring intently.

"You know you are beautiful even when you are sleep," Terrence said. His voice was low and I could feel myself being turned on.

Trying to lighten the mood, I joked, "Oh, so you were watching me while I slept?"

"I apologize but I couldn't help it," Terrence answered.

He moved closer to me and again we were mere inches apart. I suddenly felt uncomfortable. Noticing my body was tense, Terrence stood, and asked if I wanted some water.

"Yeah, that would be nice."

He left the room to get some ice from the machine down the hall and once again I was alone in his room, with his belongings, and that damn screensaver staring back at me. The boys and Stacy, smiling, looking like their daddy.

"How are you feeling now?" Terrence asked after returning with a container full of ice. He grabbed one of the glasses sitting on his desk and a bottled water from the mini fridge.

"I am feeling better."

"Rachel, there is no reason for you to get on the road until you feel 100 percent," Terrence said.

There was a bottle of Hennessey sitting on the desk right beside the ice that Terrence had retrieved. Maybe that's what he ordered from the front desk, I thought. I sat up in the middle of this huge bed and watched Terrence fix a drink for himself and a glass of water for me. Terrence still had on the same red shirt but it was unbuttoned showing a white t-shirt underneath. His shoulders were broad and his stomach was flat. He had gotten comfortable and taken off his shoes, and was walking around in his black dress socks.

"Ms. lady, I have been nice letting you use my bed and all, but now you need to slide over," Terrence said approaching the bed and handed me the water.

I slid over and he sat on top of the covers and reached for the remote that was lying on the bed. We were sitting side by side in bed with our backs against the headboard, Terrence on top of the covers and me underneath. To my surprise, this didn't feel as uneasy as when he was facing me. After a few swallows I placed the glass on the floor next to the bed.

"So let's see what's on TV," he said.

He flipped to a news channel and we talked about current events. A David's Bridal commercial came on and I became quiet. My smile disappeared. I lifted my knees towards my chest, and placed my head on them. In a matter of seconds I began to cry. Terrence put his arm around my shoulders and pulled me into his chest and for the first time in a long time, I was comforted.

He felt warm and safe. This felt different from when Kevin comforted me. My body relaxed and I exhaled and allowed his arms to shelter me.

"I thought you said that you weren't going to cry," Terrence said making an effort to stop my tears.

"I'm sorry," I mumbled in between sobs. "We have shared a lot of stories and even though I feel really close to you, I have been feeling lonely for the last three months. You already know that Corey and I have been constantly arguing and every time he says he is coming to see me he cancels." I sighed and looked up at Terrence. He held me tighter and waited for me to continue. "We haven't been intimate in a while, and I don't feel wanted or desired," I confessed.

This was a bad topic to talk about, especially with liquor still in my system, but I couldn't mask the tears or the pain. Terrence touched my face with his hand so tenderly that my tears stopped. He lifted my face and our eyes locked for what seemed like the hundredth time that night. He took his other hand and grabbed my hand and held it tight. I couldn't think. All I could see was this attractive man in front of me that was staring at me but not making a move.

"Rachel, I am sorry that you are going through all this. I can't tell you that it's going to get better but don't ever feel that you are not wanted." Terrence's eyes were steady and his voice was so low that if I was not right beside him I would not have heard anything he said.

Without thinking, I touched his hand that was caressing my face and gently kissed it. He stared at me as if to ask was I sure. I leaned in and answered his question by resting my lips on his. Terrence quickly pulled back, abandoning my kiss.

"I am sorry," I uttered, embarrassed that I thought he wanted to kiss me.

Terrence stared at me for a moment and leaned in closer.

"Shhh," he whispered in my ear as he kissed my ear, traveled down to my neck, and finally found my lips again.

In 26 years, three boyfriends, and a fiancé, I can honestly say that I had never been kissed like that before. Never been kissed so slowly and with so much passion. Never been kissed with lips that were so soft, so freeing. Lips that made me want to surrender and give him all of me. Terrence's kiss made me feel like my lips were a buried treasure that he had been seeking and at last had found. His hand still held mine as he continued to kiss me. I was hungry for his mouth and I was losing myself. This had to stop. Suddenly, I pulled back.

"I apologize," Terrence said letting go of my hand.

"There is no reason for you to apologize. I just don't want this to go too far."

"I understand," Terrence said now looking at the TV. "I want you to know that I didn't intend or expect anything like this to happen." Terrence finally looked back at me. He rubbed his bald head and gave me a weak smile. "It's getting late and I really don't want you to go anywhere tonight. Do you mind if I just hold you?" he asked.

Terrence's words echoed in my head for a moment and compelled a smile to overtake my face.

"I don't see a problem with that," I said. I couldn't even remember the last time I had been held.

Terrence went in the bathroom while I got comfortable again in the soothing, cozy king size bed. When he came out of the bathroom he had only his white t-shirt on and blue basketball shorts instead of the slacks that he wore to dinner. He climbed into bed and pulled the covers over us.

"Is this okay with you?" Terrence asked in a low calm voice.

"I am fine."

Terrence lay on his back and pulled me into his arms. I rested my head on his shoulder, wrapped my arms around him, and fell into a deep sleep.

Chapter 17

I was awakened by the whistling on my cell phone. Terrence was still lying beside me snoring softly. His gorgeous mouth was pressed together and he looked calm and content, even in his sleep. I carefully reached around him trying to grab my phone that was lighting up on the nightstand. I didn't want to awaken him since he looked so peaceful. Terrence turned on his side as I grabbed my phone and saw Monica's face flashing on the screen.

It was 8:00 Saturday morning and I would definitely have to get on the road before people began to search for me. As soon as I peeled the covers back and got out of bed, Terrence woke up and asked if I was leaving. I let him know the time and that I had to get on the road before anyone started worrying. Terrence pushed the covers back and got out of bed heading towards the bathroom.

I again attempted to comb thru my hair with my fingers and wipe the sleep from my eyes. The room was still somewhat dark, but just as before, the screensaver stared at me.

Terrence came out of the bathroom and as I passed him to go in to straighten myself up a little, our eyes met causing me to grin. I came out of the bathroom and there Terrence stood as if he was waiting on me. He had put his black slacks back on but still had on the white t-shirt.

"I enjoyed you last night," he said moving in closer towards me.

"I had a nice time as well." My voice squeaked, exposing my nervousness.

I reached out to give him a hug and what I thought would be a quick embrace became the total opposite. Terrence held me tight and without saying anything I held him the same way.

I felt the heat from his body and listened to the enticing sounds of his breathing. I wrapped my arms tighter around his masculine frame and closed my eyes.

"I don't understand why this doesn't feel wrong," he whispered in my ear.

He tightened his grip around me and for the next few seconds we stood in Room 309 in each other's arms, his laptop facing us as Stacy smiled, showing her missing teeth.

***

"Where are you? I have tried to reach you all morning." Monica's voice boomed over my cell phone. She was on speaker phone since I lost my hands free blue tooth and I didn't want my arms getting tired from holding the phone to my ear. I was on such a high from being with Terrence that even Monica couldn't upset me. Terrence's conference was concluding on Saturday with lunch and a short meeting and he assured me that he would call me before he checked out of the hotel. My heart was soaring and so light that it felt like a balloon in the Macy's Thanksgiving Day Parade.

"I been about my business," I sang into the phone ignoring Monica's twenty questions.

"Was that business with Corey?" Monica asked.

She was so determined to know what was going on in my life in order to avoid making decisions in her own.

"No, nosey!" I was getting irritated at Monica for trying to knock me off the fluffy cloud on which I was now perched, with thoughts of Terrence flying around my head.

"Oh, well, excuse me."

"Monica, I just took a little time for myself." I wanted to change the subject before she began to ask more questions. "So how are things going with you?" I asked.

"Tony is back."

I couldn't tell whether my sister was delighted about this or not; but I did know that she was not jumping for joy at the moment.

"What does that mean?" I asked trying to hide my sarcasm.

"It means that we are trying to work things out."

Monica knew that any other time I would have made a smart comment but ever since we were back on good terms I didn't want her to think that I was being judgmental, or as she liked to call me, high and mighty.

"If you are happy, then I am happy," I said.

"I am not sure what I am, Rachel. I mean, he is doing everything possible to make things better but there is this child and we still are not sure if he is even the father."

"If you want to be with him just stick by his side through it all and the truth will come out."

"You are being real mellow today. Did you get some?" Monica laughed while my thoughts went back to how gorgeous Terrence looked last night.

"No, I did not! I told you I wasn't with Corey. I had a really nice night and I have cleared my mind."

"Girl, whatever you did, maybe I need to do it so I can sound all relaxed. Call me a little later on."

"Okay sis." I hung up the phone and turned my music up full blast. The speakers rocked my car back and forth. Trey Songz was singing about not wanting to leave but he had to go. I could feel his pain.

It was almost ten and the only thing I wanted to do when I got home was take a nice hot bubble bath and get in my bed. I didn't want to talk to Corey and have him ruin my good mood. I didn't want to talk to my mom and think about the wedding. I definitely didn't want to talk to Von about her cheating ass father. I wanted to get in bed with my thoughts of Terrence and the amazing night we had together.

I arrived home and went straight to my room. I was determined not to let anyone bring me down so I didn't even stop to check my phone messages.

The light was blinking, but I could care less about that right now. I almost turned my cell phone off, too, but remembering that Terrence said he was going to call, I left it on.

Once I got out of the tub I snuggled in bed and turned on the TV that I would not watch. All I could think about was the kiss that Terrence and I shared. It was so different than when I was with Kevin. Even though it was only a kiss and what I did with Kevin was a lot more, I didn't feel the same guilt as I did before. I didn't want to run to Corey and tell him what happened like I did the morning after I was with Kevin. To me this was a secret that only Terrence and I shared. But it bothered me that I didn't feel guilty. Not only was I kissing another man months before my wedding, but this was a married man. Another woman's husband. Still the remorse did not come. The shame did not dig inside me like it did with Kevin and I was not disgusted at the fact that I spent the night with Terrence. He held me the entire night and I had not slept so peacefully in months. Was my relationship with Corey so far gone that I needed to be comforted by another man and was not ashamed that I had been?

I thought about how Terrence held my hand and how his hug was so strong, so tight as if he didn't want to let me go. Then that damn screensaver came to mind. He had three beautiful kids. Thinking about the kids, maybe that would bring about the guilt. Maybe that will force me to feel ashamed of my actions. I waited. No guilt. No shame.

I remembered the little girl's face. For some reason I keep seeing her smile in my head. I could imagine her calling out to her daddy. Telling him to come see the picture she drew for him. Could imagine them playing in the yard and Terrence kissing her. The same lips that kissed me last night. Jumping into her dad's arms. The same arms that held me last night.

My thoughts were interrupted by my cell phone. I picked it up after seeing a number that I didn't recognize.

"Hello," I answered still deeply enthralled in my thoughts of Terrence.

"Hello there." Terrence's voice was just as enticing as it was last night.

"I was just thinking about you," I said realizing that is was Terrence and the hotel's number that appeared on my phone.

"Oh really?"

I could tell that he was smiling on the other end as well and this made my heart flutter even more.

"Maybe just a little," I said, laughing at my obvious lie.

"Glad I am not alone then, 'cause you have been on my mind as well."

Everything in me wanted to let him know that I couldn't stop thinking about the kiss and him but I just couldn't. No matter how I felt I couldn't act on it, and telling him would not do anything but make me think about him even more, if that was possible.

"So how was the conference?" I asked moving on to a safer subject.

"It was cool, a lot of good information," he said laughing at my effort to avoid talks of how much we enjoyed one another

"I'm glad that you benefited from it." I flipped through the channels trying to find something to watch on TV.

"The best part was seeing you."

Not sure how to respond I sat silent on the phone for a few seconds.

"Oh sorry, we were not supposed to talk about that," Terrence said chuckling again.

"You are a trip," I laughed along with Terrence.

"Rachel I am about to get on the road and head back to Atlanta. I will be thinking of you. Talk to you first thing Monday morning."

"Sounds good."

"Take care."

Even after I pressed end on my cell phone, my old butterfly friends were at it again in my stomach. This man had no right to make me feel this way.

I placed my cell phone on the dresser beside my bed and wrapped myself up in my sheets and comforter. It was the end of September and still dry and humid in South Carolina although I always kept my apartment cool. I loved to snuggle up under the covers even if I was just cuddling with myself most nights.

I dozed in and out of sleep dreaming about being back in Terrence's arms when I heard my cell phone ring again. I looked at my phone and saw that it was Von and let it go to my voicemail. I would give her a call later. It wasn't Terrence, so I refused to let anyone else spoil my rare day of bliss.

I flipped the TV to another channel that would not get much attention from me. With my hands behind my head and sinking deeper into my pillows, I smiled as my mind went back to Terrence. I was still in shock over how I didn't feel that my thinking about him and the night we shared was wrong. In high school and college I was always the one telling Monica and Von right from wrong where men were concerned. Always the one saying that if he has a girlfriend don't even look at him because if he would talk to you then he was no good. Always the one telling them to never ever let a man dictate what you do. Always preaching to them that the things they did were wrong and were things that I would never do.

I would never cheat on my man; never be dishonest with him because I would expect the same in return. Why wasn't all the preaching that I had done to others coming into play now? Did I need affection so bad that I was not going to listen to the advice that I had given my sister and best friend for so long? This man is married and I am sitting here thinking about him like both of us are single and available. This was just senseless.

My voicemail notification sounded and I decided to listen to the message even though I knew I wasn't going to call Von back right now. In a defeated tone that I rarely heard, Von left a message saying that she had to meet her sister. She felt like she was in a no win situation between her dad and Kevin pushing her to meet this woman.

Von needed me, but I couldn't be there for her right now. I needed some time to myself to be alone with my thoughts. I knew I wouldn't be able to focus on Von and her family issues. My mind was everywhere but where it should be. The wedding was six months away, and even though my mom was doing mostly everything herself, I still had to do a lot more. I was supposed to be concentrating on that and the happy life that Corey and I had planned.

I slid down further in my bed and pulled my satin sheets over my head. I wondered if Terrence was thinking about me. I wonder if he would be thinking about me when he got home to his wife and kids. When he walked in the door and kissed his wife and told her how much he missed her, would he think about my lips that he kissed the night before? When he held her tonight in their bed, would he reflect on the fact that he held me just twenty-four hours ago? Come on, Rachel. This man is married and you are not on his mind, I admonished myself.

Maybe those feelings were just lies, infatuation. There were not years between us. It was just exciting to get to know someone new. Get over it, Rachel. This man was going back to his home, his wife, and his kids. You are his friend and you all shared a liquored up kiss because he's dealing with his home life and you're lonely without Corey. I sank deeper in my bed and replaced my thoughts of Terrence with earlier times that Corey and I shared. After all, he was my soon-to-be husband and the quicker I put my focus back on him, the better things would be.

***

I woke up the second time after my two hour nap and called Von to check on her.

"Hey girl," she said in that same crushed tone.

"Hey, are you okay? I got your message."

"Yeah, I will be alright.

It's just that there are so many unanswered questions I have right now." Von sighed deeply in the phone. My best friend was in some serious pain.

"Have you talked to your dad again?"

"Yeah, but all he wants is for all his kids to meet."

"How do you feel about that?"

"Rachel, you have known me mostly all my life and you know that I have not always done the right things. I have slept with married men, men that had live-in girlfriends and all kinds of other things, but to know that my father was going around cheating on my mother makes me rethink everything I ever did."

My heart had an anchor on it and was plummeting to the bottom of the ocean. I listened to Von talk about marriage and how she always thought that her parents were perfect for each other. She felt so betrayed that my mind went back to Terrence and our night together. Is this how his wife and daughter would feel? Is this the way I would feel if Corey ever cheated on me? I prayed I would never find out.

"You have always preached to me about doing what's right, but you know I don't listen." Von continued to talk as my heart broke for her.

"Von, we all have done wrong, so don't beat yourself up over something that your father did." I wanted to tell Von that she was not alone and everybody makes mistakes, even me, except I didn't want to make this about me right now.

"Rachel, I never told you this, but I admire you. No matter what you always seem to do the right thing. It used to aggravate the hell out of me a while back but now I respect that quality in you." Von went on about being honest, and all I saw as she spoke were flashes of Kevin and Terrence.

"I just don't know if I can handle this," Von's voice cracked.

"You don't have to do it alone, girl."

Chapter 18

I pushed my way through the heavy glass doors of Snyder & Lawry and chose to actually talk to Daria today instead of running past her or just saying "Hey girl" and ignoring her conversation about her broke ass boyfriend.

"Hey Daria, how was your weekend?"

"Hey, girl!" Daria said smiling and twisting her hair.

She had all those red curls piled on the top of her head and a few pieces hanging here and there around the edges. Her breasts looked as if they were only seconds anyway from popping out of her orange and blue blouse and hitting someone in the eye.

"My weekend was great! My boyfriend got an interview at the warehouse not too far from my house. His cousin hooked him up with it so hopefully he will get the job and we can get a place together," she announced.

She was so elated that this man she had been putting up with forever was finally getting a job that I didn't want to rain on her parade.

"That's wonderful. I hope everything works out for you two. I am going to try to tackle all this work I have, but I will talk to you later." I continued to my office hoping she wouldn't call me back to finish up our conversation.

"Okay girl!" Daria shouted, swinging around in her chair to face the door and pounce on the next employee that walked in.

Every since I was with Terrence Friday night and Saturday morning, nothing seemed to bother me much. On Saturday night, I lounged around my apartment and talked to Von about meeting her sister. She was at a complete loss about what she wanted to do. My experiences were nonexistent on those types of situations, so I was unsure of what to tell her.

If I was in her position, I am not certain that I would want to meet the child that my dad conceived with another woman. But then again that was her sister and a part of her desired to meet this woman. This stranger with whom she shared the same father. Von was reliving the day that her mom informed her about her dad's indiscretions and how wounded she felt. I listened to my best friend talk and volunteered no advice. She just needed an ear and I would provide that.

I had gone to church by myself on Sunday after Von turned me down. After service, Jerome had wanted to hold a long conversation, but I was eager to get back home and work out. I spoke with Corey as well and even though the conversation was general without getting into any heavy stuff, it was pleasant.

After unlocking my office door, I opened my blinds so that the sunlight would pour into this quaint space. I sat down in my chair, rolled around to face my computer, and logged on. The first thing I did each morning was check my email and read anything vital that was sent out by the lawyers. I looked at my inbox and the first name I saw was Terrence Walker. A grin spread over my face as I opened the email. I expected it to be some sort of inspirational phrase or a little saying just to make me laugh. As I began to read the email my heart thumped as if the little drummer boy was playing his favorite tune on it.

From: Terrence Walker
To: Rachel Simms
Subject: Thoughts of you
I know that you have not gotten in yet, but I came in early and I was sitting at my desk with you on my mind. I can't seem to stop thinking about you. I stayed up Saturday and Sunday nights and thought about you and how good it felt to have you in my arms. I feel like I am back in high school again with a crush on the prettiest girl in school. Believe me, everything in me is saying that I should not be thinking this, but I can't help myself. I want to see you again, I want to hold you again, and I want to kiss you again. I keep seeing your beautiful smile in my head and my heart does all these weird things that it has not done in years.

*Being with you and talking to you is so easy. Can we see each other again?
I don't want to pressure you and I know that you are getting married in a
few months so don't say yes unless you are sure.*
Terrence

I studied his email. I couldn't imagine that he was feeling the
exact same way I was. I clicked reply but couldn't find the
words to say. It was nice dreaming of being in his arms again,
but it couldn't happen. I had to stay true to Corey and even
though nothing transpired but a kiss, it could never occur again.
I closed the reply message and turned my chair around to face
the window.

My heart was doing all kind of flips. I envisioned this was
what Terrence was talking about in his email. This had to stop
before it got any further. There was no doubt in my mind that
enjoying Terrence's company needed to end at just that. There
was no way I was going to jeopardize my relationship with
Corey more than I already had. We weren't spending any time
together, still had not had sex, and we were barely talking, but
the fact still remained that in a matter of months I was going to
be his wife and that was not going to change. I leaned back in
my chair and thought about Corey and all the hopes and
dreams that we shared.

I turned around towards my desk and hit reply for the
second time. Once again nothing came to me. I couldn't come
up with the words to express my feelings about what he wrote
or what happened between us. Something did take place
between us that night. We didn't sleep together but a bond had
formed. Terrence touched my heart that night. We didn't have
sex but we were intimate. Intimate in a way that I had never
been with anyone other than Corey in years.

As soon as I began to type I felt my cell phone vibrating. I
dug my phone out of my pocket and saw that it was Jerome
sending me a text message.

Around your way, want to have lunch?

Perfect distraction! I quickly typed back, *Sure, where?*

***

Jerome and I planned to meet at a soul food restaurant called Mom's Kitchen, which was directly across the street from my job. I walked in the glass finger-printed door as Joe, the owner, waved and smiled at me. Joe was an older black man that knew everyone who frequented the restaurant.

"Hey Ms. Rachel!" Joe smiled so wide showing all the indentions in the back of his mouth that should have been home to maybe four or five teeth.

Mom's Kitchen smelled of greens, ham hocks, and sweet potato pie all mixed into one. The restaurant was merely a hole in the wall with five small rectangular tables facing the door and two smaller ones off to the side. There were local news story clippings and famous celebrity pictures plastered all over the walls. The beige stained counter was covered with pies and cakes, and near the register, flyers that promoters and local business owners left in hopes that someone would notice and pick up. Most people ordered their food to go, but a few came in to sit down and just enjoy the home cooked scents and conversations. This restaurant was definitely what one would call country, and no one could deny that the food was scrumptious.

I smiled back at Joe and asked how he was doing. I arrived a little earlier to get comfortable before Jerome got there. Sitting down at one of the smaller tables off to the side near the door, I wanted Jerome to see me as soon as he came in. I waited for almost ten minutes and was caught by surprise when Jerome walked into the restaurant. After being used to him in suits and church attire, seeing him in actual street clothes was a pleasing sight.

He glided in wearing a pair of blue jeans and a grey short-sleeve v-neck shirt that displayed every chest, stomach, and arm muscle he had.

All those muscles were hidden underneath the suits he wore every Sunday. I was stunned at how physically fit he was. Jerome immediately saw me and removed the dark sunglasses that covered his eyes. His grey shirt complimented his eyes in a way that made it difficult not to stare. He approached my table as I took a deep breath, remembering my reason for meeting him. I wanted to take my mind off of Terrence and get a male's prospective on why I was feeling this way. Jerome was the perfect person to talk to since he was going through similar feelings with planning his wedding and was so focused on his fiancé and church, which I should be concentrating on as well.

"Hey there."   I stood up to give Jerome a hug.

"Hey Rachel," he said squeezing me, then giving me a quick glance over.

"I was surprised to get your text for lunch," I said, sitting back down and looking over the menu.

I always ordered the croaker fish when I ate at Mom's Kitchen, but I wanted something different today. My workouts were going extremely well and the pounds were dropping like crazy. I didn't want to mess that up by eating any fattening fried fish. I adjusted my low cut teal colored shirt so that I wouldn't give Jerome an unwelcomed view of my twins.

"You were on my mind today and when I saw you on Sunday you looked like you were dealing with a lot," Jerome said after ordering an iced tea from the waitress that was hovering near our table.

The dark skinned wanna-be diva was trying her best to get Jerome's attention by smiling intensely and standing with her right leg cocked out farther to the side so he could have a clear view of her ass. Some women had no shame.

"I am glad you asked me to lunch. I needed a distraction from everything that has been going on," I said.

When the waitress realized that Jerome was paying her little attention, she frowned at me and trotted away.

Over lunch, I conveyed how I was feeling about the wedding, Corey, and the way he was acting.

I even admitted what had happened with Terrence and the night I had with Kevin. At first, I was not going to share all this with him. I didn't want anyone to judge me, but there was this surprising warmth I felt with Jerome.

I felt like I could confide in him and it would go no further than just me and him. He didn't want or expect anything from me and I felt as if I could trust him. He told me that I was wrong for treating Kevin the way I had, but he never once told me that I was wrong for what I allowed him to do. He didn't even give me a scolding look as I went into detail about the night I shared with Terrence and the email that greeted me when I arrived at work this morning.

"How do you feel about him?" Jerome asked.

"To be honest, in a different time and place, if he was single and so was I, there could be something."

"Are you having any doubts about getting married, Rachel?"

"Jerome, before we started planning this wedding, everything was great, but now I hardly see Corey and we don't even talk as much as we used to. When we do talk we always end up arguing. I know things will change once we get married, but it's so hard to look toward that day when we don't get along now."

"You still didn't answer my question." Jerome stared at me.

I played with my straw to avoid his gaze. "Maybe I am having doubts now," I said. "If things have changed so much now before the wedding, can I be so sure that everything will be perfect after we say I do"?

"You really need to talk to your fiancé because it's possible that he is feeling the same way."

Jerome was right, but why did I always have to be the bigger person and go to Corey with what I was feeling? If he was feeling the same way, why couldn't he come to me? Then again it was possible he had tried, but with the way I was so stressed out, he may have felt like he couldn't talk to me.

I sighed and shook my head. "Jerome, I've just been feeling so lonely lately."

Jerome reached across the table and touched my hand just like he had done in the car a couple of weeks earlier. "Whenever you want to talk, I am here," he said.

Once again he showed that beautiful smile that needed to be on a Crest toothpaste commercial.

"How about you come over tonight and we can brainstorm and figure out how to put your soon to be marriage back on track?" Jerome asked.

During our lunch I felt really close to Jerome, almost like another brother. A part of me was just glad to have someone I could talk to that understood what I was going though and no romantic feelings to complicate things.

"That would be nice."

"Alright lil' lady, come over around seven."

***

When I returned to my office, I checked the voicemail and sure enough there was a message from Terrence. It was Monday and I had to talk to him about the numbers for the week. His call was more business than personal now. On the voicemail he simply said, "This is Terrence. Please return my phone call." He expected me to at least reply to his email and when I didn't that must have left him just as confused as I was. As a matter of fact, this whole situation was confounding. I had to respond to that email.

I waited another twenty minutes hoping that the right words would come to me, but after hitting reply and closing out the email the third time, I resolved to call him. Maybe he wouldn't even bring the email up. I prepared myself to talk to this man that was still making my stomach jump and turn like a million Mexican beans celebrating New Year's Day. The phone rang and after the third ring right before I hung up I heard one of the most arousing voices ever.

"Terrence Walker."

My body melted in 2.5 seconds.

"Hey, Terrence, this is Rachel." My voice cracked and my face was beet red. Good thing he could not see me right now. My voice resembled a thirteen-year-old girl speaking to her crush on the phone for the first time.

"Glad that you returned my phone call," he replied stumbling slightly over his words.

Was this gorgeous man just as nervous as I was? I went over business first, and it seemed like both us of were trying to feel the other out. After his phone call from the hotel Saturday afternoon, we had no contact. He'd advised me that his wife was a very jealous woman, so I refused to call, text, or email him when he was at home with his family. Now that we both were back at work and he sent that email, neither one of us knew how to approach the other.

We went over the numbers and other business matters and I refused to bring up the email. There was enough awkwardness between us already.

"Well, Terrence that is all I have for you today. I am going to try to get all my other work done that is staring me in the face." I attempted to laugh but it came out uneasily.

Anyone could tell that it was forced and again, I felt embarrassed for that.

"So we are just going to ignore it, huh?" Terrence asked after a brief pause.

"Ignore what?"

"The email I sent and what's happening between us."

I sighed and couldn't find the words to say. Everything that I thought of sounded wrong. I had no problem telling Jerome about Terrence and how I felt, but I just couldn't tell him.

"I am not ignoring it." Wow Rachel that was the best that you could come up with? I thought.

"What are we doing then?" Terrence asked. "Rachel, I don't go around and do this all the time. I am a man so of course I find other women attractive, but never have I had someone on my mind the way you have been this weekend. I want you back in my arms."

"Same here," I mumbled.

"I know we shouldn't take it there."

"Terrence, another time, if things were different"

"Yeah, I know, and that's what I have been telling myself," Terrence interjected. "I've been saying the same thing but for some reason it's not registering with me."

"Me either," I admitted.

"Rachel, can I see you again?"

"Yes," I answered without hesitation. Throughout this whole conversation, I was having a hard time responding and finding the words, but as soon as he asked that question I had no difficulty answering.

"It will be in the next few weeks, but I will let you know when," Terrence informed me.

"Okay."

"Take care and I will talk to you later."

Terrence hung up the phone and after a second passed I realized that I still had the phone to my ear.

Chapter 19

I was delighted at the welcome change of being able to go to a man's house without having expectations and worrying about his intentions. Jerome was safe. He was in love and soon to be married and I viewed him as a friend and a brother. We were siblings in Christ as well, and a man with a voice that powerful surely lived by his anointing. I was thankful for that. Thankful he was someone I could confide in. Thankful that he didn't judge me. And just thankful he listened to me. Yes, this man was as gorgeous and fascinating as a beach sunset, but there was a pure friendship between us and I was grateful.

After lunch, Jerome had texted me directions to his house. I wanted to talk to him about the conversation I had with Terrence today and ask him his thoughts. His advice would be greatly appreciated since I didn't have the slightest clue what to do.

Jerome opened the door as soon as I knocked and I was taken aback by how appealing he looked. I noticed that Jerome had on a black t-shirt and black sweat pants as if he had just finished up an intense workout.

"Hey Rachel," Jerome said waving for me to come in.

"Hi Jerome. Did you just finish working out?" I asked.

"No, I was just sitting around relaxing."

I entered his apartment and had to admire how spotless and tidy it was. This didn't look like a typical bachelor's pad. The apartment seemed as if it has been decorated by someone's mother. There were flowers here and there that accentuated paintings, figurines and the sweet aroma of potpourri in the air. He even had scented candles placed delicately around his living room.

"You have a lovely apartment," I told Jerome.

My eyes wandered around the room in amazement at how everything was put together. I was sure that his fiancé probably helped him decorate. It had a woman's touch all over it.

"Thanks, I decorated it myself," Jerome replied.

"You really have great taste. I would have thought that your fiancé did this."

Jerome turned and headed toward the kitchen. "Would you like some wine?"

"Sure."

Home decorating and wine? Jerome wasn't the average guy and I liked that about him. He handed me a glass of Chardonnay and signaled for me to have a seat beside him on his antique couch. Even his sofa looked like it should be in someone's home décor magazine. It was vintage but still elegant and was covered with a beige and plum flower pattern that could have easily been on my grandmother's furniture.

"How was the rest of your day?" Jerome asked.

I told Jerome about my conversation with Terrence and the choice to see him again. Jerome listened attentively and asked if I thought that was a wise decision. I thought about it for a second and remained silent. Of course it wasn't a sensible choice, but I didn't want to admit it. Jerome and I talked for another hour about the what-ifs of my decision, Corey, and even about his fiancé, Tamara.

"Rachel, I think you are a spectacular woman, just like Tamara." Jerome finished his third glass of wine and placed it on one of the coasters that lined his coffee table.

"Thank you, Jerome. I enjoy talking to you. You always put things into perspective for me."

"That's what friends are supposed to do."

Jerome picked up both our glasses and took them into the kitchen. "You know, I thought about doing something wild and crazy before I say I do, but I wouldn't know where to begin. I am a little square." Jerome shrugged his shoulders and laughed.

"Do you go out?" I asked.

"Not really, I kind of stay to myself for the most part."

"You should hang out with me and Von sometime."

Jerome's eyes widened when he heard Von's name.

"Oh, I forgot, my best friend is crazy about you."

"I don't think I am her type," Jerome laughed. "Honestly if I wasn't engaged I would probably try to date you."

Stunned by his comment, I turned around to look at Jerome who was still in the kitchen washing out the wine glasses.

"And if I wasn't engaged I am sure I wouldn't have an issue with you dating me," I replied.

Our eyes met for a quick second and then I turned back around, facing the opposite direction. All of a sudden, I heard a loud thump come from down the hall leading towards the bedroom. Jerome pointed up at the ceiling and said the neighbors always get so loud. I could have sworn the thump was from somewhere in the back room but I took his word for it. He knew his apartment better than I did.

Jerome dried his hands on the flowered dishcloth and came back into the living room. He gave a quick glance down the hall and then sat beside me on the couch. It was getting late and I informed Jerome that I had to leave soon. He shook his head up and down and gave me the okay sign.

Jerome slid closer to me on the couch and once again put his arm around the back. Before I realized it I had sunk into his arm and rested my head on his chiseled chest. I nuzzled into his arms and told Jerome that he was a good friend and thanked him for the talk. I felt comforted, and I was grateful. Jerome stroked my hair.

"Anytime," he said.

Jerome innocently kissed my forehead. I closed my eyes and once again snuggled up against his warm body.

"Can I share something with you?" he asked.

"Of course," I answered. "After all the sharing I did tonight I would love for you to do the same, Jerome."

I lifted my head up and looked in Jerome's eyes. There was a sudden fear that had not been there all night. A look that dominated his mysterious grey eyes.

"I feel like we have formed a true friendship tonight and I think I want to let you in," he said in a peculiar tone.

I was confused but resisted the urge to say anything. I sat up straight. Jerome clutched my hand, pulled me up from the sofa, and guided me down the hall. Wondering what he had to show me, I hesitantly followed.

"You remember that I said I wanted to do something wild before I got married," Jerome started.

"Uh, yes but I don't think -" My words were cut off as Jerome's grasp on my hand tightened. We stood in front of his bedroom door. He turned around to face me and pulled me into him. Before I could realize what was happening, he placed his hands on my shoulders and planted a hard kiss on my lips. I tried to pull away but his hold was so strong that I couldn't. His lips parted from mine and I was lost for words. As handsome as he was, I didn't see Jerome in this light and I didn't want an innocent night spoiled.

"I want you to help me with that," he whispered.

He twisted the knob of his bedroom door, opening it to show what he had in mind. I gasped. Poised on the bed was a naked man wearing only a smile. I blinked twice before recognizing who this man was that sat on the bed waiting for both me and Jerome.

"Freddie?" I screamed. I pushed Jerome from in front of me, ran down the hall, grabbed my keys and bolted out the door.

***

I rushed home, baffled and mortified. Jerome was bisexual? Why would he want to share that with me? What would make him think I would want to join in? Those questions overwhelmed my mind. I felt disgusted. I didn't understand. This was way too much for me to handle. Then to see Freddie in the bed ready to leap, the image burned a hole in my brain. I hadn't seen Freddie in years.

He was a former member of my dad's church that came out of the closet and left after criticism from the holier than thou members. There was a lot of talking going on behind Freddie's back and at the end he felt it was his time to leave. My dad instructed the members to stop with the gossip and condemnation, but they continued, to his dismay.

My phone was blowing up between calls and texts from Jerome. I left them all unanswered for the lack of anything to say. I was appalled to say the least-and humiliated. So humiliated that I didn't want anyone to know what had just happened, not even Von.

His texts were coming in back to back and my phone showed twenty unread messages. They ranged from "I am so sorry" to "Please don't tell anyone." When I didn't reply back another text came in saying that he would keep my secrets if I kept his. How dare he try to use what I shared with him in confidence against me! He wouldn't have to worry about that. I replied back to one of the last texts and told him I had no plans of uttering what happened tonight to anyone. So much for trying to take my mind off of Terrence.

Tonight was a total disaster. I wanted to forget it ever occurred. I pushed all of the events to the rear of my mind, stuck them in a little box, and closed the lid. That's where they would remain. Gone and forgotten. I immediately took a shower when I reached my apartment and collapsed on my bed. My thoughts quickly went to Terrence and our upcoming rendezvous. Those feelings would help me get through this horrendous night.

Chapter 20

For this occasion we agreed that Terrence would come to Charlotte to see me. Guilt burned in the pit of my stomach when he informed me that he told his wife he had upcoming meetings with our company. He did need to take a look at some business endeavors, but the trip could have waited. I was more apprehensive about seeing him this time than any previous times before. So many instances I looked at my phone wanting to call and tell him that seeing each other was a mistake and that we should just leave it alone. Of course we would always think about each other but thoughts never hurt. When thoughts became actions, that's when things took a turn for the worst.

It was Friday night, and as I looked at the time on the clock, my hands began to tremble. The first two times that I saw Terrence I was nervous, but nothing like what I was feeling tonight. Maybe it was because we had essentially premeditated being together this time. All the talks of being in each other's arms and letting whatever happens happen made me comprehend that the whole idea of all of this was wrong. After the encounter with Kevin, I would not allow another man into my house, and definitely not in the bed that Corey and I made love in. So I told Terrence that I would get a room at a nearby hotel and give him directions.

The Hilton Doubletree hotel was one of the most miraculous hotels in uptown Charlotte. A doorman greeted each guest upon entering the hotel through the gigantic double glass doors. Arranged in the center of the grand lobby was a captivating waterfall that reached midway to the ceiling and created an atmosphere of romance.

It flowed down into a circular fountain, at the bottom of which resided pennies, dimes, nickels, and quarters, carrying the wishes of strangers, along with rocks and dashes of sand. I imagined parents bringing their children near the waterfall and handing them coins telling them to make a wish, then the children flinging the money in the fountain. If only it was that simple. Behind the waterfall was the hotel's restaurant. The restaurant was full of delectable dishes and cuisines that made you ignore the steep prices and order seconds.

My heart thumped as I gave Ashley, the lady at the counter, my credit card for the room. Her strawberry blond hair was tied back in a ponytail, freckles covered her face, and her breath smelled of grape bubble gum. She nodded, smiled, and handed me the room key. "Enjoy your stay, Ms. Simms," she replied.

I wonder if Ashley would have smiled at me if she knew what I was about to do. She probably would have called me every name that she could think of: home wrecker, hoe, slut, all of the above, because that was exactly what I felt like right now. Carrying a small black duffel bag filled with candles, a lingerie set, and a CD player, I glanced at the room key again and traveled towards the elevator. If I was going to go through with something like this then I would at least make it special. But how could having sex with a married man be special?

While riding in the elevator, I retrieved my cell phone from my jacket pocket and sent Terrence a message with the name of the hotel and the room number. A minute went by and I received a text letting me know that he would be here in an hour. My hands were still shaking as I slid the key in the door and turned the handle. Cold air smacked me in the face upon entering the room. I tossed the duffel bag on the king sized bed and headed to the air conditioner to turn it off.

Room 413 was beautiful and much more appealing than the executive room Terrence had in Greensboro. The comforter was shimmering black and gold with matching curtains, which were completely closed.

An exquisite picture of a morning sunrise decorated the wall and the scent of flowers filled the room as I noticed the beautiful arrangement placed neatly on the oak desk.

The smell of flowers flowed through the room now, but soon the smell of sex would overtake that. *Sex.* I repeated the word over and over in my head and finally said it out loud. For four years I had made love to only Corey and now I was about to have sex with someone that I barely knew. Just sex. No love making, no promising the future to each other, no wedding plans. Just a night full of lust and sex. I'd never had a one night stand, never slept with someone that I wasn't in a relationship with. Never met someone and just had sex with him. Why was I even doing this?

In four years I had never cheated on Corey and now, months before we were to become husband and wife, I do something like this. Was it because I was lonely or just scared of getting married? Did I have commitment issues? All these years I have never wanted anyone other than Corey but now everything seems so different. I was different. Was this a sign that I didn't need to get married right now? Maybe I wasn't ready after all.

My thoughts were interrupted by my phone. Von was calling, so I pressed ignore. Her conversation would have to wait until later. On second thought, maybe I needed her to talk me out of this. I had made up another ridiculous excuse about being sick so that I wouldn't have to go out with her tonight. I knew she was calling to check on me.

I sat on the bed for a minute and thought about the ideal person that could make me leave this room. Corey. All I needed was to hear his voice. I dialed his number and smiled. He would save me from making a grave mistake. The phone continued to ring but Corey didn't answer. His voice mail didn't even pick up. I ended the call and tried again.

This time it seemed as if the phone clicked on and then back off. Did Corey just hang up on me? I was even more puzzled and a little hurt.

I give up. I wanted to feel like I was important to someone.

I set up the CD player and listened to R. Kelly's seductive voice remove thoughts of Corey for now. I jumped in the shower, shaved and waited patiently for Terrence to arrive.

A knock on the door suspended my thoughts as R. Kelly and Kelly Rowland sang about how there was no such thing as a half mistake so we might as well go all the way. I smiled as I thought about how perfect that song was for this moment. Dressed in a red lace bra and panty set from Victoria's Secret hidden by a red silk robe, I walked over to the door in my red stilettos and slowly opened it. It felt as if it weighed a hundred pounds as I pulled it open with all my might.

Standing on the other side was the sexiest man I had ever laid my eyes on. The scent of his Armani cologne sent me in a daze and I was speechless for what seemed like minutes. Terrence's eyes explored my body and finally rested on my eyes. I motioned for him to come in but still couldn't get any words to come out my mouth.

I thought Terrence was sexy when I saw him before but this time he was beyond that. This man was ravishing. He had on a pair of stone washed blue jeans, a black button down collar shirt, and a pair of black loafers. Terrence's head was completely bald and all I could think about was getting my hands on it and rubbing slowly over and over again. Calm down Rachel, I thought. I closed the door behind him and neither one of us said anything. R. Kelly was still doing all the talking.

Terrence came toward me and hugged me ever so gently and finally he spoke. "Can I just look at you?" he asked.

I smiled and twirled around so he could get a full view of everything I was offering him tonight.

"You are amazing," Terrence said, steadying his eyes on mine.

"Thank you," I squeaked.

Terrence picked up on my nervousness immediately. "Are you okay?" he asked.

He walked towards me and took my hand in his so that we were standing directly in front of each other.

I answered by pressing my lips against his. He opened my mouth with his tongue and played hide-and-seek with mine. He kissed me gently and slowly, as if this was the first time we kissed and as if this was going to be the last time wrapped all in one. He kissed my top lip and then my bottom and let his tongue trace them until he found his way back into my mouth. Seconds turned to minutes and by the time I was able to open my eyes and realize I was not dreaming, Terrence was still kissing me like he had wanted me forever. His hands traveled up and down my body and touched every curve and dip. They moved from my shoulders to my back then rested on my behind. He gently squeezed my ass and I let out a slight moan. Guiding me towards the bed, he lay me down and stood over me, not saying a word.

"I just want to admire you," Terrence whispered.

I was nervous, and the cold air made me quiver and tense up. Terrence climbed on the bed and begin to kiss me again. So soft. So delicate like he was afraid that he would hurt me if he was too rough. His kisses left my mouth and went from my neck to my shoulders and then my breasts. Terrence carefully stripped me of my robe and unhooked my bra in the front. His hands massaged my breasts as he sucked on my nipples. Terrence's head went from one breast to the other making sure he gave each one the same amount of attention. My moans were louder now as I rubbed and kissed his beautiful bald head.

"Do you like that?" He asked lifting up his head and looking into my eyes.

All I managed to do was nod. Terrence smiled and in another quick motion stripped me of my underwear and buried his head between my legs. Just as slowly and carefully as he had sucked my nipples, his tongue found my spot and he licked me like I was the best ice cream cone he had ever tasted.

I couldn't stop myself from having an orgasm the way I did when I was with Kevin. They came too easy and back to back.

My body twitched and turned and I felt myself pushing away from him. He grabbed my legs and pulled me back into him and again ever so slowly licked me until I had tears in my eyes. I felt myself climaxing again and crying as he literally sucked everything out of me.

"Oh my God!" I screamed as I had the greatest orgasm that I had ever endured in my entire life. My body contracted and I closed my legs and turned on my side. I couldn't move. My body shook again and the tears were evident on my face.

"Are you okay?" Terrence asked as he rubbed my legs.

I held one finger up, letting him know that I needed a minute to regain my composure. I took a deep breath and my body finally relaxed. I wiped the tears from my eyes and tried to move. Terrence again rubbed my legs to soothe me but once more I asked him to give me a second. I took another deep breath and stared at this divine man that had given me so much pleasure.

His jeans and boxers were off now and I was able to view what he was presenting to me. Thick, long, and enticing, I held myself back from taking all of his erection in my mouth. I couldn't stop my hands, however, and I reached out and allowed my fingers to glide over his smoothness from the base to the tip. He watched me and then placed his hand on top of mine to follow the motion. We both smiled at each other. Once Terrence saw that I was relaxed he removed my hand, turned me on my back, and opened my legs up into the position they were moments ago. He climbed on top of me and gently entered my body.

"Wait," I said as my thoughts went to the condoms I bought from the store earlier.

"Don't worry, I have one," Terrence said reading my mind and reaching down to the floor to retrieve the rubber out of his pants pocket.

He slipped the condom on and kissed me like he had done earlier, with so much feeling. He kissed me with love and tenderness.

I gasped as he pushed himself deep into me. I grabbed onto him and he continued to push further and further in.

"Oh God!" I screamed again as his body told me that he still was not fully in.

Terrence stilled and looked at me. "Am I hurting you?"

Once again all I could do was shake my head no. Taking things easier now, he continued to push his way inside me until I felt him relax and move back and forth inside my walls. Our groans and moans were mixed together and filled the room. Terrence would slow down for moments and then move faster making me scream even more. He lifted one of my legs up so it rested on his shoulders and dug deeper inside me. The pleasure and pain mixed together so intensely that I cried, screamed, yelled, and cursed all at the same time.

In one swift motion, Terrence dropped my leg from his shoulder, turned me over on my stomach, and laid on top of me entering me from behind. I arched my back to give him the perfect entrance inside me. He thrust his body into mine, back and forth, faster and faster until my head started swimming. When I thought I couldn't take anymore, he lifted me into a kneeling position. He caressed my breasts and again entered me from behind. Moving slower now, he groaned and whispered my name. Never before had any man made me feel this satisfied. His movements became faster, and I screamed out for what seemed like the hundredth time. His hands moved from my breasts to my waist and his grip became stronger. He dug his fingers into my waist and I felt his body shake several times.

Seconds passed and slowly, Terrence kissed me on my neck and pulled out of me holding the condom in place. He stood up from the bed, and fumbled around finding his way to the bathroom.

While he was in the bathroom, I reached for the comforter realizing that it was not on the bed anymore, but balled up in a corner of the floor. My legs didn't want to cooperate as I stumbled around to recover the blanket.

Finally, I was able to get them to work and threw the comforter back on the bed. I thought of Kelly Rowland's song, *Motivation*, when she sings, *"And when we're done I don't want to feel my legs."* This must have been exactly what she was talking about.

My entire body was sore and it still felt like I was dreaming. I returned to the bed and covered my nakedness with the comforter. Terrence walked out of the bathroom, giving me the perfect view of his flawless body. Muscles ripped down his flat stomach, and his chest was picture perfect, no hair, no scratches or marks, just spotless with the exception of a bible scripture that was beautifully drawn on his left pec. He had legs that were made for running and I was in awe of how fit he was.

"Can I hold you?" Terrence asked, smiling at me, aware that I was checking him out.

"You know you don't have to ask."

He joined me in bed and wrapped those magnificent arms around me. Our naked bodies clung to each other and as I closed my eyes, I felt safe. I felt wanted. I felt loved.

***

I was awakened by tiny kisses on my back. I smiled knowing that this was not a dream at all. I was really here with Terrence, making love to him. He continued to kiss my back and then his kisses explored my entire body once again. I became instantly ready for him and when he entered my body it was prepared for him. He penetrated me and was able to feel my wetness with nothing between us. We made love again for what seemed like hours and collapsed in each other's arms afterwards. Once again sleep overtook us and sweet dreams were all I had.

Chapter 21

A month and a half had passed since the night I spent with Terrence and the emails, phone calls, and texts were exchanged every day. We talked all day while at work and then at home we texted whenever we could. This man had my nose so wide open I could smell what my mom was cooking at her house forty miles away.

Corey and I had spent last weekend together and things were slowly getting back to normal. I wasn't sure whether it was because I was stressing less since Terrence had me in a better mood or because Corey's attitude had changed about the wedding. Since Corey was with me for the weekend, I didn't get a chance to talk to Terrence as much, a text here and there, but just the thought of him put a smile on my face. All I knew was that I was in a better place. I was feeling love from Terrence, and Corey's behavior wasn't bothering me anymore.

The fighting had even ceased between Corey and me, and he was helping a little with the wedding. Although we spent the past weekend together, the visits hadn't become regular like they once were. Since he wasn't around as much, he never questioned where I was the weekend I was with Terrence; he just assumed I was with Von. I still loved Corey, but I wasn't hurt anymore when I didn't see him; I would just email or text Terrence.

The affair that I had with Terrence was exhilarating. It gave me such a rush every time I talked to him. For the first time in my life, I was living in the moment and didn't care about the consequences. We shared so much and just the talks between us sent chills up my spine.

We reminisced about the night we spent together and since we couldn't see each other whenever we wanted, he introduced me to phone sex.

His voice made me touch myself in different ways and every time I did, I had an unforgettable orgasm. He opened up a part of me that I never knew existed. I wasn't only infatuated with this man; I was falling in love with him. Five months until my wedding and my mind was always on Terrence.

***

Thursday morning I woke up feeling groggy, like I had been hit by a Mack truck. I had gone to bed at ten last night and I got my desired hours of sleep, so I couldn't fathom why I was still so sleepy and feeling so dreadful. I dragged myself out of bed and stumbled toward the bathroom.

Inches away from the bathroom my stomach did one major flip and sent me to my knees. A sharp pain started on my right side and ripped to my left as I tried to catch my breath. What was going on? I crawled into the bathroom and made it over the toilet just in time to avoid having to clean up vomit from my rug and floor. Not remembering the last time I was sick, my first notion was that I had a virus or the flu. It was that time of year and people in the office were getting it left and right. Seasons were changing and the cold front was calmly approaching the South. The beginning of November was still warm, but there was always a crisp chill in the air in the mornings.

Daria was out all last week with the stomach virus; however, I didn't have time to be sick. I picked myself up off the floor and looked in the bathroom mirror. My eyes were bloodshot and swollen like I had been crying all night. No way was I going into the office like this. I staggered out of the bathroom and grabbed my phone off the nightstand.

After calling and letting the office know I would not be in today, I flopped back on my bed, struggled to get underneath the covers, and pulled them over my head. I needed something to ease the pain in my stomach but there wasn't anything in my house to take and I refused to leave to get something.

I could call Von to bring me something that would make my stomach feel a little better. If it was a virus I would just have to sleep it off but something had to alleviate the pain. I peeked at my clock on the dresser and it read 8:15. Von was just arriving at work. I would call her in an hour to see if she could stop by.

I closed my eyes and tried to go back to sleep but the sharp pains in my stomach turned to cramps and had me balled up in the fetal position. After vomiting for the second time, I called Von and told her that I had a virus and needed some medicine.

Von walked into my apartment and called out that she was in the living room. The only response that I could muster up was a groan. Von came into my bedroom and peered down at me. She placed her hand on my forehead to check for a fever. "Girl you look a hot ass mess."

"I feel like one too," I mumbled.

"You don't have a fever, so what's hurting you?"

I pointed at my stomach. I struggled to sit up but the cramps once again took over and only allowed me to lie there.

"Is your period on?"

"No. I have been so stressed out about the wedding that I can't even remember the last time it came on," I said, grabbing my stomach.

"Uh oh, so there could be a little Corey Jr. in there." She laughed and headed back to the kitchen to pour me some ginger ale.

Corey Jr. repeated in my head as I thought back to the last time that Corey and me had been intimate. Other than this past weekend, it had been so long ago that I couldn't even remember the date. I was taking birth control pills, but had been a little slack since me and Corey weren't seeing each other regularly anymore. I would miss one here and there but I didn't think that would do any harm.

Besides Corey, the last person that I had slept with was Terrence. We used protection the first time, but after that it was lost in the sheets along with my common sense.

It's just a virus, I thought as Von came back in the room with the ginger ale and some Mylanta.

"If you don't feel any better by tomorrow you might want to take a test." Von was serious, now looking at me in that way that she always did to let me know she was concerned.

"Yes ma'am," I said, disgusted with myself.

"Girl, I might be an auntie!" Von hugged me and told me to call her if I needed anything else.

***

It took all my strength to get out of bed and put some clothes on, but here I was in the drug store staring at the home pregnancy tests attempting to figure out which one I should buy. I should not even be here. I wasn't pregnant. I didn't feel pregnant. Didn't pregnant women feel a certain way when they were carrying a child inside them? I didn't feel anything. I had never been pregnant before so I wouldn't know what it felt like to begin with. I chose an EPT test and made my way to the register. Rachel, there is no need to get yourself all worked up. You are not pregnant and you know that. I repeated this thought over and over until I had convinced myself that it was true. The cramps stopped for a while and I felt better. It's all in the mind.

After waiting for what seemed like an hour even though the clock confirmed only five minutes had passed, I looked at the little white stick I urinated on and only one line emerged. Not pregnant.

I felt like shouting and dancing all over my room. So it was just a virus.

"Thank God!" I said out loud. Now I can put all those thoughts out of my head.

***

Following another night of tossing, turning, and puking, I called into work again and tried to recuperate. I was feeling mildly well by mid afternoon so I prepared some chicken noodle soup and clicked on the television. Terrence texted to see if I was okay after I didn't respond back to his email sent to my work address. I assured him that I was fine. After texting Von and Monica that I was sick, they both called to check on me. I told them I was fine and rushed off the phone in order to avoid their many questions. I returned Daryl's call as well. He had heard through Monica that I wasn't feeling well. Daryl had recently moved to Atlanta, accepting a position with the Atlanta Falcons as a physical therapist, and I missed my brother badly.

"Hey, sis." Daryl answered the phone in a rather chipper tone.

"Hey, D."

"How you feeling, babygirl?"

"I am okay now. Stomach not hurting as much as before."

"Sis, you not pregnant are you?" Daryl asked.

"No, D, I am not, thank God," I sighed as the thought of being pregnant by another man crept into my mind.

"Well it wouldn't have been such a bad thing now, would it? You and Corey are almost married anyway."

"Yeah, I know, but now is not the right time."

"I feel ya, sis," Daryl said. "Just take care of yourself." Daryl hung up and I thought about the possibility that I could have been pregnant.

There was no way it would have been Corey's. Well, maybe a slight chance, depending on how far along I was. I have got to be more careful. I lay back down and rid myself of those crazy thoughts that were inside my head.

Chapter 22

Shouldn't I feel back to normal now? A week and a half had passed since my first sick day and my body still felt feeble. I wasn't feeling as sick as I was before, but at times I would feel sore and exhausted like I had worked out all day. I was drained most of the time and whenever I went to lunch with Von I barely had an appetite. She noticed this and the first thing she asked was whether or not I had taken a pregnancy test. I was overjoyed to tell her that the test was negative, so there was no need to start with the auntie planning.

"You need to take another one," she said in her matter of fact tone that irritated the hell out of me.

"Why?" I whined.

"It could have been wrong."

I rolled my eyes at her and stared down at my half eaten burger and fries. I tried to stuff another fry in my mouth but the fear that it might come back up made me put it down.

Von sighed and shook her head. "Rachel, if you were pregnant it wouldn't be such an awful thing. Probably would do you and Corey some good. Bring you guys closer together."

I didn't hear a word Von was saying now. All I could hear was it could have been wrong. The test was accurate, no doubt about it. It had to be. I couldn't be pregnant. Fear overcame me again and I felt like I was going to be ill.

"What's going on, Rachel?" Von asked with a worried stare.

"Nothing," I mumbled, still playing with the fries on my plate.

"Just take another test and you will know for sure. Maybe you have nothing to worry about."

I didn't respond to Von and that let her know I didn't want to talk about it anymore.

"My dad wants to have a cookout so all his kids can meet."

Von changed the subject so quickly that I had to think about what she said.

"Are you going?" I asked.

"I have to," Von said in that same crushed tone she used whenever she talked about her dad or new sister.

"When?"

"He said he wants to do it the end of this month since the weather is still warm. I talked to him this morning. He gave me her number in case I wanted to call her."

"You want me to come with you?" I asked, wanting to be there for my best friend.

"Please," was Von's simple response as her eyes watered up and she looked away.

***

As the two lines appeared on the stick I became sick again and threw my head into the toilet. The tears swelled up in my eyes and before I knew it I was curled up in fetal position once again rocking back and forth and crying hysterically. I cried as if my best friend had passed. I cried as if I had lost everything I owned. I cried as if my life was over. To me it was. Two lines. *Two lines.* I was numb. I was dreaming all this. There could not be two lines on that stick telling me that I was pregnant. I was pregnant. The words were not right. This was not right. I was pregnant? Still weeping, I sat up and reached for the dreadful stick. The stick that told me that everything was different now. The stick that told me what I did was wrong and now I have to live with that forever. The stick that still showed the two lines.

Something made me think that it would change. One line would disappear and the stick would show that my eyes had played tricks on me and I wasn't really pregnant. But this wicked stick read the same exact thing that it had ten minutes ago. No matter how much I wanted it to change it wasn't going to. Those same two lines were still there. Not fading away, not disappearing, still there.

As clear as anything I have ever seen before. Two lines. I looked at them while they stared back at me.

***

I opened my eyes and decided I wasn't going to get out of bed today. After taking five more pregnancy tests that all yielded the same result yesterday; I just wanted to sleep until this nightmare was over. I cried so much that I didn't have any tears left. I was tired of crying. I was tired of thinking. I was just tired. I was getting married in five months and I was pregnant. Pregnant. Rachel and pregnant didn't go together in the same sentence. It didn't go together in the same anything. Corey and I talked about having kids, but not until we were years into the marriage. After traveling and doing whatever we wanted to do, the kids would come. We had it all planned out and this was not how it was supposed to happen. How could I have been so stupid? I asked myself this a million times yesterday and today and still had no answer.

I needed to make a doctor's appointment. There was a slight chance that it could be Corey's baby and everything would work out. I kept this in mind. Was positive thinking that strong that it could change reality? I called into work on this Monday morning and was lying in my bed feeling every emotion known to man. I thought about it some more and changed my original plan and chose to get up instead of staying in bed. I picked up the phone and called my doctor to schedule an appointment. After telling the nurse all my symptoms she told me that they could see me this afternoon.

***

I walked into the doctor's office and signed my name on the blank sheet of paper on the receptionist's desk.

The beady-eyed elderly nurse looked up from her computer, smiled, and asked had any information changed since my last visit. Yeah, the fact that I am pregnant and I wasn't the last time I was here, I thought. I grinned back at her, said a soft no, and took a seat in a chair facing the window.

Twenty minutes passed and I started to get antsy. I despised just sitting and waiting. Having to smile and say hello to strangers and act as if I was delighted to be here was torture. The reality was that I just wanted to jump up, scream, and run out of this office, out of the building, down the street and keep running until I couldn't run anymore. I watched while a young couple sat across from me holding hands and talking to one another. He had to be about 25 and she didn't look a day over 20. Her belly was round and sticking out from under the yellow shirt that tried its best to cover it. She looked as if she was ready to pop any day and I imagined this was their first baby. They seemed excited to experience this together and it made me even more dejected that I would never get to share my first child with anyone. I took another deep breath and picked up a home decorating magazine off the table in front of me.

"Rachel Simms," the nurse said searching the room for me. I placed the magazine back on the table and proceeded to the door.

"How are you doing today, Ms. Simms?" she asked while weighing me and taking my blood pressure.

I gave her a half smile. "Fine."

"I see that we think we may be pregnant."

The nurse smiled and handed me a small cup to take into the bathroom for a urine sample. After making myself go, I returned and gave the cup to the nurse.

"The doctor will be right in to see you," she said as she guided me towards a room and placed my chart on the door.

Another thirty minutes passed and my anxiety turned into aggravation. Did it take all this to tell me something that I already knew and didn't want to hear? By the time my doctor finally entered the room I had no more fake smiles to give.

Dr. Ainsley was an attractive woman in her mid 40's with a very youthful appearance. Her auburn colored hair fell in loose curls past her shoulders and she was dressed in a beige pants suit that complimented her slender figure. She resembled the actress Debra Messer from the TV show *Will and Grace*.

"I see that we have some good news today, Rachel," Dr. Ainsley said sitting down in front of me on her metal stool.

"Is everything okay?"

"Yes sweetie, everything is looking good. It seems that you are about seven weeks pregnant and the baby is forming well. All your blood levels are wonderful. Do you have any questions?"

"I am seven weeks pregnant?" I asked. I had heard her the first time, but I wanted to make sure.

"Yes, seven weeks," Dr. Ainsley repeated.

Seven weeks ago I was with Terrence. Making love to him over and over again. Seven weeks ago we conceived a child. These thoughts repeated in my head as the doctor rambled on about the things I needed to do in order to stay healthy. She handed me a prescription for prenatal vitamins, a bag full of pamphlets, and other things for the expectant mom. Expectant mom. I was in a daze at this point and the next thing I knew I was sitting in my car sobbing again.

This was not supposed to be me. I always followed the rules, always was the one doing the right thing. I wasn't one of those females sleeping around and just doing whatever felt good at the moment. I guess one day I had to be kicked off the high horse I had been riding for so many years. Today was the day that I was not only forced off, but fell face down in the mud. My sister would love this. I thought about Monica and all her mistakes and the times she had gotten annoyed with me for acting like I was superior. She would eat this up. Everyone would.

But wait, maybe no one would have to find out. Yeah right Rachel, and when your stomach gets larger what are you going to say?

Oh I am just gaining weight? All of these thoughts made me weep harder. I rubbed my stomach and thought about the innocent life that was now living inside me. Maybe it was a boy, or maybe a little girl that looked like me. I didn't look pregnant at all but it was too soon to show. I looked a little bloated so I had a few months before anyone would realize that I was pregnant.

What was I thinking? There was no way I could keep this child. In all of my "better than thou" days I was so against abortion. Killing a child was not an option for me, but how could I carry a married man's child? I couldn't take the chance of passing this child off as Corey's. That would just be foul; no one deserves to be treated that way. I wouldn't dare tell him the child was his if it really wasn't, and better yet, Corey and Terrence didn't resemble each other at all.

My head was throbbing. I had to get myself together in order to drive home. I felt sick again. Dizziness made it hard for me to even focus on the road. Good thing I lived only about ten miles away from the doctor's office.

I pulled into the parking lot of my apartments and stumbled up the steps. Ms. Harris came out of her apartment as I was unlocking my door. I gave her a slight smile and waved my hand as I walked in my door. Another person that would be disappointed in me if she knew what I had done. But not as disappointed as I was in myself.

Chapter 23

Given that I seldom was absent from the office I had a lot of hours of paid time off. After discovering I was pregnant, I tapped into my hours again and took a few days to get myself together and determine what I was going to do. Wow. What was I going to do? Did that mean I was contemplating getting rid of this child? My child. I didn't know if I was going to tell Terrence that I was pregnant with his child or not. He had a right to know, but what would that do? Regardless of whether I had this baby or not, I would not anticipate him taking care of me or the child. He already had a family. This was a mistake. The entire relationship that we had was a mistake.

This was my second day out of the office since my doctor's appointment and I had not spoken to anyone. My phone was blowing up between Von and my mother calling, but I had no intentions of answering the phone. Corey called and left a message that he was worried about me since he hadn't heard from me in a couple of days. I texted him and told him that I thought I had the flu. He then asked if I needed him to come take care of me. I responded no, I was fine and I would call him once I felt better.

My text to Von said the same, but she didn't give me a simple okay. She started by asking did I go to the doctor, and after answering her fifth question, I just stopped responding. I could count on her call, but I would talk to her later once I felt the need to tell someone how I had destroyed my life. Monica and Daryl also called to check on me and when I didn't answer I was hoping that they would just call back later. I sent my brother and sister the same generic text that I sent Corey and Von. That would at least keep people at bay and buy me some time.

Terrence also called but I didn't answer the phone or respond to his text. I had to talk to him at some point; however, I was just not ready right now. I was leaning towards telling him I was pregnant, but I couldn't bring myself to even utter the words. When we were together, he had awakened me in the middle of the night and we hadn't used any protection after the first round. The following morning, I assured him that I was on birth control and everything would be fine. At the time I had missed taking my pills for a couple of days, but I didn't give it much thought. I just didn't think that a baby would come out of it. I had forgotten to take my pills before and caught back up. Corey and I didn't use protection and I had not once become pregnant. Why did it have to happen this time?

The picture of Terrence's children flashed in my head and I wondered if this child inside me would look like them. What are you thinking, Rachel? You can't have this child. What about Corey? You still love him and you are supposed to be HIS wife and have HIS kids, not some married man's kids. I was smarter than this, or at least I thought.

I stroked my stomach and thought about the life I had inside me. The baby hadn't asked to be here and none of this was his or her fault. I considered taking this secret to my grave. Then again, maybe Von would understand. No, with everything going on in her life, I doubt I would get a "Congrats, girl! You are having a married man's baby!" from her.

This was a tragedy and I was a wreck. I was no better than anyone else I had ridiculed over the years. I was foolish for even thinking that. Out of everyone that I thought I was greater than and everyone I felt always made mistakes, I was the biggest hypocrite I knew. I felt worse than I ever had in my whole life. I buried my head under the covers and once again wept until I fell into a deep sleep.

***

The work week was finally over and I felt a little better. I had gotten past the pity party and with all my research on the Internet about my options; I finally wrapped my head around what I needed to do. Days of solitude cleared my mind and I accepted what had transpired. Now it was time to get myself together.

Terrence was still calling and texting. His last text asked if everything was okay and why I wasn't at work. I finally replied back and informed him that yes I was okay, just dealing with a lot right now. Hearing from me seemed to calm him down a bit and the calls stopped. He continued to text saying he was checking on me and to call when I felt like chatting. I conveyed to him that it was necessary for me to see him and I would travel to Atlanta this time. He asked again if everything was okay and I said yes, but I just really needed to see him. Assuming that I was stressed over wedding plans and wanted him to take my mind off things, he told me that he looked forward to seeing me. The sooner I told him that I was pregnant, the better it would be. I would also tell him that I had made the decision to abort our child.

I made an appointment at the clinic that had the most thorough information, and after having all my questions answered by the doctors, I felt slightly at ease. My appointment was in two weeks and that would put me at ten weeks pregnant. The doctor told me that this was fine and quoted me a price for the procedure. She discussed what to do before and after the appointment and told me that I would require a driver.

The only person that I would feel comfortable having with me throughout this whole ordeal would be Von. I just didn't know when and how I would tell her what I had done and the consequences I was now facing. My appointment was after the cookout Von's dad was having, so I decided to tell her then.

My hopes were that she would hit it off with her sister and be in a gracious mood making it easy for me to tell her about the pregnancy and scheduled termination.

By the time the cookout came around, I was looking even more bloated and if someone had seen me naked they would know that my shape was changing dramatically. Thankfully, Corey had not asked to see me. His job had sent him to California for two weeks to set up a store there, and we weren't even able to spend Thanksgiving together. Thanksgiving dinner was held at my parent's house. Between my mom being the extravagant host that she always is and telling everyone "her" wedding plans, she didn't have time to scrutinize me and the fact that I was putting on a little weight. Von, on the other hand, noticed everything about me, and Saturday afternoon after lunch commented on my slightly protruding stomach. She informed me that I either needed to hit the gym a little harder or I had been lying to her for weeks.

"Let's just focus on the task at hand," I said, referring to Von meeting her sister the next day.

"I know, I know but we are going to have to talk and soon. You haven't told me what's going on in your world in a while."

"I know girl. We will talk soon." I jumped out of her truck and walked up the stairs to my apartment.

The cookout was tomorrow after church, and I still didn't want to face anyone else, so I was spending Saturday night alone in my house. I was dozing off when I heard my phone ring. At first I wasn't going to look at it, but if it was Corey, I would talk to him for a bit. Shocked to see Terrence's number on my phone, especially on the weekend, I answered with a surprised hello.

"Hey Rachel, how are you feeling?" He asked in that same sexy tone that drove me crazy.

Butterflies nestled in my stomach once again and I thought about the fact that they now shared space with his child. *Our child.*

"I am feeling much better," I lied.

"Well, I am actually in town right now and I wanted to know if I could see you for a few minutes tonight or maybe tomorrow?

It will only be for a little while because my wife is here and we have some family business to take care of. Would you like to get some coffee or something?"

"Is everything okay with your family?"

I truly didn't want to see Terrence right now, and I was shocked that he hadn't told me about any family affairs. But then again, with all the sick days I had taken, we hadn't talked much in the past few weeks. I knew if I saw him he would definitely be able to tell that I was looking a little pudgy about my mid section.

"Yeah everything is fine," he said. "We haven't talked in a while and I miss you."

My heart fluttered. "I don't think that seeing each other would be a good idea, Terrence, especially with your wife here." I wanted to avoid him at all costs, especially now. After I had the abortion, I would make the trip to Atlanta and maybe then I could finally be honest with him about everything.

Terrence was quiet for a second and then said that was cool. I could tell he was disappointed. "Are you still planning on coming to Atlanta soon?" he asked anxiously.

"Yes, within the next few weeks."

"Perfect," he replied. "See you then!"

Chapter 24

"I like that one," I said for what seemed like the hundredth time.

"Well I don't," Von huffed and stomped back to her room.

If I didn't know her real age, I would have sworn she was five and getting ready for the first day of school. After seeing seven outfits, I was fatigued and starving. I wore a white lace baby doll shirt that camouflaged my bulging stomach, black pants, and a pair of black and white loafers. Von was pleased with my outfit but was catching hell trying to find something she thought was appropriate to wear. It was the end of November and still quite warm outside. There was no stifling humidity that Charlotte usually produced during the warmer months, but a delightful autumn day. This was a day where the brown, gold, red, and yellow leaves swayed timidly and the breeze whisked by to blow your hair out of place every few seconds.

Von had spoken to her sister briefly. Her sister and family were from Georgia, and looking forward to meeting everyone. She was married with kids and Von was eager to meet her niece and nephews. I was content that Von was finally accepting she had a sister and that no matter how she felt about it there was nothing she could do to change that.

"I am hungry!" I yelled hoping this would put some fire underneath Von and hurry her up.

"Okay, okay. I think I am going to go with this one." Von paraded out of the room, stunning as always, dressed in a mid-length orange dress that hit every dip and curve God gave her and camel colored knee high boots.

"Perfect," I said as I rushed her out the door.

***

Von and I were rocking to one of Monica's earlier CDs on the way to her dad's house. I wasn't a huge fan of the R&B singer, but I had to confess that this CD had my head bobbing and fingers snapping.

When we arrived at Von's dad's place, there were more people than I expected. Mr. James lived in the next city right after Fort Mill. The city of Rock Hill was larger and more developed than my little town. Mr. James' brick ranch style house adorned with black shutters was surrounded by four acres of crisp green grass in the front yard and rich red clay in the back. The manicured yard was freshly cut and the hedges were impeccably trimmed. This vision was the epitome of country living at its best.

Rolling onto the gravel driveway, I inhaled the rustic scents in the air and let go of my ever-present animosity for a while. Today, thankfully, was not about me, and for the next few hours I didn't have to be constantly reminded of my woes. We hopped out of Von's truck and strolled over to where her dad was standing by the grill.

Mr. James was in his sixties and Kevin resembled him a lot more than Von did. He was once a muscular man, but after the hard life he lived, those muscles had been replaced by fat and, of course, the infamous old man belly. His gut was covered today by a white t-shirt and pair of old faded blue jeans.

"Hi Mr. James," I said giving him a big hug. His 6'1" frame towered over me.

"Well aren't you just a pretty young woman, all grown up and getting married. Corey is one lucky man," Mr. James said warmly.

"Dad, is Kevin here?" Von asked after giving her dad a weak hug. She still had issues with him and I hoped for her sake they would at least have a heart to heart before the day was over.

"Yeah, he got here a few minutes ago. I think he went inside," he replied pointing towards the house.

Von and I walked past everyone that was sitting outside underneath the shade tree and the picnic tables and headed towards the house. Kids were running all over the place and I thought back to the little boy or girl in my stomach growing by the day. I remained on the porch while Von disappeared inside to find her brother.

"Excuse me ma'am." A pretty little girl ran up to me trying to catch her breath and talk at the same time.

"Yes sweetie?" I smiled at her and thought about how wonderful it would be to have a little girl one day.

The girl's pink and purple flowered dress hung past her knees and her hair held what seemed like a thousand small bows and ribbons. She bounced up the porch steps, pointed at the cooler in the corner, and asked if she could have some water. She grinned, showing me her missing front teeth.

"You sure can." I opened the cooler, gave her a small bottle of water, and watched her gulp it down.

"Thank you," she said, wiping her mouth with her hand. She jumped down the steps and ran off.

As she darted towards the other kids, I felt that there was something so familiar about her. I just couldn't put my finger on it. I had probably seen her at one of Von's family cookouts, but I was surprised that she didn't know my name. Then again, she looked about five or six, and at the age it was hard for kids to remember anyone's name.

Von and Kevin came out the house and stood beside me on the porch. I realized that it was time to be nice and squash things with Kevin. I was at fault for my part in what occurred and I shouldn't make anyone pay for the poor decisions that I made. I glanced down at my stomach again.

"Hey Rachel," Kevin said blandly without looking at me.

"Hey Kevin, how are you?" I tried to sound upbeat to let him know that we were cool. I gave him a slight push on the arm hoping that he would look at me. I would apologize to him later, but right now I just wanted him to know that I wasn't going to act weird today like I had before.

He glanced at me and once he saw that I was smiling, he returned the gesture.

Kevin turned towards Von and touched her on the shoulder. "You ready to meet her, sis?"

"I'm here now," Von whispered as she and Kevin walked down the steps. I followed behind them. Von glanced back at me to make certain I was there. I nodded my support.

The little girl I had given the bottle of water to ran past me to a lovely woman in a long flowing red shirt and fitted black pants that displayed her slender frame. Her hair stopped right above her shoulders and was styled in a bob cut that complimented her round face. Her complexion was bronze and the red shirt looked stunning next to it. That must be her mother, I thought. I saw two older boys run up to the little girl, playfully hit her, and run off as she chased them.

Von and Kevin stood next to their dad at the grill. I remained a few feet off to the side so I wouldn't disturb this rather delicate family moment. Von noticed that I wasn't beside her and reached out her hand telling me to come towards her. I walked up and grabbed my best friend's hand, reassuring her that I was still there. Mr. James called out to the woman in the red shirt and signaled for her to come over. That must be Von's sister. I noticed how pretty she was and how much she favored Mr. James. Kevin, Von, and I stood there while this lady approached us and introduced herself.

"Hi my name is Vivian," she said timidly, reaching out her hand.

Mr. James placed his hand on Vivian's shoulder and turned to Kevin and Von. "Vivian, this is Kevin and Yvonne."

He smiled and waited for his children to say something. Instead of Kevin shaking Vivian's outstretched hand, he opened his arms to give Vivian a hug and they embraced. A few seconds later Von joined them. Vivian seemed ecstatic that she was finally meeting her family and she squeezed both Von and Kevin tightly.

"I want you to meet my kids," she said finally letting loose the grip she had on her newly found brother and sister. "Stacy, get your brothers and come meet your uncle and aunt."

Stacy? *Stacy?* My eyes stretched as I watched the same little girl with the head full of bows pull two boys by the arms toward her mom. Now I knew where I remembered her from. The missing front teeth. The picture of her and the two boys. *Terrence's screensaver.* My legs felt like mush and couldn't hold me up. I needed to sit down. I needed to lie down. This couldn't possibly be true. Okay, Rachel, get yourself together. This was just a coincidence. It had to be. How many little girls named Stacy were there in the world? There were thousands so just because she resembled the Stacy on the screensaver didn't mean it was really her.

The kids scurried up to Vivian and as Vivian introduced little Brandon, David, and Stacy my legs started to wobble.

"My husband is somewhere around here" I heard Vivian say. "Stacy, where is your dad?"

"Here he comes, Mom," she said pointing to a man walking towards us.

At that moment my legs couldn't hold me any longer. The last thing I remember was Von screaming my name before I hit the ground.

***

When I came to I was sitting in Mr. James' living room. I had an extreme headache and I can't remember exactly what happened. The scent of moth balls and ribs was driving me insane and making it hard to breathe.

Von emerged from the kitchen holding a bottle of water. She handed it to me and told me to drink it.

"Rachel, I am worried about you, hon," she said in her motherly voice. "For the last few weeks you have not been yourself, you haven't been eating, you've been sick, and just now you fainted.

Please make a doctor's appointment because if you are not pregnant then something else is going on with you."

"I think it was the heat," I said, sipping the water then placing it on the coffee table in front of me.

I tried to remember exactly what caused me to faint, but it was a blur right now. My head ached too awfully for me to try to explain why I had passed out.

"Sweetie, it was more than the heat. Trust me, we are making you a doctor's appointment next week."

Von was standing over me now and in order not to fight with her today, I nodded my consent. I put my hand over my head and asked Von to get me something for my headache. As she was walking back in the kitchen, there was a knock on the screen door.

"Come in," she yelled.

My head was still in my hands and my eyes were closed. I heard a man say that he was sent in to check on the lady that fainted. That voice was all too familiar to me and once again my heart skipped a beat.

"So that's what did it," I whispered as it all came back to me. I rubbed my head again and wished this damn headache would go away.

"Terrence this is my best friend Rachel, and Rachel this is Vivian's husband, Terrence, so I guess this would be my brother-in-law," Von laughed and gave Terrence a hug. Terrence embraced her and then turned his attention towards me.

"Hello Rachel, are you feeling better?" he asked, looking just as shocked as I was.

I nodded and told him that it was nice meeting him and apologized that he had to see me this way. It took everything in me to contain myself and mumble those few words.

Terrence's hunter green long sleeve shirt and khaki pants made him look even more handsome than the last time I saw him. I blinked several times to make sure he was really standing in front of me.

"No need to apologize, just wanted to make sure everything was alright in here."

Terrence turned toward Von and asked her where the bathroom was. She directed her new brother-in-law down the hall.

"Rachel, I am going to run outside real quick. I will be right back," Von said walking out the screen door and closing it behind her.

Terrence waited until Von was outside and walked back into the living room.

"Terrence please tell me this is a dream," I pleaded. My hands begin to shake and my eyes filled with tears. I looked at this man that I had slept with a few months ago, this man that I was in love with, this man whose child I carried.

"I wish it was." He shook his head and frowned. "Rachel I had no idea that my wife's half sister would be your best friend."

"Neither did I. You never said anything about your wife having a sister here."

'This was all laid on us a few months ago." Terrence whispered and watched the door. "My wife and I were constantly fighting and this came up. By the time I was going to talk to you about it, you had gotten ill. Are you sure you are okay? Maybe you need to go to the doctor."

His sincere concern for me was touching. I adjusted my shirt to make sure he didn't notice anything.

"Yes, I am fine," I said not looking at Terrence. "I think you need to go back outside with your wife."

Terrence frowned again. He hesitated at first and then moved closer to the door. "Rachel…are you…."

When he saw that I was not looking up, Terrence walked out and closed the screen door behind him, leaving his question half asked.

Chapter 25

For the remainder of the cookout I stayed in the house. Mr. James offered me his bed and since that was the safest place to be I disappeared into his room and took a nap. I woke up woozy and confused. My eyes searched around the room and reality set in. I hadn't dreamed about today's events, and that only made me feel worse. Coming face to face with Vivian, Terrence's wife, was a bit too much for me to handle. My stomach was cramping and my heart felt like a punching bag.

I rolled out of bed and wobbled into the kitchen to see if the food was inside now. There were hamburgers, hotdogs, ribs and fish scattered on the counters and table. The cookout was probably over by now since all the food was in the house. I hoped that Terrence and Vivian's visit was over, as well. I didn't want to chance having to see him again and run the risk of him noticing my plump stomach. I made a hamburger and expected that to settle my stomach a bit until I got an opportunity to fix a full plate.

I felt the need to walk outside and check things before I sat down and fed my face. Maybe Von would be ready to go and all I would have to do was walk to the truck. That way I could avoid everyone. I didn't feel like people asking me if I was okay and what happened when the answers were "No, I am not okay" and "I am pregnant by this woman's husband." My best friend's brother-in-law. I felt like the biggest slut in the Carolinas. Not only had I slept with Von's brother, however briefly, but now I was pregnant by her brother-in-law. The phrase "small world" came to mind. Too small for me. Way too small.

I stumbled out of the kitchen, into the living room, and peeked out the screen door.

I witnessed a few people still standing under the big tree in the yard. I stepped out on the porch and spotted Von and her dad. As soon as she saw me she waved her hands and motioned for me to come over. Standing there with them was Kevin, along with Vivian, Terrence, and their kids. I forced a smile and slowly made my way over. When I finally reached them, everyone asked if I was feeling better.

"Yes, I am feeling a lot better," I muttered glancing at the ground and then back at Von. I struggled to avoid any eye contact with Terrence.

"It's probably all the stress of the wedding and the fact that she is not taking care of herself that has her like this," Von said looking at me then at my round stomach.

Terrence's eyes were focused on Von. He caught her staring at my stomach and followed suit. He frowned as he had done in the house. Stacy tugged on her dad's pants leg and he patted her head and gave her a dry smile.

I crossed my arms in front of me. "Von are we almost ready to go?"

"Yeah, here are the keys." Von handed me the keys and I told her that I would be sitting in the truck.

"It was nice meeting you all," I said glancing at Vivian, again avoiding Terrence's eyes. Head down, I slowly walked to the truck.

After about fifteen more minutes of chatting, I watched Von practically skip towards the truck and jump in. "Okay, chick, what's going on with you?"

"Nothing." I gazed out the window. I could feel the tears swelling up in my eyes and I didn't want her to see them.

She turned on the truck and Monica's voice blasted, " *Ain't you tired of being on the sideline, tired of getting yours after I get mine, baby second place don't get a prize, when you gone realize you wasting your time.* "

With all the hormones that were raging throughout my body and after seeing Terrence, I couldn't control the tears.

Von caught a glimpse of my wet face and pulled her truck into a Burger King parking lot.

"I am a sideline ho," I bawled pointing at the radio where Monica was still singing and asking, *"Have you been to his church and do he ask you to pray? No, because Sunday is family day."*

"Rachel, what are you talking about?"

As I cried, I told Von everything about Terrence and how he works with me and when we met. I even told her that I was sitting in her car pregnant. I confessed to her about the night I spent with Kevin and how I mistreated him afterwards. I never once thought about telling her about Kevin but once I started talking I just couldn't stop.

Between sobs I told her that I felt that I was just worthless and Corey couldn't possibly want to marry someone like me. I just wanted to feel wanted. I just wanted to feel loved. After spilling my guts, the tears subsided a moment and I peeked up at my best friend.

"I am just tired," I sighed.

Von stared at me in disbelief and for a moment said nothing. After digesting everything Von finally broke the silence and placed her hand on my stomach.

"Everyone makes mistakes," she told me with tears in her eyes. "I am just upset that you didn't come to me before."

"I thought you would look at me differently. I am the one always preaching about not doing this and that and now look at me."

Von smirked. "Yeah, you are. After everything I have done in my lifetime, there is no way I can judge you, girl. What are you going to do about the baby?"

"Abortion."

The word came out cold and dry and sent chills up my spine. For the first time I realized the decision I had made.

"Are you sure?" Von asked removing her hand from my stomach.

"I have no other choice."

***

My appointment was at 9:30 Tuesday morning and I asked Von to come with me. I needed my best friend to help me through this nightmare. The entire time I envisioned Von scolding me, but not once did she even utter one word that would make me feel bad about myself. My best friend was being there for me like no one had ever done before. I looked to her to get me through this and she was proving that she would.

When we arrived at the Sanyer Clinic I felt nauseous all over again and puked my breakfast out in the parking lot. Between the time of the cookout and coming to the clinic, I had begun to experience fluttering in my stomach. Through my internet research, I learned this was the very first movements of the baby. I didn't quite know how to feel about this. In the past when I thought of being pregnant I imagined sharing this with my husband. Never in a million years had I expected to be alone and pregnant. And even though Von was with me now, I still felt alone.

I signed in with the dark haired receptionist and told her how far along I was. Without looking up, she instructed me to have a seat and said the nurse would be with me in one minute. I felt nauseous once again and waited for Von to tell me that I shouldn't go through with this. Von grabbed my hand and said nothing.

A part of me wanted her to say that somehow, some way, everything would work out and I could keep my baby. My eyes wandered around the waiting room. I spotted a young girl that could be no older than 18 with her head down, sitting on her hands. She sat motionless. Her black stringy hair rested over both shoulders and she never raised her head. Three chairs down from her were a woman and a man. The woman looked like she was in her 30's with red hair and bags under her eyes. The man sitting next to her was bald with a weary cruel expression on his face as if he really didn't want to be here.

I thought about it, and neither did I.

"Am I doing the right thing?" I whispered. I glanced at Von and then back at the young girl.

"Only you can answer that question," Von replied squeezing my hand tighter.

The receptionist called me back up to her desk to obtain my payment information for services rendered. As I was about to tell her cash, I felt myself becoming sick again. Everything inside me was screaming out, Don't do this! I couldn't kill an innocent baby that didn't ask to be here in the first place. I was so against this. This was not me. I didn't even know who I was anymore. I wanted to cry. I wanted to run out of this dreadful place and never look back. I turned around and stared at my best friend for what seemed like minutes.

"Ma'am?" The receptionist asked again, becoming impatient.

I turned away from the desk and walked towards Von. "Can we leave?" I whispered.

"Whatever you want to do," Von said.

Von grabbed my arm and led me out of the office. I stopped for a moment, glancing back to see the young girl lift her head and look at me for the first time. Our eyes met. Her eyes told me she wanted to leave, too. I nodded, and without saying a word, let her know it was okay to leave.

Von let go of my arm, grabbed my hand and ushered me the rest of the way out of the office. I walked out and wondered if the girl had taken my advice and found the courage to leave, too. As soon as my feet hit the pavement outside, I suddenly felt a hundred times better. All before my stomach was twisting and turning and now it was settled.

"What now?" Von asked. Her face showed both relief and worry.

"Take me home," I replied.

Chapter 26

I returned to work following a week of being absent. After the failed abortion attempt, I decided to take the rest of the week off to figure everything out. Now that I was back at work, my objective was to submerge myself in business to take my mind off things. My stomach was poking out just a bit and I had reached eleven weeks without anyone suspecting that I was pregnant. My resolution was to keep my baby. Aware that this would end my relationship with Corey, I had to tell him immediately. Our wedding was four months away and I was about to devastate him.

I called Corey and invited him to come up for the weekend. To my surprise, he agreed. He inquired about any wedding tasks I had to complete and if I wanted help. He continued on about how we only had four months before the wedding, and then we would be off on our honeymoon, which would be his favorite part. He even spoke about Christmas being a few weeks away and that he would try to take off some days so we could spend time together. Any other day I would have appreciated hearing this from him, but now his excitement tormented me.

I was sorting through the work I neglected last week and noticed there was a new email in my inbox. It was from Terrence. It read, "Can we talk?" I considered it for a minute and then replied back that I was about to go to a meeting and would call him when I got out. I really didn't have a meeting to go to, but I just didn't know what to say to Terrence now. He is my best friend's brother-in-law. There could be no more us. I still had very strong feelings for this man, but I had to let it go. I was doing this on my own and I didn't have it in me to tell Terrence that I was carrying his baby.

Yes, he deserved to know but I wasn't ready to let that cat out of the bag yet.

I was feeling lightheaded. I had to take better care of myself. I wasn't eating right and not once had I taken a prenatal vitamin. Once I concluded that I would have the abortion I did not feel the need in taking the vitamins. However, now that I had changed my mind, I regretted not at least taking one or two. As I sat at my desk, cramps begin to ripple through the lower part of my stomach. Perhaps I just needed to eat something.

This whole pregnancy thing was no joke. If I missed one meal this kid was making me feel the consequences. These pains started last night while I was in bed, and as soon as I ate a piece of cake, they regressed. I leaned back in my chair and rubbed my stomach assuring my little "it" that I would eat better. I referred to him or her as little "it" until I learned the sex.

I marched to the vending machine in the break room down the hall from my office and bought a pack of peanut butter crackers. This would hold me until lunch. Immediately the cramps subsided. My plan after work was to go home, unwind, take a long hot bath, and plunge into my bed. No interruptions or no errands. I would dig up a good book from my book stand, sink into my pillows, and get lost in whatever fantasy world I desired. I was looking forward to that. Fantasy was much more appreciated than my reality right now.

Time went by extremely fast and before I realized it, the work day was done. I avoided calling Terrence by emailing him a spreadsheet of the weekly numbers. He responded, again asking if we could talk. I couldn't bring myself to talk to Terrence today, so I replied that I would call him tomorrow. The only thing I wanted to do was go home and relax. I danced out of the office so delighted to be leaving. Today the traffic didn't even disturb me. I swerved in and out of cars and bounced from one lane to the next without getting my usual road rage.

I arrived at my apartment and removed my black and white blouse, black dress pants and kicked off my heels. I jumped in my tub and took a long, soothing, hot bubble bath. After my bath, I put on my pink and white flannel pajamas, fixed a big bowl of butter pecan ice cream, and snuggled in my bed.

A sharp pain awakened me from an hour of sleep. I wasn't hungry, so I didn't understand why this pain was so unbearable. I stirred around in bed lessening the pain, and got up to go to the bathroom. I dropped my pants and rested on the toilet, noticing a few spots of pink in my underwear. Recalling what the doctor said about spotting during pregnancy, I didn't give it much thought. I would call the doctor if I saw more blood, I thought as I wiped and pulled up my pajama pants. The tissue was also a light pink, but the pain was gone. I scrambled back in my bed, settling in with the intent of going back to sleep for the night.

***

The week was flying by, and as Thursday approached, I was more frightened than a sixteen year old girl that had missed her period. I planned to tell Corey I was pregnant and break his heart. Initially, I expected him to be surprised and happy thinking that he was the father, but once he saw my expression, I would have to watch his heart shatter into a thousand pieces, and then deal with his anger. I was not emotionally ready to handle this but I couldn't delay it any longer. The baby was not his and there was no getting around that fact. I would not pass it off as his, either. That wasn't even an option.

The spotting had stopped and the pains were coming and going. Every now and then I would get a sharp, knife life twinge, but if I stayed still for a few minutes, the pain would pass. I called the doctor and informed her of the aches. She advised me to monitor it and if it persisted to come in as soon as possible.

Pacing around my living room and reciting the speech that I would give Corey was how I spent most of Thursday night. He was excited about seeing me. His apparent enthusiasm ripped into my heart and I felt queasy once again. I threw up my lunch and couldn't fathom the notion of eating dinner. Stress wasn't good for me or the baby but I couldn't put all the anxiety and fright behind me. I repeated out loud over and over what I was going to divulge to Corey. I would begin by acknowledging how much I loved him. This would be a dead giveaway that something was wrong. Most people opened this way when they had something dreadful to convey to the other person. Perhaps I should just give it to him, no sugar coating. Just shoot straight from the hip like Daryl always said.

The mild cramps came again causing me to halt the excessive pacing and sit down. I sat on my couch, in front of my TV, and watched Derwin on *The Game* struggle to explain why he cheated and beg Melanie to work things out. I felt distraught again once I realized I didn't have it in me to plead with Corey to work things out. I didn't warrant his love. The best thing he could do was walk away from me. All this brainstorming and attempting to get my story straight for tomorrow night was strenuous and tiring me out.

The clock on the wall displayed 9:30. I pressed the off button on the television and left Melanie crying. I had enough of *The Game*; I needed something that was going to make me laugh instead of worry more about my situation. Kevin Hart was recorded on my DVR in my bedroom. This would be a great pick me up. His stand-up routine was sure to make me chuckle if nothing else could. I giggled so hard at Kevin that he sent me right into a sound deep sleep.

Chapter 27

Today was the day that I told Corey the truth. The truth about the baby and my transgressions. The day that everything came out in the open and I watched the man that I had loved for so long walk out the door and out of my life. I felt repulsed at the idea of confessing my sins to Corey and dealing with whatever response he gave me. Every action had a consequence and it was time for me to face mine.

My stomach did flip flops all day and I was unable to eat anything. I was miserable and sick. This little person was really demanding. I used the bathroom for what seemed like the hundredth time today. The lower section of my stomach throbbed and the only thing I yearned for was a few Aleve to get me through the day.

I started cramping slightly while at work, and on my one hundred and first trip to the bathroom, I saw light pink spots in my underwear. I called the doctor and she instructed me to monitor it yet again and come in this afternoon for a checkup. I was convinced it was stress from the events that were about to happen. Not having eaten anything also played a big role in why I wasn't feeling well.

Around noon I ended my work day and went home to rest until tonight. Corey texted that he couldn't wait to see me and he loved me. I considered cooking dinner, but I didn't feel up to it. My stomach still ached, and from the time I got off until about five I laid in the bed trying to ease the sharp pains that controlled my stomach. It was worry and fright getting the better of me and I couldn't help it. I had messed up and I didn't even want Corey's forgiveness.

I just wanted to tell him the truth and be done with it. I didn't deserve his mercy or his pity. I deserved to be a single mother raising my child alone.

That was the reality of my situation and it was staring at me like a child beaming at a big bowl of cake and ice cream. Without blinking, without looking away, in my face, gawking.

Monica called and I realized that being so wrapped up in my drama-filled life, I hadn't spoken to my sister in almost two weeks. I had been extremely busy, but my rationale for not talking to her was that I was ashamed of what I had become. I was not the same little innocent Rachel that tried to steer everyone in the right direction. I was not the same Rachel that someone could come to when they wanted to know the appropriate thing to do. I was not the same Rachel at all. Not the high and mighty Rachel that never did any wrong and turned her nose up at people. The Rachel that knew her shit didn't stink. I was different.

The alarm clock on my nightstand changed from 5:59 to 6:00. I dragged myself out of bed to clean up before Corey arrived. I pictured my vase and little figurines scattered all over the floor after I told Corey that I was pregnant with another man's child. He was not the violent type, but after hearing news like that I really couldn't say what he would or wouldn't do. On the way to the kitchen a pain stopped me mid-stride. I needed to eat, but I was too weak to go anywhere right now. I called Von to bring over some food, hoping that her Friday night hadn't started already.

"You know I got you girl," she replied right before she hung up the phone.

I was still spotting but I didn't want to go to the ER and I had slept thru the time Dr. Ainsley had set aside for my checkup this afternoon. No hospitals or doctors tonight. Not when I had to tell Corey the truth.

Von picked up some good home-cooked food from a restaurant called Down South. She knew exactly what to bring me. Baked Chicken, green beans, corn, rice and gravy, and cornbread weighed down the plate. I didn't realize how hungry I was until the first drop of gravy hit my lips.

"Girl, I needed this."

My mouth was full and my entire face was in the plate.

"I can tell. You don't look so good," she said squinting her eyes and examining me.

"I haven't been feeling that well today, but I think it's because of my nerves and what I am about to do."

"So you still telling Corey tonight?"

"Yeah," I said with a mouth full of food. The thought of having to tell him almost made my food come back up.

"Rachel in your state I don't think ---"

I cut Von off, fully aware of what she was going to suggest. "This is something I have to do." I stopped eating and my eyes pleaded with Von just to support me.

"Don't look at me like that. You know I will back you up no matter what. I am always a phone call away."

Von reached over and gave me a one armed hug before leaving the room. I heard her lock my front door and once again my apartment was silent.

***

Time crept by until I heard Corey's keys unlock my front door. He trotted in with a smile on his face that I hadn't seen in months.

"Hey baby!" he exclaimed

I was poised in the kitchen, still contemplating on how to deliver the news. He ran up to me and scooped me in his arms like the leading man in a romance movie. Our situation was anything but romantic, I thought trying to hide the pains that were rippling through my stomach.

I peeped out a "hey" and hugged him back the best I could. I wore a large t-shirt and sweat pants so that Corey wouldn't start asking questions before I had a chance to sit down and talk to him.

"I have missed you so much, baby," Corey said still hugging me.

He finally let go and gazed at me.

He detected that something was wrong. I might as well go ahead and tell him so that he could leave before it got too late. After I finished what I had to say there was no way that he would want to stay with me tonight.

"Corey, I need to tell you something," I said.

I pointed toward the couch hoping that we could sit down and talk. Still staring at me he didn't move.

"Rachel, whatever you have to tell me will have to wait until tomorrow," Corey touched my hand and drew me back into him.

"It can't wait," I said louder pushing back from him.

Again he pulled me into him, grabbing both my arms. "It can and it will."

He tilted my face up towards his and placed a kiss on me that made my entire body weak. I had almost forgotten how it felt to kiss Corey and be in his arms. I let his tongue enter my mouth and I temporarily disregarded the anticipated speech for tonight. Maybe it could wait until tomorrow. While we were kissing Corey's phone began to vibrate in his pocket.

"Baby your phone is going off," I whispered. I pulled away from him assuming he would reach into his pocket to answer it.

"That can wait, too," he demanded.

As we headed to my bedroom my thoughts of the conversation we were supposed to have returned. It can wait, I thought to myself over and over again as we made love and fell asleep in each other's arms.

***

Pains slashed thru my stomach, awakening me from a deep slumber. Corey was sound asleep next to me and didn't feel me move when I crawled out of bed and crept to the bathroom. The pain that I was feeling was different than anything I had felt before. Instead of the rippling cramps, these were knife like stabs all through my stomach.

"Oh God," I growled, falling to the floor of the bathroom before having a chance to make it to the toilet.

Dismissing the attempt to actually use the bathroom, now all I wanted to do was lie back down. I inched across my bedroom floor on my hands and knees hoping that lying down would stop the pain or at least ease it a bit.

I had asked Corey to take it easy when we made love, but his excitement mixed with pleasure had caused him to be rougher than usual. I was frightened that Corey would see my changing body but he seemed so anxious to get his hands on me that he never even noticed. After hours of lovemaking, I had fallen asleep with just my t-shirt on, not bothering to put on a gown or my satin pajama set.

I made it back to the bed and kneeled on the side. Now that the pains had ceased a bit I noticed that my legs were wet and sticky. The moonlight shone on Corey's face and lit the bed where I had been asleep. I tried to pick myself up, but as I caught a glimpse of my side of the bed the revelation of why my pain was so severe sent me back to my knees.

"OH, NO!" I screamed as I stared at my sheets drenched in blood.

Chapter 28

My back hurt from resting in this cold stiff bed all night. I was tired of looking at this same bright plain white wall and this lifeless picture of an orchid plastered on it. I wasn't concerned with the TV that was perched above me dangling from the wall either. I didn't want to answer the nurse's questions as they poked and prodded. And if one more person asked how I was feeling, I swear I was going to start yelling at the top of my lungs.

Corey finally left the room to get something to eat and all that crowded my mind was the look on his face when the doctor informed us that I had a miscarriage. He looked horrified but at the same time saddened. All I could do was weep. I didn't want to even look at him. He asked me did I know I was pregnant and I confessed that was what our conversation was going to be about. Stunned, he didn't say anything else.

After I got settled in the room, I called Von to come to the hospital. I told her what happened and that the miscarriage occurred so fast that I didn't get a chance to tell Corey about the baby. I didn't even feel like having the conversation anymore. She agreed and thought maybe it would be best not to tell him any more details. I was still in bed when the nurse came in and told me that all the tests had come back okay and I was free to leave.

Once I got home, after having both Corey and Von take care of me, I was exhausted all over again. I fell in and out of deep sleep. When I woke up, I heard the tail end of a conversation that my best friend and fiancé were engaged in.

"I don't think she can handle that right now, and I can't believe you are saying this, Corey," Von hissed.

"Okay but she has to know. I can't hide this from her," he whispered.

Corey was pacing around the kitchen and I wondered what it was that he needed to tell me. My eyes became heavy again, and as I speculated about what my best friend and fiancé were discussing, I fell into another deep sleep.

I was awaken by a light kiss on my forehead. Corey told me he had to go and he would be back later on in the week to check on me. He advised me that Von was still here and he would call me as soon as he got home. I mumbled ok and told him that I loved him before he walked out of the room. My head was throbbing and I was so hungry that I could have eaten everything on the pig, from the mouth to the feet, or like my granddad used to say, from the roota to the toota.

Terrence called several times throughout this hardship and sent several texts saying that he just wanted to talk. I needed to end things with him and let it be that. It had to be over. I sent him a text message and let him know that I was okay and agreed that we did need to have a face to face talk. My mind told me this might not be a good idea but my heart wanted to see him and let him know how I felt about everything that happened. I wanted him to comprehend how I felt seeing his wife and that I had loved him. I had actually been pregnant by this man and had decided to have the baby. I yearned to tell him everything and close this chapter of my life.

After eating, I told Von that I would be fine and even though she didn't want to leave I insisted that she go home, at least for a few hours. I loved my best friend but I really needed to be alone with my thoughts right now. I was a mess and the only person that I could talk to about this was God. I had to pray. I didn't believe that anything happened just because; nothing was a coincidence or just came to be.

It was all a part of a bigger picture, all part of a larger plan and I needed understanding as to what was to be. I needed comfort.

In all my months of looking for this in other people, especially men, I realized that I had been looking to the wrong source.

I wanted to feel loved, so first I went to Kevin, and then Terrence. That didn't satisfy my need and I still felt empty inside, and now that my baby was gone, I suffered an unbearable void. I wanted to cry but that's all I had been doing for the last few months. Crying and making mistakes. My wedding, if there was still going to be one, was a few months away and here I was sitting in bed having just lost a married man's child.

I acted so superior with Monica and Von about all the crazy situations they got into and here I was in an impossible state. It was time for me to decide what I wanted, but first I had to pray. I gradually edged out of my bed and fell on my knees.

"Lord," I repeated five times before anything else came out. I let out a heavy sigh and released everything in me that I had done and thought about. After twenty minutes on my knees, I cried. I cried for hurting Corey, I cried for hurting Terrence and his family, and most of all, I cried for hurting myself. The tears didn't stop, and I cried for hurting God. For disappointing him and not being who I should have been. I prayed for him to show me the way and to heal me. "In Jesus name, amen."

After kneeling for what seemed like an hour, I pulled myself up and toppled back on the bed. I was determined to sleep and get some rest without having all those feelings of depression and sorrow. God would work it out and I was going to leave it in his hands.

***

Two months had passed since the miscarriage and I was beginning to feel like myself again. My relationship with Corey was getting back on track and we were becoming more and more like we used to be.

I was concerned about the far off look in his eyes that he would get at night when he didn't think I was paying attention. I questioned him about it once, but he assured me nothing was wrong. I didn't pressure him about it. For all my sins and secrets I couldn't really hound him for not telling me every thought that was on his mind. I am sure that it had to do with the miscarriage. We moved the wedding back two months just to give us some breathing room and now we were three and a half months away from becoming one. The drama in my life had subsided for a while and for that I was thankful.

Von formed a relationship with her sister, and they were trying to get to know each other. She told me that Terrence had no problems with that and even helped when he could. Von could see that they had deep problems in their marriage, and that her sister was a lot for any man to handle, but they were trying to work at it. I felt for Terrence because he did have a place in my heart, but I wanted to see him and his wife work things out. When we used to talk, he would always say he just wanted to be happy. That's all I wanted for him as well.

"You ready to go, baby?" I hollered from the bedroom. It was Saturday night and Corey and I had reservations at my favorite New Orleans style restaurant. I was highly anticipating the spicy gumbo sauce and the sweet flavor of my favorite shrimp and chicken creole dish. I stumbled into the living room still trying to press my foot down in my boots so I could zip them up. Corey stood with his leather jacket on in the middle of the living room, frozen, staring at nothing.

"I was drunk," he said softly, so softly that I could barely make out the words.

I noticed the same distant look on his face that I had seen so many times at night.

"What's wrong, Corey?"

"I was drunk," he repeated still not looking at me. He looked like a mannequin in a department store, just still. I waited for a second to see if he was going to say anything else, but he didn't.

"When were you drunk, baby?" I asked, finally able to zip up my boots. I walked towards him so I could hear exactly what he was saying.

"One night, months ago," he replied.

Corey turned to me with tears forming in his eyes. He took the back of his hand and wiped one tear before it could roll down his face. "We were arguing so much and I was confused," Corey began.

My heart dropped and I just knew I wasn't going to like what he had to say.

"She didn't mean anything to me," he continued. He stood with his shoulders hunched over as if he had been carrying this weight on him for months.

I didn't say anything. I couldn't say anything. It was not because I didn't have anything to say. It was merely because I was desperately hoping that at any minute I would awaken from this ghastly nightmare, roll over in my bed, and go back to sleep to begin a more enjoyable dream.

"Please don't hate me." Corey's eyes pleaded with mine.

I still couldn't say anything. I needed to sit down before I ended up falling down. Corey expected me to interrupt him at any second. Interrupt him with a million questions like I always did but I wasn't going to do that. I didn't feel like doing that. Not this time. This time I was going to let him say whatever he needed to without any input from me. One of his many nicknames for me was "Insert" because he said that I couldn't let anyone tell a story without inserting something into it. Well, Ms. Insert was just the complete opposite today. Silently, I sat on the edge of the couch and braced myself for what I was about to hear.

Corey told me about some woman that he met and began talking to about our wedding and the concerns he had. He also confided in her about our constant disagreements and the issues he was facing on his job. He said she was just a friend that was there for him and one thing lead to another, and things happened. I asked him what things.

At first, he just looked at me and then dropped his head. "You know," he mumbled. I knew what things he was talking about and I don't even know why I wanted him to say it. His words were tearing my heart to shreds, but all I could think about was the baby that I miscarried. Here he was telling me about cheating with some woman, and just two months ago I was pregnant by another man.

Before I knew it, tears were streaming from my eyes and I couldn't look at Corey. Somewhere in the background Corey was apologizing and saying that he loved me. It sounded as if he was a million miles, his voice a light whisper. The tears kept coming, and no matter what I did I couldn't stop them. I couldn't say anything. I heard him say, "Baby, just look at me." I couldn't even do that. My head felt so heavy that I couldn't lift it up. It felt as if I had a cement block on the back of my neck forcing my head down. He sat beside me on the couch and grabbed my hand. My first instinct was to snatch my hand back, but I was too weak.

"Rachel, I just want you to know that I love you and I always will. I know you need time to digest this so I will give you that. She meant nothing to me and we don't talk anymore. I love you and you are who I want to spend the rest of my life with."

Just as he was saying this I heard my phone beep indicating that I had a text message. My phone was the last thing I wanted to look at right now. Corey leaned over and kissed me gently on my cheek. He walked to the door and called my name once again, maybe twice, but I still couldn't raise my head. The cement block was still there, pressing down on me, locking my head towards the floor and making it impossible for me to move. I heard his footsteps disappear into the breezeway and the click of him locking the door with his key.

Finally, I was able to look up. I reached for my phone to check the message and it was Terrence letting me know that he was thinking about me.

"Cruel joke," I said through tears as I looked up at the ceiling.

Chapter 29

A week went by and I had communicated with Corey through texts only. I needed time and space and he provided me that. The first few days after he told me what happened I didn't talk to him. He texted to check on me and told me that he loved me but didn't press when I didn't respond back. Truth be told, he still had my heart. I should have come clean to him about Terrence and the baby like he did about his indiscretions, but I would never want to hurt him like I was hurting. Selfish on my part, maybe, but I didn't want that for him. Then again, maybe I just didn't want that for me. I wasn't going to let him believe that I was this perfect woman that did no wrong like I had tried to be my entire life, but at the same time I couldn't crush him like I knew my honesty would.

I spoke with Von about it since he had confided in her the night that I came home from the hospital after my miscarriage. Those were the whispers they had exchanged in my living room while I was in and out of sleep. I was somewhat distraught that Von knew and had not told me, but at the same time, it was not her place. Corey needed to tell me that secret, yet I still couldn't tell him mine.

When I finally responded back to his text messages, I shared with him that he wasn't the only one that looked for comfort in another person. Before I said too much, he cut me off and told me that he didn't need to know anything else. All he wanted was to put this behind us and try to start fresh. That is what I wanted, too, but wanting it and actually being able to do that were two different things. There was one thing I needed to do before we could start anew. I had to talk to Terrence and tell him everything - how I felt for him and about the baby.

For the last few weeks I was able to tell Terrence that I was doing okay and that's all.

I learned through Von that things were so severely damaged in his marriage that they were at the point of separation. My heart went out to him. Despite our illicit encounters, I knew that he wanted his family to stay together.

While at work, I sent Terrence an email asking if I could see him so that we could talk. He responded that he was relieved to hear from me and he would love for us to sit down and discuss things. I would make the trip to Atlanta this weekend. The sooner, this whole ordeal was behind me, the better. I could have just forgotten about Terrence and moved on with my life but my heart wouldn't allow it. I wanted more than anything to move forward and to me this was the best way. All of my loose ends needed to be tied up. Corey was still allowing me time to process what he had told me; therefore, he didn't hassle me about seeing one another. He texted and informed me that he was working an extra shift this weekend.

Terrence and I desired privacy, so I would get a hotel room in order for us to talk. This would be an emotional discussion and I didn't want to chance us being in public and breaking down in tears. Terrence was happy that I was coming to Atlanta. I was far from sharing those same feelings, knowing the dreaded conversation that would take place.

***

After arriving in Atlanta, I checked into the Holiday Inn downtown and texted Terrence to let him know that I made it safely and my location. As expected, he was still at work. I had taken a half day in order to make the drive and be settled when he got off. There was nothing romantic about this meeting. No soft music or sexy lingerie. I didn't get dolled up or make sure I was flawless for Terrence. I was a woman that was carrying around too many secrets. That burden alone made me feel like I had a 500 pound man resting on my shoulders.

Terrence texted letting me know that he was on his way and I felt a wave of nervousness sweep over me.

I wasn't fearful about seeing him but about what I had to tell him. I hadn't seen him since the cookout and my bulging stomach from that time was now gone along with my pride. My words would hurt him for sure but this endless circle of pain had to stop somewhere. My heart was a bed of torture from what Corey told me about his unfaithfulness, even though parts of me didn't feel like I had a right to be upset.

Three small taps on the door informed me that Terrence had arrived. My first thought was to leave him standing on the other side of the door and text that this was a bad idea. However, if I wanted to start over, I needed to come clean about everything and end this. It was bizarre how I felt convicted to reveal myself to Terrence but not to Corey.

I answered the door and was not prepared for what was standing on the other side. Terrence was once again gorgeous and breathtaking. My heart sank into my stomach and rested among the butterflies that were back for a visit. His head was not entirely bald this time; there was slight fuzz growing on the top. This look made him more handsome and virile than before. Since he was coming straight from the office he was dressed in navy blue dress slacks complimented by a sky blue shirt and a blue and grey tie. In one hand he held a dozen long-stemmed red roses and in the other a medium sized white gift box. He looked tired and uneasy, as if sleep had missed him for several days, but he was still so attractive.

We stared at each other for seconds and then I moved to the side to allow him into the room. His footsteps were short and controlled as he placed the roses and box on the small metal desk beside the TV. He turned back toward me in order to give me a hug. I gave him an uncomfortable hug and let go quickly.

"Rachel, you look beautiful," Terrence said taking notice of the jeans and white blouse that I had on.

He stared at my stomach a few seconds too long. I turned toward the bed and asked him to sit next to me so that we could talk.

"I want you to open your gift first." Terrence moved toward the table and grabbed the box.

He handed it to me and sat down on the bed facing me. Smiling, almost unable to contain himself, he instructed me to open the box. I untied the white ribbon from the box and opened it. Inside was a miniature book titled, *Inspiration and Love Quotes.* A smile formed on my face as I opened my gift and browsed through some of the quotes that the book included.

"Page 53," Terrence ordered.

I quickly turned to the page requested and read the quote aloud that was highlighted in yellow.

"Love is the flower of life, and blossoms unexpectedly and without law, and must be plucked where it is found, and enjoyed for the brief hour of its duration.' D. H. Lawrence."

I was still and couldn't say another word. I felt the tears swelling in my eyes and attempted to hold them back with all my power. Terrence grabbed my hand. His touch was so warm, so soothing like it had always been.

"I love it," I whispered still staring at the quote.

His fingers caressed my knuckles as his grip became stronger. "I hoped you would," he breathed in and continued stroking my hand. "I know we have a lot to talk about."

"He cheated," I blurted out. I had no plans of telling Terrence what Corey had done since I was no better than him, and I don't know how these words escaped my lips.

I told Terrence about what Corey had confessed to me, and the shame I felt for doing the same things but not being woman enough to tell him. Terrence allowed me to rest my head on his shoulder as he wrapped his athletic arms around me. He held me for what seemed like an hour and let me release all the agony from both my actions and Corey's.

His sky blue shirt was now stained with my tears and I apologized for the obvious mess that I had become. Sitting beside each other, my head nestled into his chest, he ran his fingers through my hair and breathed in. His body visibly relaxed as he closed his eyes.

"Rachel you are not a mess," he whispered, one arm around me while his hand continued to run through my hair.

My crying finally ceased and I relaxed in his arms, the arms that provided my solace. I looked at this man that could make me feel comfort in one hug, in one hour by just holding me, and our eyes locked. He leaned down and kissed my forehead. I looked up at him and he leaned in once again and kissed me like he had months ago, with more passion and desire than I had ever felt before. My head was saying no but my heart was leaping for joy and I succumbed to its wishes. I couldn't think or talk, all I could do was feel. No matter how wrong I was, I still wanted this man. My heart took over and just like the quote said, I enjoyed the brief hour of love's duration.

***

As he let out a lingering sigh, I opened my eyes and hesitantly glanced at this man on top of me. His body shook once again and I felt his chest rise and then fall as he took another deep breath. Both our bodies were sticky and moist from the sweat that had us bound to each other.

"Are you okay?" he asked, relieved that I had finally opened my eyes. I looked around the room for a moment, his body weight pinning me to the bed. I tried to form my mouth in order to produce something, but I was speechless.

So many thoughts were running through my mind, but none of them made any sense to me right now. Almost simultaneously, we slowly glanced at the gold and black condom wrapper lying on the nightstand.

"Damn," I said, thinking out loud.

I attempted to focus on something else, anything else. The hotel room was dark except for the flickering light from the muted television. Not remembering who had turned the TV on or whether it had been my idea to mute it, I cocked my head to the side imagining what the girl on the Aleve commercial was saying.

The small room contained a queen sized bed draped with a shabby ivory-colored blanket, a TV stand the size of a card playing table, and the tiniest metal desk ever. It captured the smell of sweat, sex, and a mixture of our colognes and gave me such a headache that I wished I had some of the advertised pain reliever.

His damp body still lay on top of mine; his sculpted chest pressed against my heavy bosom as he began to stroke my now wet hair. I could still smell the spearmint gum on his breath. My muscles relaxed as he carefully pulled himself out of me and rolled over onto the other side of the bed. Lying on his back, his eyes shifted to the ceiling and he exhaled loudly.

"Damn," I repeated again, looking at his muscular dark brown frame, then focusing on his sexy almond colored eyes.

We had just finished a session of love making that lasted for at least two hours, and to my own surprise I wanted more. I wanted to feel him inside me again; pleasing me while I in return did everything I could to make sure he was satisfied. As we lay in silence, reality slowly reared its ugly head and I remembered the big event that would be taking place in my life in a little more than eight weeks.

My wedding day was quickly approaching, and my heart dropped at the mere thought. The Aleve commercial was gone and two women were now fighting on *The Jerry Springer Show*.

One lady who looked like she weighed close to three hundred pounds swung her dirty blond hair back and forth before lunging toward a frail pale girl dressed in daisy dukes shorts and a halter top.

I turned my focus back to the man that lay beside me. Noticing the worried look on my face, he turned on his side and leaned over to place a tender kiss on my forehead.

"Rachel, I will not cause any problems for you, all I want is for you to be happy," he whispered.

I stared at him wondering if he was as confused as I was. I turned on my side with my back towards him and faced the wall.

Maybe if I just closed my eyes I would wake up and all of this would be a dream. The room was silent except for his breathing, and even that turned me on. He placed his arms around me and squeezed me tight like I was his and he never wanted to let go. And at that moment I felt like his. I tried to wrap my mind around what had just happened and how I could allow myself to do this once again. This was so *wrong*. So dishonest and devious, yet here I was again, indulging in him once more.

I cautiously turned to face this married man and kissed the tattoo on his right arm. My lips traveled over each letter of his son's name that was carefully sketched into his skin and I slowly inhaled his scent. Jay-Z's Gold engulfed me and made my nipples harden. I looked deep into his eyes and was honest with him and myself.

"I love you," I whispered, burying my sweat glistened face into his chest, knowing that this one night had changed my life forever.

***

I drove home with the events of the night a blur to me but still fresh in my mind. After riding for about thirty minutes in complete silence I realized that I had not turned on the radio, which I always do as soon as I get in my car. My shaking hand fumbled around the silver knob as I tried to find a station. My heart stopped when I heard Kelly Price belt out her rendition of "As We Lay". It felt like she knew exactly what I had done and was singing this song for me.

Its morning, and now it's time for us to say goodbye. You're leaving me I know you got to hurry home to face your wife.

I sang along with Kelly and her words cut me so deep that I barely heard my cell phone ringing. I took a deep breath and reached down into my red Ralph Lauren purse.

"Hey, lil' mama," he said in his most seductive voice.

Flashes of him on top of me filled my head and I squeaked out "Hey" without trying to sound like I had a million things on my mind. I tried to remain calm, but my voice told on me. It was the voice of someone that did not know what she wanted anymore.

"Where are you?"

His concern caused a huge smile to spread across my face, but it quickly disappeared as my mind went back to tonight's actions. My voice was a mere whisper as I informed him that I had just crossed the Georgia state line, leaving me with a few more hours to drive.

"Rachel, I understand that we can't see each other anymore. I know that soon you will be a married woman and I don't want to stop you or distract you from your plans."

I swallowed hard. These were the exact words that I needed to hear to get my mind focused on the reality of our situation. My palms began to sweat. My two carat princess cut diamond engagement ring slid around on my finger as I tried to get a good grip on the steering wheel. Just talking to him on the phone made me nervous. Rachel, stay in control, I thought.

He went on about how he realized that our situations would not change. His voice was steady and without feeling when he referred to his own marriage. Usually, I never have any difficulty telling people how I feel and what I want, but for some reason, this man did something to me that made me become a different person.

I became someone that listened to her heart without thinking about the "what ifs."

"Are you there?"

"Yeah, I'm here," I replied flatly, my stomach twisting into knots. "This wasn't supposed to happen, we should have just talked," I said remorsefully.

He sighed as silence overtook our conversation. After a few seconds he finally spoke. "I know," he said. "I didn't plan on this happening again. I just had to see you."

Why can't I let him go?

I wanted to scream feeling the tears well up in my eyes. My stomach continued to turn and that meant I was going to be sick at any moment. I held my cell phone in my dripping wet hand and struggled to concentrate on the road.

"How do you feel about me?" I asked quickly.

"You know I love you. How could I not love you?"

His answer made the tears fall uncontrollably and I began to tell him what was in my heart. As I began to speak, he cut me off and said the one thing that I did not want to hear.

"Rachel, you know how I feel about you, but I want to talk about the one thing that you have not told me."

He can't know about that. He can't know my secret. That was the reason for us meeting tonight but I still couldn't bring myself to tell him.

"Sweetheart, I'm sorry," was all that I could manage to say.

"Please tell me the truth."

He knew. He already knew. Before I could say anything else, I glanced at the road and slammed on brakes. I felt the car slide from right to left. My cell phone fell from my hand as I tightened my grip on the steering wheel, trying to gain control of the car, but it was too late. The car jerked forward. Still pressing the brake with all my power, I finally came to a complete stop. I looked up and saw that I was now on the side of the road. Before I could blink twice the brightness of two lights on high beam blinded me. I couldn't move and the lights were coming straight for me.

"Oh Jesus!" I screamed, and braced myself for the impact.

***

After the loud honking had stopped and I realized that I was still intact, I opened my eyes. The truck swerved just enough to avoid direct impact with my car, only swiping the side.

"Thank you, Jesus," was the only thing that I managed to say.

I reached for my phone that had landed on the passenger's side floor and said a little prayer before continuing on my way home. I had no intentions of sleeping with Terrence today and since it had happened anyway, just hours ago, I knew God was not pleased. I was pretty sure that was the reason I had just had a near death experience.

As I pulled back onto the highway, heart still racing, hands trembling, I thought about what happened and the events that led up to my accident. I still had not told Terrence about our baby, but once again, we had made love. Passionate love that pierced my soul and made me utter the words I love you to this married man. I left the hotel room with so many thoughts swirling around in my head.

Glancing at my phone, I saw there were three missed calls from Terrence and a text asking what happened and was I alright. I texted back and let him know I was okay and that I would call him when I got home. This had to be over. Almost losing my life was enough of a wakeup call for me. Tonight had to be the last time I ever saw Terrence Walker.

Chapter 30

After a long, tiresome, four-hour drive, I was finally back home. Once I got settled in my apartment and stopped the excessive shaking I was still doing, I sent Terrence another text and told him that tonight was a mistake and there didn't need to be any further communication between us with the exception of business matters. My text prompted a call from him and after another long drawn out conversation about what had happened tonight, the accident, our feelings, and so forth, he finally agreed that things needed to end, but not before telling me that he loved me. I felt the same but it didn't mean anything; we could never be together and had injured too many people in the process of feeding our desires. Right before I hung up the phone, Terrence asked again the one question he never got his answer to.

His voice was raspy and shaking, and the words crept from his mouth like he didn't even want to say them. "Rachel, are you pregnant?"

At first I didn't respond. Even though I knew that this was the reason for our meeting today, I was still hesitant about revealing the secret about the baby, about our baby. After my traumatic near death experience, I was worn out emotionally and I dreaded having the conversation. I was so weary and all I could do was sigh into the phone.

"Rachel?" Terrence repeated.

"I was," I whispered.

"What happened?"

"I lost the baby."

"You lost our baby?" Terrence asked softly. His voice went in and out. "Our baby?" he repeated.

"Terrence, I wanted to tell you, but I didn't know how.

Then when I saw you at the cookout it was just too much to handle."

"Our baby," Terrence said again. "Rachel, we could have been a family."

His response caught me off guard. "Terrence, you have a family," I insisted.

"I want you. I love you. Don't marry him, Rachel." Terrence's voice was clear and crisp now.

Surprised by what he was saying, I fell silent.

"Did you hear me?" Terrence asked.

"How can you ask me not to marry him? You are married. We just agreed to stop seeing one another," I demanded.

"That was before I knew. Before I knew about our baby. Give me some time. Just don't marry him. Wait on me."

"Terrence, the baby is gone and I love Corey. You can't tell me not -"

Terrence cut me off again, and there was more anger in his voice than sadness now. "Don't marry him."

Before I could say anything else, Terrence hung up the phone. I couldn't believe what he was asking me to do, or better yet, not do. He had not once requested that I wait on him during our entire affair. We often played with the idea of being together, talked and laughed about what it would be like, but we both knew that it could never happen. I debated on calling him back, but I decided against that. I was already spent from today and I just wanted to sleep.

***

After tossing and turning all night, I spent the better part of Saturday in bed. I was drained from last night's events and needed some time to myself. Von called to see how my meeting with Terrence went, but I didn't feel like discussing it. Corey texted to tell me he loved me and I responded back saying the same. No matter what Corey had done I still loved him.

After watching a rerun of *The Real Housewives of Atlanta*, I decided to get up and try to eat something even though I wasn't particularly hungry. I ate half of a turkey sandwich and returned to my safe place, my bed. My thoughts went back to Terrence and the last thing he said before he hung up on me. Don't marry Corey and wait on him. Terrence had to be delusional if he thought that I was going to wait on him to leave his wife, something that may or may not happen.

I rolled over on my side to get in a more comfortable position in bed and heard my phone beeping informing me that I had a text message. I retrieved my phone from the charger on my nightstand and turned it over to check the message. I closed my eyes and took a deep breath when I saw Terrence's name flash on my phone.

Did you end things with Corey yet?

Again I was stunned at what he was asking me to do.

I replied back as fast as I could. *No, and I cannot believe what you are asking me to do! Haven't we been through enough? After everything, don't you want me to be happy?*

After a few seconds another text came through.

You have a few weeks to end things. End it or I will.

What the hell? Was Terrence threatening me? I pressed call on my phone so fast that the phone was ringing in my ear before I had a chance to even think about what I was doing. I didn't care if Terrence's wife was in front of him and she saw me calling. He had the audacity to threaten to end things between me and Corey and I needed to talk to him.

After the fifth ring, Terrence's voice mail picked up. I refused to leave a message so I hung up my phone and threw it down on my bed. Why did Terrence believe he had the right to make me end things with Corey? After staring at my TV for minutes, my ringtone began to play. I scurried for my phone once I saw Terrence's name flashing on it.

"What the hell, Terrence?" I screamed in the phone.

"Rachel, you know I love and want to be with you," he said calmly.

I lowered my voice. "Terrence, I am going to marry Corey and that's the end of it."

Terrence sighed. "Rachel, please just think about it. I promise I am working on getting out of my marriage and then we can be together."

"Terrence, we can never be together! Your wife is my best friend's sister for God's sakes! Think about that for a minute."

Silence overtook the conversation and for a moment I thought Terrence had hung up.

"Rachel, when I am with you I am happy. I feel like we fit and I haven't felt that way for a long time. Just think about it, please."

I didn't want to go back and forth with Terrence anymore so I told him I would give it some thought, even though I knew that my answer would still be no. I had to get him to understand that I wasn't going to leave Corey for him. It just wasn't possible and my heart still belonged to Corey. I had to find a way to make Terrence comprehend that.

***

A week crawled by and every day I received a text from Terrence asking for my decision. When I didn't respond he would follow with more threats. This side of Terrence frightened me and I believed that he would tell Corey about our affair. There had to be a way to get through to Terrence but I didn't know how. This ravishing man that had been there for me and loved me was turning into someone I didn't know. Maybe I didn't know him as well as I thought I had. He called my office constantly. At one time, I had thought this was endearing, but now it only troubled me. After sending a heartfelt email pleading him to stop with his obsession about us being together, he called once again.

I was in tears and I just wanted it to be over. Every time I talked to Terrence it reminded me of the day I lost our child. The sorrow was still there.

While on the phone, sobbing uncontrollably, I begged Terrence to let me go. I told him how I thought about our child every time we spoke and I wanted to be free of him. God had given me a second chance with Corey and after making so many poor choices I wanted to make the right one.

He begged me not to cry and sat quietly on the phone listening to my every word. There was so much pain in my voice that I couldn't hide it and I didn't try to. He needed to hear how I felt. He finally spoke and told me that he was sorry and he would give me what I asked for. Finally, I had gotten through to Terrence. He still had pieces of my heart, but the reality was we could never be together. It was time for both of us to face that.

***

The following morning, after a sleepless night I decided to move forward and get my life back together. As Tamar from the reality show *Braxton Family Values* would say, "Get your life," and that is exactly what I planned on doing.

Still not talking in great detail with Corey, I sent him a text asking him if he would go to church with me. It took him a while to respond, but when he did he inquired about spending the weekend together. My reply was, *"No. Just want to go to church together."* At this point Corey was going to take whatever he could get so I wasn't surprised by his agreeable response. I tossed my phone on the bed and said a little prayer that whatever happened, let God's will be done.

***

Corey arrived at my house especially early so we could ride to church together. Handsome as always, his attire included a grey suit with a pink shirt topped off with a pink and grey tie. Most men couldn't pull this look off, but my Corey could. My Corey.

My Corey that I still wanted to spend the rest of my life with. Despite his infidelities and my own, I still aspired to be with this man. In spite of everything, I felt love for him and a bond that neither one of our mistakes could sever.

Corey entered my house with slow strides and was cautious about what he said and did. Sitting on the couch he clicked on the TV and nervously starred at it without really watching. This was our first time being together since he told me about the affair. I didn't want to focus on that, so I pushed the thought out of my mind. I caught him stealing glances and trying to figure out from my body language if I was still upset. We hadn't talked about what happened and I didn't want to. Part of me knew he didn't want to discuss it and have to relive those moments either. I wasn't going to put either one of us through that again.

I waltzed out of my bedroom in a fitting heather grey sleeveless dress and silver and black heels. A silver matching earrings and necklace set that was a gift from my mom and dad decorated my neck and hung from my ear lobes. I grabbed my black Coach purse which was hanging from the knob of my bedroom door and turned to face Corey, letting him know I was ready to leave. Corey stood up and walked towards me, taking my hand and leading me out my front door.

***

As we entered the church I glanced at the front where the choir was located and spotted Jerome heading to the microphone to lead a song. He had been absent from church a few Sundays and I guessed it was because of what happened between us. I flushed as embarrassment struck every nerve in my body. A sick feeling erupted in my gut. Remembering my tendency to show all my emotions on my face, I forced a smile and looked away. I searched around the crowded sanctuary for my sister.

I spotted Monica sitting close to the back so I proceeded over to where she was.

After waving at my sister, Corey and I found seats beside her, and I saw Tony sitting next to her. He looked rather handsome dressed in a black suit, tan shirt, and a black tie. I was almost certain that my sister helped pick out his outfit. Then again every loser and user at least had a black suit. Tony smiled and waved as Corey and I took our seats beside them.

Church service had been going on for an hour now and the Holy Spirit was flowing through each pew in New Zion Baptist Church. I listened to the choir, decked out in their red and grey robes with NZBC imprinted on the front, and all the songs about God being all we need and encouraging yourself. Hearing these words of praise made the tears start flowing once again. Corey was watching me and once he saw the tears, he put his arm around me and pulled me close to him.

I am sure that he thought I was crying for us, but God knew I was crying for me. Weeping for the baby I lost and all the mistakes I had made in the last few months. I just wanted to stop it all. Stop the hurt and tears. I was tired of constantly hurting myself and others.

Corey touched my hand. His touch was gentle and calm and it soothed me. I let his hand sit on mine for a second, then grabbed his hand and moved closer to him. I felt peace with Corey and I wanted our life back, absent of Terrence and whatever her name was that he slept with. How did my perfect relationship get to this? Maybe because it wasn't as flawless as I thought and neither was I. It was so fitting that my dad preached about forgiveness today. God sends messages any way he can and we have the choice to ignore them or listen.

After the sermon, the choir sang "Break Every Chain," which sent the church into an uproar of screams. The tears came harder and I couldn't control them any longer. I heard a man whimper beside me. Assuming that Corey felt the spirit as well, I held his hand tighter. However, it was not his cries that had caught my attention.

Tony was now standing, hands raised in the air crying and calling on God over and over again. I peeked at my sister and the expression on her face was one of shock as well. She was staring, mouth open, unable to take her eyes off of Tony. He stomped his feet and rocked back and forth as the spirit took control of his body.

My father stood in front of the church with his hands reaching out towards the congregation. "Today is the day to give your life to God. Tomorrow is not promised," Pastor Simms recited over and over. He paced back and forth in front of the church beckoning for someone to ask God to direct his or her life.

Tony slid out of the pew and began to walk toward the front of the church. His walk was as if he had no control over his movements, like he was a puppet controlled by his master. He staggered down the aisle still crying out to God, arms waving in the air. Dad saw Tony coming toward him and shouted out, "Thank you Jesus!" He continued his speech about giving your life to God. Tony finally reached my dad at the front and by this time Monica, Corey and I were standing up in the back, arms raised in the air, praising God. Shouts of hallelujah and amen rang out from our pew.

Pastor Simms greeted Tony with a hug and whispered something in his ear. He motioned for the choir to stop singing as he began his speech about having one person come to give his life to God and that he was old enough to speak for himself. Pastor Simms handed Tony the microphone, urging him to say what was on his heart.

"I know I have been living foul and I am tired of going through life without a purpose," Tony stated. He looked toward the ceiling and shouted out, "I don't want to just exist anymore. I want to live for God."

Still standing, Monica cried out and wrapped her arms around her body, holding herself and rocking back and forth. Tony then invited Monica to join him at the front of the church.

Sliding out of the pew and almost running, she approached the front to stand next to Tony. He turned to face Monica and grabbed both of her hands.

"I apologize to you and God for the mistakes I have made and I want both of us to live for him."

My heart was overflowing with so many emotions that I couldn't stop crying. Never in a million years would I have thought that Tony would give his life to God. For once I was proud of him and happy for Monica that they were together. People were shouting from the front of the church to the back. Shrieks, shouts, and wails filled this house and there wasn't a dry eye in sight.

I couldn't contain myself and before I knew how I got there, I was positioned in front of the church standing with my sister and Tony. I had no idea what to say now that I was in front of everybody. Was I going to confess my sins about the affair, the baby, to everyone? I didn't know but I just knew that I had to get this off of me. The heavy weight that I had been carrying around for so long somehow had to be lifted. I couldn't bear it any longer.

"I use to think I was perfect," I started. I glanced up through tear filled eyes and saw Corey advancing toward the front to stand beside me. "No one is without sin, especially not me. I have made so many mistakes in my life and I don't want to go into a marriage without God." I glanced at Corey now standing beside me and saw the tears trickling down his face.

"I want to rededicate my life to God so that whatever me and Corey go through, we have God in the midst."

Corey wiped his eyes with his hand. "I want to do the same," he announced.

The church exploded in hallelujahs and thank you Gods. My dad was so caught up in the Spirit that he just raised his hands. He handed the microphone to associate Pastor Clemmons who was now standing beside him and began to dance and rejoice down the aisle.

I had never seen my dad shout before and seeing him jump like he was twenty instead of sixty sent chills throughout my body.

Another associate pastor, Minister Richards, followed my dad's lead and jumped from the pulpit to run up and down the aisles. She would pause for a brief moment to shout and then start running again. To a non-believer, this would have seemed like a three ring circus, but to everyone that attending New Zion Baptist Church today, this was just God moving and saving souls.

I hugged Corey, and for the first time in months it felt like we were together. He embraced me and whispered in my ear that he loved me and God would see us through. I believed him.

Chapter 31

I rolled over on my side and slowly opened my eyes. Yawning, I squinted at the sun that shone brightly, lighting up my room and beaming directly on my face. I laid there for a moment and closed my eyes again in an attempt to go back to sleep. However, that was impossible due to the pounding headache that would not abandon me.

"Wake up, sis!" Monica yelled opening the door to the bedroom suite we shared that night and jumping on the bed.

Her constant leaps made my headache worse. I groaned and turned on my stomach to ignore her screaming.

"You have a hair appointment in an hour so get in the shower and throw on some clothes."

Monica hopped off the bed and rummaged through the clothes in my suitcase. She pulled out a pair of white shorts and a pink shirt, and tossed them on the bed.

"Get up and put this on, Rachel!" she demanded now standing beside the bed shaking me.

"Wait, sis, please," I moaned turning on my back and away from her.

I lifted myself up slowly into a sitting position and wiped the sleep from my eyes. Monica went back into the living room of the deluxe suite still telling me to get in the shower and listing everything I had to do today. As she rambled on and on it dawned on me what today was. Finally, after all the months, the fighting and the never ending battles, the day was here. It was my wedding day!

As this thought registered into my mind I bounced out of bed and ran into the bathroom.

"Be out in 15 minutes!" I screamed.

Excitement took over and my pounding headache subsided. It was still there, but it didn't matter anymore.

My wedding day was at long last here. The day that seemed like it had taken forever to arrive was finally here and I was thrilled. I didn't care what went wrong. I didn't care who was late or not there. I didn't care about anything as long as Corey was waiting for me at the front of the church. At the end of the day we would be husband and wife. Nothing else was of importance.

Last night my sister had reserved a suite at The Plaza Hotel downtown for us, and we partied most of the night with friends and family. Of course there were strippers, three of the sexiest chocolate brothers that I had ever rested my eyes upon. Flipping me in the air, and gyrating between my legs, they made my last night as a single woman unforgettable. Now, hours after that, I was on my way to get my hair done and then back to the hotel to dress and head to the church.

There was a light breeze on this 9th day of June but the sun was shining bright and a beautiful cloudless sky floated above. It was a perfect 70 degrees outside and in my mind the day was exactly how it should be. Exquisite.

***

The doors of the New Zion Baptist Church swung open, and as I had envisioned in my dreams, 500 pairs of eyes stared at me. Flowers and decorations were arranged from the pulpit to the pews and candles highlighted the interior of the church. The colors of sage and cream with splashes of peach came to life and dazzled this splendid sanctuary.

Smiles and whispers continued as I glided down the aisle with my dad by my side. My strapless satin white gown embroidered with beads and a long flowing train gave me the princess appearance that I had desired. Corey's cousin, Tyrone, belted out the words to "Beautiful Girl" by Kenny Lattimore, the ideal song choice for this moment.

Corey looked more handsome than I had ever seen him dressed in a black tuxedo that made him look like a model waiting to be photographed.

At the moment, he looked at me with tears in his eyes, I felt like an angel. All the fights, all the distress and pain were a far off memory and this was the life that was waiting on me. It was worth it all.

***

Dancing and laughing with my sister and brother at the reception, Monica handed me my phone and informed me that I had a million text messages, probably congratulations from my friends and family. Sure enough there were text messages and phone calls from co workers and friends that were unable to attend the wedding, all saying congrats to me and Corey.

I beamed as I realized that finally, I was Mrs. Rachel Perkins. The last text message on my phone was from Terrence. It read, *I hope that today is everything you want it to be. Love you always and forever...pg 53...and you look beautiful.*

I stood there for a moment and stared at the floor as the message tugged at my heart. How did Terrence know how I looked? Was he here? I scanned the ballroom and recognized only family and friends. I hadn't talked to Terrence at all since I rededicated my life to God. Terrence's law firm finally hired a business manager, no longer burdening me with having to speak to him. The threats had stopped as well, and I felt that he had finally accepted that it was over between us. I took a deep breath and calmed myself before anyone noticed my apparent anxiety. As I breathed in and out trying to relax my worried mind, I caught a quick glimpse of a man walking out of the reception hall. The walk was familiar, the bald head even more recognizable. Could it be? Could Terrence be here?

Corey walked up behind me, startling me and breaking up my thoughts. I took another deep breath in and released it. Rachel, you have nothing to worry about, I told myself.

He placed his warm hands on my strapless shoulders and whispered in my ear. "Is my wife okay?"

I cleared the text from my phone and turned to face Corey. His smile eased my nervousness.

"I am better than okay. I am wonderful." I tilted my head up, gave my husband a kiss, and grabbed his hand to lead him to the dance floor.

John Legend's "All of Me" played as we danced, Corey's arms wrapped tightly around my body. I couldn't control my smile and my heart overflowed with love for this man. Flaws and all, I loved Corey with all of me. He was not perfect and neither was I, but we were perfect for each other.

"I love you," we both said at the same time.

I giggled and gazed at my new husband. My husband. My Corey. I placed my head on his chest and closed my eyes. This is where I am supposed to be. Not for a brief hour. Not for a short day. But for an eternity. Thank you, God.

Please enjoy on the following page a sample chapter from my next book Divided Souls. Catch up with all the characters that you loved in Before I Say I Do. Divided Souls will be released Summer 2015.

Prologue

"NO, NO, NO! I will not condone that kind of talk in MY church! Everyone calm down right now!" Pastor Simms shouted. The veins bulged in his neck as he frantically waved his lanky arms up and down. The New Zion Baptist Church Friday night meeting was wrapping up, but there was one issue that the members were openly at odds over and the crass words that were being thrown around the holy building were enough to enrage the pastor. Pastor Simms stood in front of the burgundy and metallic gold altar, desperately trying to get the congregation's attention as they continued to talk among themselves.

"Pastor, I know we are supposed to open our doors to everyone, but wrong is wrong!" Sister Lucille rolled her thick neck and beady eyes at the same time. Her tight, greasy, jet black curls shook as she stood up to say her piece. She looked around the room, waiting for agreement from her church family, and then plopped her 250-pound frame back down on the wooden pew.

"Mmm hmm," Sister Margaret and Sister Patricia said in unison.

"It just don't go with what we believe, Pastor." Deacon Jeter stood with his cane and tapped it on the brick-colored carpet. "I can't believe that we gonna let some lil' sissy back in this place. Young men walkin' round with them tight ole jeans on and lil' flower shirts wantin' to be gals just ain't right!" Deacon Jeter said, showing his obvious disdain. He sat back down as Sister Margaret gingerly patted him on the back to quiet him.

Pastor Simms closed his eyes, rubbed his temples, and in a calmer voice this time asked the church members to settle down. "We are not God; therefore, he is the only one that can judge this young man. Who are we to turn him away?"

Pastor Simms was not completely for bringing Freddie back into the church, but he couldn't tell him no and turn his back on him. No matter if he was gay or not, God still loved him. Freddie had spent many years at New Zion Baptist Church, leading the youth ministries and singing in the choir. Many suspected his homosexuality; however, no one judged him until he had officially come out by bringing his lover to church with him. Once Freddie confirmed that he was indeed in a relationship with a man, some church members candidly ridiculed and chastised him so much that they eventually drove him away. Pastor Simms did everything in his power to stop the condemnation, but it continued and Freddie left New Zion. That was almost five years ago and Pastor Simms still didn't understand, even after their meeting a few days ago, why he was so determined to come back.

"We don't turn anyone away from God," Pastor Simms continued. "Deacon Jeter, what if this was your son? Sister Lucille, what if this was your grandson? Are you saying that you would tell them God does not love them and they can't come to church and worship Him?"

Silence descended upon the sanctuary and everyone's full attention was now on the pastor. Pastor Simms removed the black wired reading glasses that covered his face and stared intently, giving each member eye contact.

"Who will cast that first stone? What we have to do is pray for this young brother that God will take that spirit from him.

We all have sinned; we can't become too holy to stop feeding others the word. That is not what New Zion Baptist Church is about."

There were a few rumbles and moans, but no one dared to debate with Pastor Simms. Relieved that everyone had finally quieted down, he took this moment to conclude the extended session. After prayer and dismissal, Pastor Simms retreated back to his study to get his belongings together before traveling home. Tonight had been one of the toughest church meetings that he had endured in a while and, to say the least, he was drained.

He sat down in his black leather swivel chair, loosened his cobalt blue silk tie, and exhaled. He thought about earlier this week when Freddie came to him asking to join the church again. Pastor Simms stroked his gray and black beard and thought about the speech he had given. It very well could have been anyone's son, even his own. He picked up the family portrait off of his L-shaped harvest cherry wood desk and allowed his middle finger to trace over the sterling silver picture frame. He smiled at his three lovely kids, Monica, Rachel, Daryl, and Deborah, his beautiful wife of forty-three years. He was swollen with pride of the responsible adults that his children had become.

Glancing toward the ceiling and thanking God that it wasn't Daryl, Pastor Simms set the picture down and slowly got out of his chair. He placed both hands on the side of his mahogany briefcase that was positioned on the edge of his desk and gently closed it.

Out of all his children, Pastor Simms was closest with his son.

Daryl was the spitting image of his father and even carried himself with dignity and respect, as if he should have been a preacher as well. Even though Daryl didn't follow in his dad's footsteps by being in the ministry, Pastor Simms still boasted about his career as a physical therapist with the Atlanta Falcons. He was elated that finally after chasing all the fast women in the church, Daryl was settling down and getting married tomorrow. Not only was Saturday Daryl's wedding day, but also his twenty-seventh birthday, a cause for great celebration.

Pastor Simms thanked God again for a heterosexual son. He grabbed his briefcase and walked out of his study door. Turning back around to lock the door, he heard faint footsteps coming toward him. Everyone should have been gone by now, but maybe Deacon Jeter was still here locking up the church, Pastor Simms thought. He turned around and proceeded down the hall towards the back door where his pewter gray Cadillac CTS was parked.

The footsteps were behind him now and getting closer. Pastor Simms stopped abruptly, turned around, and peered into the darkness.

"Deacon?" he nervously called out. The footsteps stopped. This time Pastor Simms demanded, "Deacon Jeter?"

Still nothing. Pastor Simms pace quickened as he headed towards the door once again.

As he put his hand on the door knob, a scream invaded the darkness, causing him to let out a light yell and turn around.

"Who's there?' Pastor Simms boldly insisted.

The footsteps were coming towards him faster now, but still he could not see down the dark hallway.

He reached in his pocket and gripped the gold tarnished handle of the butterfly pocket knife that he always kept on him.

New Zion Baptist Church was located near several dangerous neighborhoods that were homes to a few gangs, therefore; he always carried some sort of protection. Pastor Simms grew up in the grimiest part of Charlotte, and even though he was a minister now, there was still some hood in him. Like the saying goes, you can take the person out the hood, but not the hood out of the person.

He took two steps forward and gasped as a man ran towards him, grabbed his shirt and fell to the floor. Pulling his pocket knife out now, he braced himself, ready to fight off any more attackers. After a few seconds, Pastor Simms slowly peered down at the man on the floor. The man began to shake in convulsions, groaning and moaning, slicing through the eerie silence of the darkness. Trying to identify the man and also watching for any assaulters, he reached for his cell phone from his shirt pocket.

"I'm calling the police!" Pastor Simms shouted, noticing the bloody handprints on his shirt that was made visible by his cell phone light.

Hands trembling, he glanced down again, and dropped his phone. Suddenly, he realized who the man was that now lay lifeless on the floor.

"Freddie?" Pastor Simms whispered.

About The Author

TARA L. THOMPSON, a native of Chester, SC, graduated from the University of South Carolina in Columbia, with a degree in Information Technology. She works as an Application Engineer in Charlotte, North Carolina. Tara has had a passion for writing since elementary school and always knew that this was her calling. Tara resides in Rock Hill, South Carolina with her daughter. Readers can visit her website at **www.taralthompson.net**

CPSIA information can be obtained at www.ICGtesting.com
Printed in the USA
LVOW06s0226250914

405787LV00001B/23/P